the further adventures of

SHERLOCK HOLMES

THE SEVENTH BULLET

the
further
adventures of

SHERLOCK HOLMES

THE SEVENTH BULLET

DANIEL D. VICTOR

TITAN BOOKS

THE FURTHER ADVENTURES OF SHERLOCK HOLMES:
THE SEVENTH BULLET

ISBN: 9781848566767

Published by
Titan Books
A division of Titan Publishing Group Ltd
144 Southwark St
London
SE1 0UP

First edition: October 2010
10 9 8 7 6 5 4 3 2

Names, places and incidents are either products of the author's
imagination or used fictitiously. Any resemblance to actual persons, living
or dead (except for satirical purposes), is entirely coincidental.

Visit our website:
www.titanbooks.com

What did you think of this book? We love to hear from our readers.
Please email us at: readerfeedback@titanemail.com, or write to
us at the above address. To receive advance information, news,
competitions, and exclusive Titan offers online, please register as a
member by clicking the 'sign up' button on our website:
www.titanbooks.com

A CIP catalogue record for this title is available from the British Library.

Printed in the USA.

For Norma
To me she will always be "*the* woman."

"The treason of the Senate! Treason is a strong word, but not too strong, rather too weak, to characterize the situation in which the Senate is the eager, resourceful, indefatigable agent of interests as hostile to the American people as any invading army could be, and vastly more dangerous; interests that manipulate the prosperity produced by all, so that it heaps up riches for the few; interests whose growth and power can only mean the degradation of the people, of the educated into sycophants, of the masses toward serfdom."

–David Graham Phillips
The Treason of the Senate, 1906

Acknowledgements

For their help in editing the manuscript, I would like to express my gratitude to Richard Evidon; Robert MacDowell; Christine McMullen; Norma K. Silverman; Barry Smolin; Peter Turchi; and my parents, Alfred and Ruth Victor. I would also like to thank Jane Cushman. It was her faith from the start that enabled this project to succeed.

Preface

A ny manuscript purporting to be a newly discovered case involving Sherlock Holmes deserves a word of explanation. When such a manuscript also casts a controversial light on well-established historical events, a naturally sceptical reading audience is entitled to know how its discovery came about.

In June 1976 I completed my doctoral dissertation on the little-known American novelist David Graham Phillips. Although few people today even recognise Phillips' name, many are quite familiar with the title of "Muckraker," which an angry President Theodore Roosevelt pinned on him for the writer's attack on members of the United States Senate in 1906. My particular interest in Phillips focused on the dichotomy in his nature that resulted, on the one hand, in the kind of political dissent that so enraged Roosevelt and, on the other, the eccentric and stylish mode of dress that earned Phillips the label of "dandy." My dissertation, entitled "The Muckraker and the Dandy: The Conflicting Personae of David Graham Phillips," studied the impact of this psychological split on Phillips' fiction, fiction that, at least during his own lifetime, garnered him comparisons to Tolstoy, Balzac, and Dickens.

The library at Princeton University houses the primary collection of manuscripts related to David Graham Phillips. Because the fact is well documented that the great bulk of his work changed very little between its creation in longhand and its publication, I felt comfortable in bypassing the Princeton collection during my doctoral studies. Besides, as a struggling graduate student on the West Coast, I didn't have the money to travel to New Jersey anyway. But three years ago I finally did get to make the pilgrimage; and while investigating the aforementioned handwritten papers of Phillips, I discovered—to my amazement and joy—at the bottom of one of the eleven cartons of documents pertaining to Phillips, the battered and water-damaged manuscript tied with twine that, thanks to the university's gracious consent, I have been allowed to edit and present here to what I assume is an eager audience.

When I first saw Dr. John Watson's account of Phillips' murder, I had no idea of the report's explosive—not to mention priceless—contents. It had no title (I confess to generating the present one thanks to the suggestion of a friend at the National Endowment for the Humanities). The original first page simply showed "David Graham Phillips" scrawled across it in a handwriting different from that which covers the rest of its pages. Although the library research department claims no knowledge of how or when the manuscript actually arrived, I surmise that some good Samaritan who knew of the Phillips collection at Princeton must simply have sent Watson's narrative to the University where an unsuspecting librarian no doubt mistakenly placed it among the compositions written by Phillips himself.

I cannot, of course, vouch for the authenticity of the manuscript. In general, it appears to be historically accurate. References to Phillips' role in reporting the naval collision, for example, or Hearst's generous offer of employment or the testimony of the numerous witnesses Watson cites can all be found in various biographies of Phillips' life. However bizarre and contradictory, even the details surrounding Phillips murder–including the passages from the assassin's diary–are consistent with the journalistic and scholarly accounts I have researched. But because Dr. Watson himself confesses to clouding some of the more controversial aspects in order to protect those who were still in power when he wrote the memoir shortly after World War I, it is difficult to determine exactly how definitive his narrative really is. For the reader seeking to try, I have included a selected bibliography following the text.

But accurate or not, the manuscript demands to be made public. Let historians and critics more qualified than I be the final judges. I can surely attest to its contents' conforming to all the vagaries of human nature and the political process that I myself have come to regard as true. I have taken the liberty of adding the chapter titles and headnotes and clarifying those transitions and explanations that were illegible, lost, or omitted in the original.

Learn from history or be condemned to repeat it, Santayana admonished. Judging from the success of the political assassins subsequent to the events marked in the history that follows, we have done very little learning. I present Dr. Watson's narrative, therefore, with the hope of making better students of us all.

–D.D.V.

Los Angeles, California

June 1992

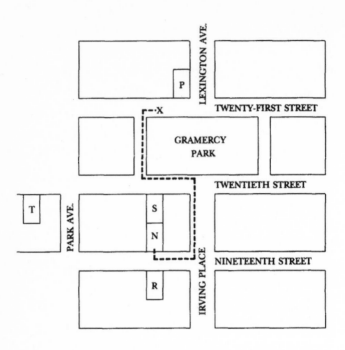

N: NATIONAL ARTS CLUB

P: PRINCETON CLUB

R: RAND SCHOOL

S: SAMUEL J. TILDEN'S FORMER HOME

T: THEODORE ROOSEVELT'S BIRTHPLACE

X: ASSASSINATION SITE OF DAVID GRAHAM
   PHILLIPS

–: ROUTE OF D.G.P. ON 23 JANUARY 1911

One

୧

THE AMERICAN LADY

"As between knaves and fools, I incline towards knaves. At least, they are teachers of wisdom in the school of experience, while fools avail nothing, are simply provokers and purveyors of knavery."

–David Graham Phillips, *Light-Fingered Gentry*

Even now, some thirty years later, it seems difficult to imagine that one of the worst disasters in British naval history, a tragedy occurring more than two thousand miles from our native England, could have so greatly affected the lives of my good friend Sherlock Holmes and me; but that is exactly the case.

In June of 1893, during manoeuvres forty miles off the coast of Syria in the Levant, Vice Admiral Sir George Tryon, commanding the fleet of eleven warships from the oaken bridge of H.M.S. *Victoria*, issued his fateful order to turn about. Despite the protests of Rear Admiral Markham aboard the nearby H.M.S. *Camperdown* that there was not sufficient room for the double file of ships to execute a turn, the *Camperdown* was commanded to proceed.

Giving truth to the appropriateness of Admiral Markham's fears, the *Camperdown* rammed into the *Victoria*, which, owing to a gaping wound in her side, plummeted downward. There was created, as the pressman David Graham Phillips reported, "a vortex, at the bottom of which whirled the great blades of the screws. Into this maelstrom, down upon those frightful, swift revolving knives, were drawn several hundred British sailors, marines, and officers. They were torn into pieces, the sea was reddened all around, and strewn with arms, legs, heads, trunks. Then the boilers, far down beneath the surface, burst, and scores of those alive were scalded to death—and the sea smoothed out again and began to laugh in the superb tropical sunlight of the summer afternoon."

In addition to the enormity of the disaster—386 brave seamen lost their lives—a significant aspect to the story was the profound silence of Fleet Street on the matter. Sceptics even went so far as to suggest collusion between the Admiralty and the government in keeping the details secret. In fact, when the full account of the tragedy was finally published, the world learned—much to the dismay of the British press—that it was an American, the aforementioned Phillips, who, with timely telegrams and fortuitous connections, had secured the story for the newspapers in the United States.

An American member of my own profession, Dr. Ira Harris, happened to be in the telegraph office in Tripoli when Phillips's daring request to anyone at all for information on the naval collision arrived.[*] Ascertaining the facts from an unidentified seaman who

---

[*] Author's note: During the period referred to by Dr. Watson, Tripoli was located in Syria. Following the geopolitical changes of World War I, however, the city found itself within the borders of Lebanon. (The Tripoli in question is not to be confused with the Libyan city of the same name.)

had witnessed the event, Dr. Harris relayed the account in detail through a Turkish clerk back to Phillips in London.

Needless to say, the journalistic community was amazed. How a mysterious sailor, a medical practitioner, and a non-English-speaking telegrapher could combine to report a story of such importance with such accuracy seemed nothing short of a miracle.

It was not until three years later, when Phillips himself visited us at Baker Street, that I learned the solution to the puzzle. Following his presumed death at the hands of Professor Moriarty at the Reichenbach Falls in Switzerland in April 1891, my friend Sherlock Holmes spent three years touring distant localities. The summer of 1893 brought him not only to the Holy Land, as Holmes explained in the case my readers know as "The Adventure of the Empty House," but also to the environs of the ill-fated naval manoeuvres. The nameless sailor who had relayed in such fine detail to Dr. Harris the narrative of the collision at sea had, of course, been Sherlock Holmes; but it was only the photographs accompanying the newspaper stories of Holmes's reappearance in 1894 that enabled Dr. Harris to learn the true identity of the anonymous witness who had furnished him with the account. Upon making this discovery, Dr. Harris informed Phillips, who, during his next trip to London, came to Baker Street to thank personally the man responsible for providing him the means to establish his international reputation. Ironically, it was this celebratory encounter between Holmes and Phillips that resulted in our personal enquiry into the writer's brutal and bizarre assassination more than ten years later, an atrocity so strange that it actually sent echoes of vampirism reverberating through the corridors of the American Capitol in Washington, D.C.

Holmes and I had been involved in portentous cases before, but none besides his role in bringing Von Bork to justice at the start of the Great War held such worldwide implications as Phillips's shocking murder. Nonetheless, because in 1906 Phillips had so successfully attacked the evildoers in his government that he brought down upon himself the wrath of many who to this very day still command power at its highest echelons, it is with great trepidation even now—more than a full decade after Phillips's death in 1911—that I dare set my pen to paper. In the name of propriety as well as prudence, therefore, I have taken the necessary care to obfuscate not only those incriminating details that might yet give rise to embarrassment, but also the specific identities of those less-easily recognised dignitaries who could still have cause to be distressed by certain particulars being made public for the first time in the narrative that follows.

It was early in the spring of 1912 when I first met that most inimitable of American ladies, Mrs. Carolyn Frevert. As I have chronicled elsewhere, Sherlock Holmes and I had by this time been going our separate ways for many a year. After retiring as a consulting detective, Holmes had taken up the tending of bees in a quaint cottage in Sussex. I, happily settled into my most recent marriage, was receiving patients in my Queen Anne Street surgery. In point of fact, we scarcely saw each other. Although he might come up to London to hear some celebrated violinist at the Albert Hall, or I might journey to Sussex for what he termed the "occasional weekend visit," these were social engagements; inevitably, the continuous occupation of ridding England of her miscreants and rogues had passed to younger men. Sherlock Holmes, after all, was now fifty-eight; I, his frequent partner in combating lawlessness and crime, fifty-nine. We no longer had the physical stamina or the energetic enthusiasm to pursue the denizens of the underworld. Indeed, the sole substantive link to our days at what my generous readers assure me will become a world-famous address was the person of Mrs. Hudson, our ever-faithful housekeeper, who, despite the opportunity to rid herself of her most untidy boarder, had given up her Baker Street lodgings to look after Holmes and his bees in the Downs. Her only real fear, she constantly repeated, was that her friendly former rooms would be razed and supplanted by some blocks of dour office buildings.

On a clear, blustery mid-March afternoon—Friday the thirteenth, to be exact, if not ironically macabre—the specific events that would carry us halfway round the world actually began. Since I had no patients scheduled after the gouty Mr. Wigmore, I entertained high hopes of beginning my weekend early. As no-one else was seated in my waiting room when I ushered the limping patient in for his examination, I was looking forward, on such a beautiful day, to a constitutional and then tea with my dear wife. It was to my great surprise, therefore, that when I escorted Wigmore out of my consulting-room door, I saw perched rigidly in one of the bowbacked chairs a raven-haired woman who despite her middle age was still quite handsome. Dressed entirely in black, she sat perfectly motionless except for the constant flutter of the black lace fan she was holding. Since it was not hot enough to warrant such an action, I took it to be the outward show of some inner agitation.

"Are you ill, madam?" I asked.

"No, Dr. Watson," she replied, looking up at me. Even in those few words, I was able to detect her American accent. "In fact, I really did not come to consult you as a doctor at all. I'm rather afraid that I'm here under false pretences since it's not even you whom I really wish to speak with."

"I don't understand," I said, feeling a little chagrined.

"I've come all this way, Dr. Watson, to see your friend, Mr. Sherlock Holmes."

I must confess that, as I had not seen Holmes for quite some time myself and since his person did not figure in my every waking thought, I was completely taken aback by the reference. After all, only moments before, my deepest thoughts were of the cakes and biscuits my wife would be serving at tea.

As we were alone, however, I sat down in the chair beside her. About to inform her of my friend's retirement, I began, "Sherlock Holmes, madam–"

"Mrs. Frevert," she informed me. "Mrs. Carolyn Frevert. In fact, Dr. Watson, I believe you knew my brother Graham."

I thought for a moment, but could not recognise the name.

"David Graham Phillips," she said slowly.

Of course, I now saw the resemblance. It was the eyes–dark, piercing, commanding–the same keen eyes that had revealed her brother to be an inquisitive, aggressive newspaperman the first time I met him when he had come round in 1896 or '97 to thank Holmes for the account of the naval collision. That had been a few years before Phillips had begun writing novels and well before, as the world now so sadly knows, Phillips was shot and killed in New York by one who at the time had been described as a deranged assassin ranting of vampires.

It had taken only a moment for these thoughts to course through my mind, but the look of concern exemplified in Mrs. Frevert's dark-knitted brow made me feel guilty for my silence, however brief.

"I beg your pardon," I said. "I was lost in memory. Do accept my apology and also my condolences on your brother's death. Holmes and I were both deeply saddened. To think, a writer with such innate ability and promise–"

"Thank you, Dr. Watson," she broke in. "All of us at home were terribly grieved, as you can imagine." Mrs. Frevert paused to take a deep breath. Then she continued, "I first learned from Graham's letters how much he had enjoyed meeting you and Mr. Holmes. And once he returned to New York, he always spoke of his encounters with you both in London as the highlights of his stay in England." It was only now that her worried expression began to fade. Indeed, the hint of a smile crept in at the corners of her red lips, and she began to slow the wave of her fan.

"Graham never really liked leaving New York," she explained. "I know he called it 'the damned East' in one of his books, but it was where so many important things were happening that he hated to be away–from them, from me. We were so very close, you see." She closed her eyes for a moment. "In fact," she said, as if trying to regain her earlier optimism, "to Graham, 221B Baker Street was one of the landmarks of London. He wrote about his visits there at great length."

Desirous of keeping her mood buoyant, I ventured recounting the rather amusing narrative of her brother's initial encounter with Holmes. Discoursing so gaily about Phillips seemed a better tonic for his sister than those therapeutic medicines for depression we physicians sometimes have to prescribe.

"When your brother first arrived at Baker Street, Mrs. Frevert, I must admit to being quite put off by his flamboyant manner of dress. Despite the politeness with which he introduced himself, he seemed quite the popinjay to me. Still, since I had grown accustomed to all types of visitors, I simply told him that Holmes was not in and suggested he come round at teatime as I expected my friend back by then.

"Your brother called again just as Mrs. Hudson, our housekeeper, was bringing up the tea. I offered him a chair; but not wishing to eat without Holmes, we quietly sat staring at the sandwiches and cakes, both of us eagerly awaiting Holmes's return. At last, after an uncomfortable three-quarters of an hour, your brother rose and asked for his hat. He was in fact glancing at his pocket watch one final time when Holmes entered the room. I was about to introduce the two of them, but Holmes interrupted. 'Allow *me*, my dear Watson,' he said. My friend remained silent for the briefest of moments observing the stranger standing before him.

'Regard the appearance, Watson,' Holmes instructed as if I had not noticed the eccentric figure with whom I had just spent close to an hour. 'The great height, the boyish grin, the hair parted in the centre. Note the distinctive apparel: the boater rakishly perched on the back of the head, the pink shirt, the cutaway suit of brightly flowered silk, the pearl-button boots. But especially note the collar.'

"Holmes was referring to the tallest and stiffest celluloid collar that I had ever seen. Indeed, it was nearly smothering the staid dark-blue cravat below."

"I know, Dr. Watson." Mrs. Frevert laughed. "Graham prided himself on having the largest collars in New York City."

"I can well believe it." I chortled, and then continued my account. "Leaning forward to admire the white chrysanthemum in your brother's lapel, Holmes glanced down at your brother's right hand.

'Indian ink on the middle finger,' Holmes murmured.

'Amazing,' I said. I had spent all this time with your brother and never noticed the telltale smudge.

'I believe, Watson,' Holmes proclaimed with a triumphant sparkle in his eye, 'that I have the honour of making the acquaintance of an American newspaperman. To be precise, Mr. David Graham Phillips, the celebrated journalist for Joseph Pulitzer's New York *World*.'

'Really, Holmes!' I exclaimed. 'This is too much. You have been in the room mere seconds, and you have deduced his identity. Your powers never cease to amaze me.'

'Watson, Watson,' he replied, 'surely you know my methods by now. The calloused finger stained with ink suggests a professional man of letters; the conspicuous costume typifies the writer who enjoys public attention, not the sort who honour their muse in some private writer's den. No, I think the description quite fits a newspaper man.'

'But how did you know he was American?' I asked, still mystified by Holmes's success. 'He hasn't spoken a word, and however distinctive his clothing, such apparel can certainly be bought in London.'

'And *was*,' your brother added.

'True, Watson. The apparel, as we have just heard, was indeed bought in London, but only an American—no offence intended, Mr. Phillips—would dress so ostentatiously. Why, the most daring Englishman would consider that flowered silk for a waistcoat at best. Our American friends, not confined by British sentimental attachment to conservative taste, display themselves in all the hues of the rainbow. No, I feel quite confident in identifying our guest as the man the newspapers call "The Dandy from Manhattan" and the "The Dude from Indiana."

"A bright-red blush had been washing over your brother's face throughout this discussion, Mrs. Frevert, but 'That's swell' is all that he said with a self-conscious grin.

"I, however, was not yet convinced by Holmes's reasoning. 'What about Oscar Wilde?' I reminded him. 'Whatever you may think of *him*, he is most certainly British.'

"Holmes sighed in mock exasperation. 'The watch,' he said. 'Mr. Phillips's pocket watch is a Waltham, a distinctive and precise instrument made in a small town not far from Boston in the state of Massachusetts. Really, quite elementary, my dear Watson."

Mrs. Frevert clapped her hands in approval. "How wonderful!" she exclaimed.

"To be sure," I said. "By this time in our friendship, I had become used to being shown by Holmes what I myself had failed to see, but even I was not prepared for Holmes's final display of wryness.

'Anyone,' he proceeded to explain, 'with a modicum of knowledge about current affairs could not help identifying this most distinctive of young writers. I, Watson, who, as you know, sustain little interest in the political world, have accomplished the feat. But if such an uninformed person did exist, my good friend, he need only review our notes on the *Victoria–Camperdown* incident'– and here he pulled down from a shelf cluttered with files his great index volume of past cases, turned to the letter *V*, and extracted a likeness of your brother from within it–'to find a newspaper drawing of the Mr. Phillips in question staring right back at him. A most remarkable similarity, would you not agree, Watson?'

"Feeling crushed, I could barely mumble a faint 'I suppose so,' but your brother was so taken by our familiar repartee that he broke into the richest cachinnation that I believe ever filled our rooms.

'I think, Mr. Holmes,' your brother said when his laughter had subsided, 'that you've been pulling my leg.'

'Did you hear that, Watson?' Holmes replied with a chuckle of his own. 'It is the true man of letters who can distinguish satire from sarcasm.'

'I'll take that as a compliment, Mr. Holmes,' Phillips said.

'As intended,' Holmes countered, offering his hand. 'Now what brings you round to Baker Street?'

'Actually, Mr. Holmes,' your brother said, accepting my friend's grasp, 'I've come here to thank you personally for your help in reporting the story you just alluded to about the collision at sea.'

'Just a moment–' I interrupted. You see, it was the first time I had learned of my friend's complicity in securing the story. But the scowl on Holmes's face told me he wanted no more of this conversation.

'It was Dr. Harris, I presume?' he asked of your brother, referring–I now understood–to the only man who could possibly have identified for Phillips the role of Holmes in the matter.

"Your brother nodded.

'I accept your thanks,' Holmes said quickly to him. Addressing both of us, he added, 'If the tragic event has led to stricter naval regulations, so much the better. But not another word on the subject.'

"Then indicating a seat at our humble table, Holmes said to your brother, 'Now, if you'll be kind enough to join us for the repast you so far appear to have resisted ...,' and the two of them seemed immediate friends. For my own part, despite my initial reluctance, I too confess to being charmed by his warm and affable manner."

"Yes," Mrs. Frevert said wistfully, "that was Graham. Always ready with a thank you and friendly to a fault." Suddenly she became silent and gazed beyond my left shoulder, as if someone were standing behind me. In fact, I turned to locate what she might be staring at but saw only the familiar hat stand with my favourite bowler hanging from one of the wooden pegs. When I turned round to face my guest once again, a sombre, sober look had clouded her countenance.

"What is the matter, Mrs. Frevert? What could you possibly want to see Sherlock Holmes about? In fact, he scarcely knew your brother."

Mrs. Frevert began fanning herself again. "It is about Graham's death that I wish to speak to him, Dr. Watson."

"Whatever for? He learned of the events surrounding your brother's death only through the newspapers."

"That is why I have come all the way from America, Dr. Watson. At Scotland Yard I was told Mr. Holmes had left London but that, since you were still in public practice, I might meet with you and appeal to your sensitivities to gain me an interview. It was from the police that I received your address; it is why I am here. I want you to take me to Sherlock Holmes, and quite frankly I'm not prepared to be turned down."

She spoke with such determination that it was hard to dissuade her. But ever the guardian of my old friend's privacy, I did my utmost. "I don't understand, Mrs. Frevert," I protested. "Your brother was killed by a fanatic. All the papers said so, and the New York City police agreed. What mystery can there possibly be in so well-publicised a story to trouble Sherlock Holmes about?"

"It is just because it is so well-publicised a story, Dr. Watson, that I am so concerned. The truth is, for almost a year I'd been agonising over the fact that I didn't believe the police report about my brother's death. As a consequence, on January 23, the anniversary of Graham's murder, I vowed to convince Sherlock Holmes, my brother's friend, to come to America and prove to the world that Graham was *not* the victim of some madman but rather the target of a cleverly conceived, nefarious plot to silence him."

Needless to say, I was stupefied. But I was not yet ready to violate the privacy of my friend's seclusion. After all, he had left London purposely to avoid such encounters.

"Dr. Watson," she said, "I have read your accounts of your adventures with Sherlock Holmes. I know you are a man of conscience. I am a lady in distress."

Did I need to hear more? Whatever evidence or theories she possessed were not intended for me that afternoon; they were destined for Sherlock Holmes. The sincerity and determination of the dark-haired woman intensified my conviction. Whether or not Holmes was interested in hearing about such matters should not, I felt, be left up to me. We both had enjoyed Phillips for his charm and forthrightness. News of his journalistic gibes at the powerful in America had reached us in England—indeed, had affected us in England—and anyone who ever championed the cause of freedom had to respect him. Particularly reported was how President Roosevelt had tried to insult Phillips with an epithet from Bunyan. After the character in *The Pilgrim's Progress*, he had called Phillips "The Man with the Muckrake" only to find the label turned into a kind of meritorious badge worn with honour not only by Phillips but also by his reform-minded colleagues. In life, I reasoned, Phillips deserved his day in court; certainly, his attractive sister with her unflagging concerns about his death deserved hers. I knew not whether her hypothesis was worthy of Holmes's time, but I did know that *he* should be the one to make that decision.

It was agreed, therefore, that, following the receipt of an affirmative telegram from Holmes, Mrs. Carolyn Frevert and I would find ourselves at Victoria Station that Sunday morning two days hence where, according to my Bradshaw, at 10:45 the Eastbourne Pullman departed that would take us to Sussex and the retirement cottage of Mr. Sherlock Holmes.

A VISIT TO SUSSEX

"It isn't easy for an intelligent human being to say as much as three sentences without betraying his intelligence."

–David Graham Phillips, *George Helm*

The day after my encounter with Mrs. Frevert, I exchanged telegrams with Holmes establishing our welcome at his cottage. That Sunday morning, therefore, I bade an early farewell to my wife, who, knowing as much as she did about her husband's exploits with Sherlock Holmes, was not completely surprised by my impulsive trips to see him. Following a brief hansom ride to Victoria, I found Mrs. Frevert, attired in travelling garb of black and looking much like a bereft widow, settled in one of the handsome Pullman carriages ready for the ninety-minute, uninterrupted journey. At Eastbourne, we would catch a local omnibus for the nearby village of Fulworth, where a wagon and driver might easily be appropriated to traverse the distance between the town and what Holmes enjoyed calling his "villa."

Our departure from London passed uneventfully. Gently rocking and swaying its way over the points in the station, the train lumbered through a flickering display of sunlight and shadow conjured by the blackened brick arches of diverse railway bridges. Minutes later, having put behind us the waves of gabled red roofs and columns of grimy chimney pots that mark the confines of London, we began to gain speed.

Once beyond the outskirts of the city, we easily contented ourselves by watching the countryside of southeastern England fly past. Indeed, there was much satisfaction to be gained from our vista. Although I had made this same journey to the South Downs on not a few occasions myself, I never tired of the halcyon beauty of the Sussex landscape in which Holmes had chosen to retire.

It was an early spring that year, and a potpourri of wild-flowers greeted us with a riot of colour. Yellow primroses, blue wood anemone, purple violets, and pied wind-flowers framed rolling green fields occupied by grazing white sheep and mottled Herefords. Within minutes these pastures gave way to intermittent woods of oak, antique remnants of the mighty forests that once covered the area. Slicing through little hills and wealden valleys, the rails carried us farther south until near Lewes the earth became that more familiar greyish white that marks the chalky cliffs overlooking the English Channel.

It is near just such a cliff that Holmes's small house sits. He occupies a whitewashed cottage near Beachy Head that we reached with no difficulty after making the proper connections in both Eastbourne and Fulworth. Motor cars being scarce in that part of the country, we relied on a dog cart to take us the final few miles of our journey. By the end of the bouncy jaunt, I was quite pleased to see the spiralling smoke from Holmes's red-brick chimney and the winding path of noisy grey gravel that leads to his front door. Of his precious beehives we could see very little, for they were situated a good hundred yards beyond the house.

"Oh, Dr. Watson," Mrs. Hudson greeted me even before the door was fully open. "It's always a pleasure to see you again." Beneath her grey hair pulled back into a chignon, wrinkles creased that familiar face, but the twinkle in her eyes whenever I appeared always made me think she was recalling those exciting, earlier days in Baker Street—those days in which Holmes and I so often entertained colourful personages whom she never failed to scrutinise when bringing up the tea. Indeed, as she awaited the introduction of Mrs. Frevert, I saw those eager eyes taking in the handsome figure of the American woman before her. It was more than mere feminine approval, I thought, that was responsible for Mrs. Hudson's fulgent smile. It was the sense, so long lying dormant, that a case might yet be at hand, a case that—in addition to whatever else—might somehow transport us all back to a more youthful time.

Mrs. Hudson led us through Holmes's extensive library. I saw many a familiar tome of chemistry and law on the sagging shelves, not to mention the two unidentifiable books lying open on the leather desk chair or the tower of eight more volumes precariously perched at the edge of the low butler's table. Magazine cuttings on a desk already cluttered with pens, scattered papers replete with Holmes's precise handwriting, numerous Petri plates, and a half-dozen upright test tubes no doubt responsible for the malodorous smell of sulphur lingering in the air—all reassured me that, despite Mrs. Hudson's repeated attempts to curb Holmes of his incredible untidiness, he still remained unfettered. It was testimony to the loyalty of his housekeeper that for so many years she had continued picking up whatever his Bohemian nature would allow.

We followed Mrs. Hudson to a pair of open French windows at the rear of the cottage. Through the casements we could see four dramatic horizontal stripes: the cloudless, azure sky; the slate-blue sea highlighted intermittently with tiny white horses like frozen dollops of cream on a gelatinous dessert; the chalky white earth; and the broad green lawn directly behind the house into which the chalk melded.

Suddenly, as if making his entry on stage from the wings, Sherlock Holmes stepped into the scene. Except for the flecks of grey in the receding hair at his temples, he looked unchanged from his Baker Street days. It is true that he navigated more slowly and that on his perambulations he often carried a walking stick out of necessity rather than as a nod to any current fashion; but, tall and lean, he appeared ready to spring into action when so summoned. Holmes was robed in his favourite dressing gown, once royal purple now a faded mouse colour. In his left hand was a copy of the T.W. Cowan *British Bee-Keeper's Guide Book*, in his right, the graceful amber curve of a calabash. The latter was a recent gift of the American actor William Gillette, who, in his theatrical impersonation of Holmes, had found the large pipe a more dramatic prop than Holmes's smaller ones made of bentwood or clay. Although the colour of Holmes's amber-hued calabash had not yet metamorphosed into the more familiar henna, a thick halo of blue smoke wafting heavenward from the creamy meerschaum bowl suggested it soon would.

"My dear Watson!" Holmes exclaimed. "How good it is

to see you. And this must be Mrs. Frevert about whom you telegraphed." Setting the book on a nearby table and the pipe in a large, iridescent abalone shell which seemed set out for just such a purpose, Sherlock Holmes stepped forward to take her two hands in his. "May I say, Mrs. Frevert, how saddened I was to hear of your brother's death. On occasion, Dr. Watson and I would join him for a tankard of ale at the Royal Larder, his favourite public house. His death was a great loss to your family, of course, but perhaps an even greater loss, if I may be permitted to say so, to that brotherhood of modern knights errant who do their jousting with pens rather than with swords."

"Thank you, Mr. Holmes. You may indeed be permitted to bestow such compliments upon my brother. As I have told Dr. Watson, Graham had only the kindest words for you both. Such faith in his work from so valued a source means a great deal to me."

Holmes smiled in response. Then, while exchanging his dressing gown for a Norfolk jacket, he announced, "Mrs. Hudson has prepared a luncheon for us. Since the winds have subsided, she insists that we eat outside. Afterwards we will discuss the matter that has brought you here."

As the long journey to the Downs had awakened in both Mrs. Frevert and myself a hearty appetite, we immediately followed Holmes's lead through the open French windows. We proceeded to discover waiting for us on the terrace a wooden table, its rusticity softened by the white table covering upon which Mrs. Hudson had placed her dishes and silver. The salmon mayonnaise, cucumber salad, *petit pois à la française,* and champagne sorbet provided the perfect afternoon meal. Indeed, dining in such an idyllic setting with the sea stretching to the horizon, one could almost forget that the reason for our outing that day was to talk of murder; but just as the undulatory ocean looked calm only from a distance, and the thunder of the waves breaking not so far beneath us reminded one of its violent force, so the persiflage at the luncheon table belied the terrible seriousness of the thoughts that were roiling just below the surface of our spoken words.

Once Mrs. Hudson had cleared the table and Sherlock Holmes had filled the calabash with his favourite shag still kept in the Persian slipper, we all seemed ready to confront the business that had been hanging just above us.

"Pray, Mrs. Frevert," Holmes said, exhaling a cloud of sweet-smelling smoke, "tell us, if you would, what you think was wrong with the publicised account of your brother's death."

From the brocade black reticule that she kept on the floor by her side, Mrs. Frevert extracted her black lace fan and began fluttering it once more. "Thank you for the invitation, Mr. Holmes," she said. "Let me refresh your memory of that darkest of days. Much of what I know is, of course, from what I myself read in the newspapers or even from what the police have told me. And I imagine I should say at the start that I have little reason to contradict most of what they all have reported. It is rather with their conclusions that I am forced to differ."

Holmes nodded. "Please, go on," he said. At Baker Street he might have closed his eyes as he pulled on the pipe and took in the narrative. Here on the South Downs, however, he stared off at the hazy conjunction of sea and sky. The raucous crying of the terns and gulls overhead and the angry pounding of the surf far below were the only counterpoints to Mrs. Frevert's story.

"It's a bizarre tale, Mr. Holmes. Even though Graham was my

brother, it doesn't make me unable to see the strangeness of the events leading up to his death. I myself learned of the shooting while I was out shopping. I was selecting the bill of fare for our dinner that night when the butcher, who obviously had already heard the tragic story, said that I wouldn't be needing anything to eat at home that evening. I'm sure I didn't know what he meant at the time. And how he had gotten the news so quickly I never did discover."

"Quite," said Sherlock Holmes impatiently. "But what about the tragedy itself?"Mrs. Frevert returned to the black bag on the floor. This time she removed a handkerchief of Irish linen framed with delicate lace. She held it in the same hand with which she gripped the fan. No-one need have told us it was for the ineluctable tears that would accompany the most wrenching part of the story.

"My brother, Mr. Holmes," she said firmly, "received a telegram on the day of his death. It was addressed, as you might expect, to David Graham Phillips. It was dated January 23, 1911, and it read: 'This is your last day.' But here is the really strange part, Mr. Holmes—it was signed 'David Graham Phillips.'"

Both Sherlock Holmes and I had heard of this peculiarity before. If we had not, it surely would have aroused Holmes's curiosity more than it did on this occasion; for after first reading in *The Times* of the strange happenstance, he had observed with not a little admiration that a self-signed death threat delivered to the victim on the day of his murder was a plan demented enough to be worthy of the late Professor Moriarty himself. Today, however, he kept his judgements to himself.

"How did your brother react to the message?" Holmes asked simply.

"He took very little notice of it, I'm sure, Mr. Holmes. You see, ever since Graham had written those articles on the Senate back in 1906, the receipt of threatening letters and telegrams had become a way of life."

"*The Treason of the Senate* the series was titled, if I'm not mistaken," Holmes said.

"That's right," Mrs. Frevert replied. "I'm flattered that its title is familiar here in England."

"The topic is very much a part of *our* history too, Mrs. Frevert. The Tower of London is a grim reminder of our own bouts with treason, isn't that so, Watson?"

"Of course," I replied, but I confess in these pages that I recognised the title of Phillips's articles that day only because I remembered at the time of their publication that they were written by a friend–not because I had ever actually read them myself.

"At any rate," Mrs. Frevert continued, "Graham took little notice of these threats. He'd grown accustomed to such rubbish and had long since vowed not to let himself be vexed by messages of that kind or by the sick minds who composed them."

"But surely," Holmes said, "a telegram addressed *to* and signed *by* oneself is unique enough to cause even the most inured recipient to take some notice?" This last comment was more of a statement than a question.

"It was not the first of its kind, Mr. Holmes. Graham thought them the work of a crank. I have already learned that material only becomes evidence in retrospect–*after* the crime has been committed–however unspeakable the deed."

At the word "crime," Mrs. Frevert seemed to shudder. Clutching the white handkerchief and black fan more tightly, she intensified her waving.

"Graham left our apartment shortly after receiving the telegram. He was bound for the nearby Princeton Club in Gramercy Park where he picked up his mail. It was a cold day, and I can still see him walking out the door in his black hat and great raglan coat." Mrs. Frevert smiled. "It seems pointless now to recall that I was worrying he might not be warm enough."

"Yes," Holmes said quietly. His pipe having extinguished in the brief silence that followed, he extracted from his dressing-gown pocket a silver match container. It was the one I recalled him receiving as payment for his help in returning the abducted son of a London mortician and was fashioned to look like a skull. Holmes had always enjoyed the responses it provoked. In this instance, however, he concealed it in the palm of his hand as best he could. Striking a Vesta, he held the flame just above the pipe's bowl. Again, the smoke wafted upward.

"How was your brother travelling?" he asked when both he and his guest were ready to resume.

"Graham was on foot," Mrs. Frevert answered with renewed vigour. "He loved to walk whenever he got the chance. He thought it was good for his health."

"Ah, yes," Holmes observed. "The carriage is the vehicle of the rich, I believe he wrote. Stick to the pavement and you'll never lose touch with the masses."

"Exactly, Mr. Holmes. I see you are familiar with my brother's writing."

"I try to keep up with current trends, Mrs. Frevert," Holmes surprised me by saying. He tended to shun contemporary literature unless of the most sensational variety. Examining the latter provided him with a perspective altogether foreign to his nature. Of *belles lettres*, he had always been surprisingly ignorant; but, as he himself went on to explain, his retirement had enabled him to alter his reading habits. "Since I am rather isolated here in Sussex," Holmes said, "my idle moments have provided me with the opportunity to keep abreast of many a modern novelist. But, pray, continue."

"My brother started for the Princeton Club that horrible afternoon, but just before he reached his destination, that wretch Goldsborough–Fitzhugh Coyle Goldsborough–accosted Graham–shot him six times–and then immediately turned the gun on himself. Goldsborough was dressed like a vagrant; and Graham, poor soul, was about to offer him a coin. The police said that Goldsborough had stretched his arm out rigidly and fired in a circular manner to hit as many parts of Graham's body as possible. After he was wounded, Graham held himself up against the fence as best he could until he was carried into his club by some of its members. Finally, an ambulance took him to Bellevue Hospital. And would you believe that during that night his condition actually improved? But late the next evening he died."

If the tears were going to come, I expected them now, but despite the ever-ready square of linen, they did not flow. Like her brother the journalist, Mrs. Frevert reported–bravely–the story as she knew it, her only display of greater stress the tighter clenching of her white handkerchief. Unlike many others of the fair sex who in our old sitting room had told similarly heart-wrenching stories of grief, Mrs. Frevert did not require comforting. That she was neither frail nor fragile seemed to give greater credibility to her account.

"After he was shot, Mr. Holmes, he said, 'I could have beaten four bullets, but six were too many.'"

Holmes nodded, allowing the remark to register. Then he asked, "Did he say anything else?"

"Only that no-one should tell our mother, who was living in California at the time. Graham feared the news would kill her. That was Graham, always thinking about someone else–even when he was mortally wounded. And, do you know, she did die less than half a year after hearing of her son's murder?"

"A tragic story indeed, Mrs. Frevert," Sherlock Holmes said. Then, propping his pipe back in the abalone shell and placing the fingertips of both hands together, he looked at her with his hawklike eyes and proceeded to ask her the paramount question: "Since all these details are known to the police, why do you believe that there is any more to be examined?"

The sky was beginning to darken, a reminder that, if we were to catch the 5:15 train from Eastbourne back to London, we would have to leave the cottage shortly. But here was the crux of what had brought the determined Mrs. Frevert to see Sherlock Holmes in the first place. She was not about to squander the opportunity.

Awaiting her answer, Holmes leaned forward in his chair, chin now resting on his interlocking fingers.

"Some people might call it women's intuition, Mr. Holmes–"

Her response, obviously deemed meagre by Holmes, caused him to lean back with an audible sigh.

"–but," she continued, "I just cannot for the life of me ignore the numerous and, I might add, powerful enemies my brother had. Too many people in high places had threatened him–to his face or indirectly. He even reported them to the police."

"I'm sure that is the case, Mrs. Frevert, but I'm afraid it's hardly enough to dispute the official findings. If, as Watson informed me, you were seeking my advice, I fear I'm going to have to disappoint you. Now, as you have a train to catch–" Holmes rose and indicated with a sweep of his arm the direction back into the house.

Mrs. Frevert, too, stood up, fixing her eyes on my friend. "Mr. Holmes," she said, "do you take me for a fool? I didn't travel all the way from New York to tell you about intuition. What's more, I'd thank you to at least extend the courtesy of hearing me out."

Holmes's humble smile and nodding head, an attitude he seldom displayed–especially to a woman–righted the moment. "Pray be seated," he said softly, and they both resumed their chairs.

"There is also the question of the bullets," she announced triumphantly.

"Bullets?" I repeated.

"The number, I mean."

"He was shot six times," Holmes reminded us.

"Precisely!" Mrs. Frevert exclaimed. "All the reports agree. Six times! And then the assassin pointed the gun at his head, firing once."

"I see," Holmes said slowly. He appeared to possess some sense of the direction in which her argument was going. For my part, I must admit to having been a bit startled to hear a woman of Mrs. Frevert's refined nature speaking so intimately about firearms.

"Don't you understand, Mr. Holmes? That's seven shots! Fitzhugh Coyle Goldsborough, my brother's alleged lone assassin, carried a single revolver that held only six bullets."

One needn't have been Sherlock Holmes to see the anomaly once the facts were made known; but allowing himself a restrained smile, my friend got up, walked into his library, and returned a moment later with a small box full of as-yet unfiled newspaper cuttings. He rummaged through them for a moment until he found what he was looking for. "Allow me to read the following, Mrs. Frevert, from your own *New York Times* dated January 24, 1911:

"David Graham Phillips, the novelist, was shot six times yesterday afternoon by Fitzhugh Coyle Goldsborough. ... After sending six bullets into Mr. Phillips's chest, abdomen and limbs with a .32 calibre automatic revolver, Goldsborough put the weapon up to his own right temple and fired one of the four remaining bullets in the magazine, killing himself instantly."

"A ten-chamber, automatic revolver quite satisfactorily accounts for the six wounds to your brother and the assassin's suicide, I should expect."

"It would, Mr. Holmes, except for Algeron Lee, the witness who said Goldsborough had been firing a six-shooter."[*]

For a brief moment Holmes was speechless. Only the cries of the birds above seemed a commentary on Mrs. Frevert's assertion. "Even so, Mrs. Frevert," he said finally, "the number of bullets could have been miscounted. Perhaps the doctors weren't sure."

"They tracked the paths of all six bullets, Mr. Holmes. They were *quite* sure. And nearby witnesses confirmed there were six shots. As did the most authoritative witness of them all—my brother! Remember, he said that he could have beaten four bullets but that six were too many."

"An interesting theory, but merely hearsay," Holmes said.

"There is also the matter of Goldsborough's diary, Mr. Holmes.

---

[*] Author's note: For confirmation of Mrs. Frevert's argument, see Louis Filler, *Voice of the Democracy: A Critical Biography of David Graham Phillips* (University Park, PA: Pennsylvania State University Press, 1978), p. 201, chap. 13. n. 4.

The evidence that the police used to identify Goldsborough's motive came from his journal, a notebook that was found by some person on the street."

"Yes," Holmes said, "careless detective work. The journal presented the singular notion that Phillips was some kind of literary vampire sucking out Mr. Goldsborough's identity. Phillips was becoming Goldsborough or Goldsborough, Phillips. I forget which. Hence the peculiar telegram your brother received. A belief based on the melodramatic novel *The House of the Vampire* by one George Sylvestre Viereck, I think."

"You're absolutely correct, Mr. Holmes. And that diary, which was so conveniently found at the scene of the crime and in which all of this nonsense was discovered, was then handed over to an assistant district attorney who kept it the entire day of the murder. He held it so long that even the coroner was furious. What's more, Mr. Holmes, the diary was written in a crooked and shaky handwriting sprinkled with blots of ink. Those jottings could have been made by anyone."

This latest charge certainly seemed a possibility to me. It also seemed to have piqued the curiosity of Sherlock Holmes. Instead of replying immediately as he had been doing, he sat rapt in thought.

Sensing his vulnerability, Mrs. Frevert was quick to exploit her advantage. "Say you'll help me, Mr. Holmes. Graham was too courageous a man to allow his murder to be dismissed so casually. In point of fact, he ruined the careers of many a fraud and changed the course of American history. Oh, that Goldsborough shot my brother I have no doubt. But that he acted alone I cannot believe. At the very least I want to know who put him up to it. Who hired him? And that seventh bullet raises an obvious question: If Goldsborough shot himself with one of the six, and Graham was struck six times, who fired the seventh? Who was the other assassin? The authorities are no longer interested. Trust me, I've asked. The police have gotten their killer. Why should they reopen an investigation that I believe might implicate some prominent people after they've already closed the case? I've come to you, Mr. Holmes, with the hope of appealing to your regard for my brother to help clear up the mystery surrounding his death."

At last she was finished, and I knew my friend well enough to know that her importuning had reached him. Holmes leaned forward and took one of Mrs. Frevert's hands.

"My dear lady," he said, "I appreciate your intentions. And I sympathise with your desires. But, as I am sure my former colleague and ever-faithful friend Dr. Watson has told you, I am retired. Even if I wanted to help you, what could I do? For the past eight years I've done very little detecting—save for the most singular death of a neighbour. I'm too old. My most constant endeavours lately have been to solve whatever puzzles surround the tending of my apiary. Composing a monograph on the segregation of the queen bee has been consuming all of my time, certainly not the study of the criminal mind, and especially not the criminal mind in America. No, I must protest. I grant you the grounds for your concern, but I am not your man."

Holmes had voiced his reservations with an earnestness befitting the situation, but there was something about his manner—perhaps the way he continued to lean forward at the edge of his seat—not the position of one who was backing away—that suggested otherwise. Mrs. Frevert must have sensed his ambivalence as well. I do believe that had she accepted his words as he spoke them,

Holmes might have escaped his involvement in the case; but she did not and, therefore, I knew he could not refuse her.

"Mr. Holmes," she said, "I live quite comfortably, and in addition to your usual fees I will be more than happy to pay for your voyage to New York and for hotel accommodations while you are there."

"It is not the money, Mrs. Frevert," he replied. "In truth, I have always wanted to see New York. And yet–" Despite his trailing voice, I began to detect that keen energy in his spirit that always shone in his eyes when he was on the hunt. Mrs. Frevert must have seen it as well.

"For my brother," she pleaded.

"And the principles for which he stood," Holmes affirmed softly. "Very well, Mrs. Frevert," he said at last, "if you're satisfied with an old veteran like myself on unfamiliar terrain, I will accept your offer."

"Thank you! Thank you, Mr. Holmes!" She beamed. "When will you begin?"

Her electric enthusiasm contrasted with my own sense of melancholic exclusion. After all, I had brought her here, and I, too, wanted to see New York. In our younger years, I reminisced, Holmes would have–

"I'll need some time to get my things in order," he was saying, "but I shall remain in touch with Watson and–" A glance at my downcast face caused him to stop. "Why, Watson," he laughed, "you certainly don't expect me to work on my own!"

I was dumbfounded. I was not prepared to go to America however much I might desire it. To be sure, my practice on Queen Anne Street had been dwindling since I myself had begun considering retirement. I had in fact already sent a number of my patients round the corner to Dr. Larraby of Harley Street, a most reliable colleague, but I still had a few remaining to whom I owed some loyalty—and, of course, I was also married.

"You're right, Watson. I have no right to ask. Just as Mrs. Frevert should not have asked me. But this is no ordinary case. I share Mrs. Frevert's concern that some very important people may be involved, and thus I could use your tactful guidance, old fellow—that is, if Mrs. Watson could spare you for some weeks."

It was true that my wife had spoken to me of wanting to visit an elderly aunt who lived in Lincolnshire. Perhaps my absence would provide her with the perfect opportunity for such a trip; at the very least, I would encourage her to go. Holmes needed me, after all, and the invitation to America, which Mrs. Frevert had likewise extended to me, seemed very alluring indeed. I therefore offered Holmes tentative affirmation of my decision to join him.

Her preliminary business completed, Mrs. Frevert joined me in bidding *adieu* to Holmes and Mrs. Hudson, and together we mounted the dog cart that had reappeared some time earlier. It would return us to Fulworth from where we would retrace our path to Eastbourne and then back to London. The afternoon had grown darker, but I sensed that the American lady's effervescent appreciation of Holmes's willingness to help her could brighten the gloomiest of journeys.

After depositing Mrs. Frevert in her Kensington hotel, I returned wearily to Queen Anne Street. Numerous arrangements needed to be made, not the least of which was pacifying my wife. A journey by rail to the Midlands could not compare with a voyage to New York; but as she detested sea travel, I had little doubt that I would triumph in the end. Would that I could have been so certain about the outcome of the investigation into political assassination upon which we were about to embark—an investigation, I noted sardonically, that was beginning on the Ides of March, the anniversary of the sanguinary murder of Julius Caesar on the floor of the Roman Senate.

Three

FROM QUEEN ANNE TO GRAMERCY PARK

"When intelligence permeates the masses, then out of the action and reaction of the common and the conflicting interests of an ever-increasing multitude of intelligent men there must begin to issue a democratic self-government."

–David Graham Phillips, *The Reign of Gilt*

Mrs. Frevert began her return to New York by steamship the following day with the understanding that Holmes and I, since my wife had reluctantly but graciously consented to let me go, would join her across the Atlantic within a fortnight. Two days after Mrs. Frevert's departure, however, I received a letter by early post announcing a meeting that was destined to alter our plans. It was from Holmes, and it requested that I join him at the Diogenes Club that afternoon at 4:45. Such an invitation could mean but one thing: a rendezvous with Holmes's older brother Mycroft, a founding member of that institution that prided itself on offering refuge to those unsociable or diffident gentlemen seeking a temporary haven from the vicissitudes of daily life. Such a man indeed was the reclusive Mycroft Holmes, whose involvement with the inner workings of His Majesty's government was quite well known to me and, of course, to his brother, but to few others. Moreover, since (as I have noted in the tragic affair concerning the Greek interpreter) Mycroft only attended his club from a quarter to five till twenty to eight each evening, that his brother Sherlock and I had been summoned at the very start of his sojourn suggested a meeting of some consequence.

Unable to secure a cab at my door and with a concern for the time, I made my way on foot that rainy March afternoon to Regent Street, where I hailed a hansom to take me to Pall Mall in which the Diogenes Club was situated. The rain washing down the grey-stuccoed façade of the old building did nothing to render the cold interior any more inviting. Upon hearing my name at the great oaken door of the cavernous entry hall, the hall porter took my umbrella and mackintosh and pointed me in the direction of the Strangers' Room, the only chamber in the entire building in which talking was permitted. Fortunately, the distance to traverse was but a few yards, for the echoing footfalls I couldn't avoid making as I trod the black-and-white chequered tiles seemed to announce my presence to every niche of the sepulchral edifice. Only a minute late, I rapped lightly at the door and heard a familiar voice say, "Come in, Watson." At first glance, Sherlock Holmes and his brother Mycroft, who were both standing by a meagre fire in the grate, seemed as physically different as any two figures could be. Holmes was lean; Mycroft, quite stout. Despite his age, my friend looked wiry, agile; Mycroft, seven years his brother's senior, appeared lethargic, almost sluggish. It was only when one regarded the heads of the two, the erect and noble bearing, and then the keenness of the steely eyes, that one recognised the adumbrations of mental prowess that united the brothers. The analytical Sherlock himself said of his brother that, had Mycroft not been employed in God-only-knew-how-many machinations for the government, the elder Holmes could easily have outshone his brother as a mastermind in solving criminal puzzles. My friend, in fact, often consulted him on cases which Mycroft was happy to scrutinise as long as the latter was not required to leave the immediate environs of Whitehall.

On a small mahogany butler's table a glass of sherry awaited each of us, but Mycroft's coldness was not thawed by the wine's consumption. After a few halfhearted pleasantries, Holmes announced to me the change in our plans.

"Watson, it would appear that you will have to make the initial part of our trip to New York on your own," he said.

The rain pelting the lone window in the room punctuated his statement with finality. The intimidating thought of undertaking so great a journey and so major an investigation by myself was obviously reflected in my open-mouthed expression.

"Come, come, Watson. I'll be joining you as soon as I can. But after some brotherly prodding, Mycroft has presented me with information on the Phillips matter that cannot be ignored."

I looked at Mycroft who was now impassively leaning an elbow on the marble mantel.

"Mycroft," his younger brother cajoled, "be so good as to fill Watson in on the history of some of the principals in this story."

"Very well, Sherlock, although I have already told you that I believe the less mentioned of this affair the better."

Holmes nodded. "Please, begin," he said.

"This Goldsborough chap," Mycroft said in short bursts that made speaking seem like an exertion he preferred to avoid, "quite an interesting fellow, really. From a good Washington family. Father's a doctor. He himself was a musician. A violinist. Once played in the Pittsburgh Symphony. Quite a temper, I'm told. Broke his violin over the pate of someone who didn't like his poetry. For all Goldsborough's sins, one hopes that he might serve as a model as far as Sherlock and his own fiddle are concerned."

Since neither brother was laughing at this thrust, I allowed myself but the most trifling nod. I hoped it would be construed by both parties as indication of my following the conversation but not an endorsement in front of my old friend of his brother's musical criticism.

"Goldsborough had a sister," Mycroft continued. "Anne. Was engaged to be married at the time of Phillips's murder to an American in the foreign service here in England."

"You can be sure, Watson," Holmes interrupted, "that no-one connected with any government office who works on British soil goes unnoticed by my brother."

"If I may," Mycroft said, removing his arm from the mantel and standing up to his full height like a wounded soldier attempting to overcome his hurt, "the American in question, one William F. Stead, is attached to the American consulate in Nottingham. Unfortunately, both he and his new wife are somewhere on the continent at present–Rome, I believe–on consular business and are not expected to return before some time next week."

As the rain began to diminish, the more the darkness outside the window lessened, and the more superfluous seemed the dim glow in the fireplace. Nonetheless, message completed, Mycroft turned to the grate and held his hands before the dying red embers.

"I do believe, Watson," Holmes said, "that before we both go running off to America, I really ought to see if this American and his wife who are both so closely tied to one of the principals in the case have anything of interest to tell me."

I was forced to concur, of course, much as I didn't relish travelling to New York to begin the investigation on my own. Still, the charming Mrs. Frevert, who promised to be so very hospitable, would be waiting, and I could begin gathering information for Holmes as I had done so many times before.

Suddenly Mycroft turned from the fire to face me.

"Since you seem determined to get yourself implicated in my brother's rashness, Doctor," he said, "I feel compelled to tell you what I have already told him. Mrs. Frevert's point about the seventh bullet? Absolute poppycock. Typical fancy of an overactive female mind. I can understand my quixotic brother falling for that kind of nonsense, Dr. Watson, but I was counting on you, a man of science, to be more sensible. I had hoped of talking you both out of this fool's errand, but I see now that I was sadly mistaken."

Having finished speaking, Mycroft turned his back on us and resumed facing the grate, a position that Holmes and I rightly took as his announcement that our meeting had ended.

At least, by the time we left the Diogenes Club, the rain had disappeared.

Thanks to Mycroft's arranging my travelling papers, the preparations for the trip went smoothly. Within two days, I had been able to send my wife on a month's visit to Lincolnshire, refer all of my patients to Harley Street, provide the appropriate instructions to our maid Polly, and pack the various clothes and necessities I thought I would be needing on such an adventure, including my old Eley's No. 2. "Be sure to carry a pistol, Watson," Holmes had warned me. "You're going to America, after all."

Despite the distance of my impending voyage, our leave-taking was hardly a sentimental affair. Holmes gave me my instructions: to gather information on as many of the personages involved with Phillips's death as I could before his own arrival, which he estimated at about a week after mine. Just before my departure, however, he did offer me some final thoughts on the enormity of the crime we were about to scrutinise, and these he pronounced with the greatest degree of seriousness. "Murder is a monstrous act, Watson," he said, "but political assassination is more heinous still; in a political murder, not only is the victim destroyed, but also the aspirations of those whose ideals and dreams he champions."

With those words still reverberating in my mind, I found myself about to travel south for the second time in less than a week. On this occasion, however, my ultimate destination was not the southern coast of England but rather the eastern seaboard of the United States of America, a prospect that filled me with both excitement and trepidation.

The boat-train for Southampton left from Waterloo. This, the largest railway nexus in London, was in the throes of reconstruction. Over the first six platforms, workmen were toiling on a mammoth glass and steel roof that allowed a hazy morning sunshine to flood the hall.

Although many compartments in the first-class carriages were crowded, mine was occupied by only a solitary traveller, an ageing, bespectacled vicar whose balding head was fringed with grey. Reading a well-fingered Bible, he looked up as the warning whistle sounded, but returned to his text once the train had lurched into the start of its eighty-mile journey.

Rattling past shops and warehouses and later suburban gardens filled with crocuses and daffodils, we soon left London. Indeed, even before the slate-roofed houses of the city had given way to the thatched cottages of the countryside, the vicar had propped his reading glasses on his forehead, closed his eyes, and allowed the soporific swaying of our coach to lull him into a snore-filled sleep. I, however, entertaining images of New York City and the intrigue of a murder case rather than the fantasies conjured in some far-off dream-world, was too filled with anticipation to enjoy a similar repose.

We streaked past woods of fir that, as the train rumbled through the grassy knolls and dells of northwestern Surrey, were interrupted by clusters of spruce and birch and oak. Then, after skirting ice-blue lakes and reflecting pools with the Hog's Back in the distance, we started the climb through the tree-shrouded embankments beyond Basingstoke to our highest elevation.

Having completed my medical training at the large military hospital in the nearby village of Netley, I was familiar with much of the terrain. Consequently, after racing through Winchester and Eastleigh at seventy miles per hour, I recognised the downward sweep towards the coast. Soon we were traversing the distinctive chalk cuttings of the Hampshire Downs and then, parallel to the Itchen, approaching the fields of the coastal plains and the cottages at the outskirts of Southampton. Finally, at no more than a walking pace, we passed the imposing South Western Railway Hotel and crossed Canute Road. Only at the whining full stop of the carriages did the vicar, snorting gruffly, awaken.

Eager to disembark, however, I responded with only the quickest of smiles and, collecting my bowler, swung my scarf round my neck, nodded farewell to my still disoriented travelling companion who was rubbing the remains of sleep from his eyes, and stepped onto the platform. Trunk in tow thanks to the help of a porter, I made my way across the recently opened White Star Dock (renamed Ocean Dock in 1919) to R.M.S. *Majesty* looming in her berth just beyond the railway terminus.

Inside, I could feel my heart pumping excitedly; outside, against my raw cheeks, I could feel the cool March breeze blowing off the Solent. Above me in a sky turned grey towered the steamer's three black funnels, great clouds of dark smoke wafting heavenward from each. Blue Peter, the azure flag with a white square at its centre, hung from a forward yardarm indicating, so the porter advised, that the ship was ready for departure.

Within minutes after I had climbed the gangplank and made my way to C Deck, the tugboats took their positions, the ropes were thrown free, the siren wailed its final warning, and we began to move. The deck shuddered briefly; then, almost imperceptibly at first, the gap between ship and pier began to widen, and *Majesty* inched towards the entrance to the docks. At no-one in particular, I waved my bowler, joining in the camaraderie among the friends and relatives of other travellers standing on the quay blown about by the wind as they saw their loved ones off to America.

Soon we were steaming down Southampton Water, passing familiar Netley Hospital and various beaches, then slowing to turn to starboard around Calshot Spit, entering Thorn Channel, and next turning to port round a buoy to enter a deeper channel, past Egypt Point, past Cowes, past Spithead, and past the long pier at Ryde. Before we left the Isle of Wight behind us, the harbour pilot climbed from *Majesty* to a cutter, leaving us on our own to steam past Culver Cliff with only a single call at Cherbourg across the channel before we reached the open sea.

Since the purpose of my journey was so serious, I paid little attention to the first-class accommodations available to me. To be sure, had it not been for the slow rolling of the deck, I might easily have mistaken my berth for a room at the Savoy or the Cavendish. It was elegantly furnished in Jacobean decor and included a private bath. Panelled in oak, the social halls were even grander, especially the smoking lounge in whose leather chairs I enjoyed an occasional after-dinner cigar.

I had little desire for such amenities, however. Excluding my early-morning walks round the deck in the bracing cold and my encounters with the rowing machine in the ship's gymnasium, I spent most of my time familiarising myself with the mind of the man whose murder we were about to investigate. Holmes had furnished me with a modest library: two novels by David Graham Phillips, *The Cost* and *The Plum Tree*, as well as a collection of all the articles in *The Treason of the Senate*. Moreover, before beginning my literary adventure, I was to peruse the biography of Phillips that Holmes had tucked between the pages of *The Cost*. Written on a folded piece of yellowing foolscap in Holmes's meticulous script, this life of Phillips had been compiled by my friend once he had begun his index entry on the *Victoria–Camperdown* collision. He had revised it the first time after meeting Phillips in Baker

Street, but had not touched it again until after agreeing to help Mrs. Frevert investigate her brother's death. Varied shades of ink differentiated the three instalments of Phillips's history.

In summary, Phillips had been born in Madison, Indiana, on 31 October, the eve of All Hallows Day, in 1867. He had three older sisters, one of whom we had met, and a younger brother. Instructed by his father—a bank cashier, Sunday School teacher, and occasional substitute for the Methodist pastor—young Graham was reading the Bible before he was four. By the time he was ten, he had been tutored in Greek, Latin, Hebrew, and German; by the time he was twelve, he had read all of Hugo, Scott, and Dickens. In 1882 he attended Asbury University in Greencastle, Indiana, but spent his final two years of college life at Princeton. Following graduation, he was employed as a reporter first for the Cincinnati *Commercial Gazette*, then for the New York *Sun*, and finally for the New York World. From 1901 until his death in 1911, he wrote primarily novels, completing more than twenty, including the two-volume *Susan Lenox, Her Fall and Rise*, which was published some six years after he was killed.[*]

Enveloped in a steamer rug on a deck chair for the next few days, I immersed myself in the lives of the characters in *The Cost* and *The Plum Tree*, fictional inhabitants of the equally fictional St. Christopher, Indiana, a midwestern town much, I surmised, like Phillips's birthplace. No-one in reality, however, could be expected to equal the moral stature of the protagonist of these two novels, Hampden Scarborough. Elected Governor in *The Cost* and President in *The Plum Tree*, he countered the exploiters who preyed

---

[*] Author's note: In 1931 Susan Lenox was made into a movie starring Greta Garbo and Clark Gable.

upon the poor and helpless. With a handsome profile and piercing eyes, here was a powerful figure who must have embodied all that Phillips believed was good in the world. Exhibiting a pragmatic faith in man not as a "falling angel, but a rising animal," Scarborough traced his ancestry back to those anti-Royalists who served with Cromwell and who enabled their descendant to champion a new kind of royalty, "the kings of the new democracy." "Over him," Phillips had written, "was the glamour of the world-that-ought-to-be in which he lived and had the power to compel others to live as long as they were under the spell of his personality." Scarborough wore "the typical Western-American expression—shrewd, easy-going good humour." He revealed a "magnetic something which we try to fix—and fail—when we say 'charm.' What's more, like the sartorially elegant Phillips himself, this modern St. George, ready to engage the dragons of the plutocracy, was "dazzling to behold."

I confess to being moved by Scarborough's impressive and noble political victories, but these fictional exploits could not prepare me for the direct assault Phillips himself made on the real American government in *The Treason of the Senate*. Holmes was right to suggest that I familiarise myself with the articles that had ignited so much ire. Little did I suspect that, armed with my newly acquired righteousness from Hampden Scarborough, I could be so aroused by a six-year-old diatribe against a foreign institution; but as Phillips laid out his charges, the more indignant I became.

He had begun with a clarion call to arms: "Treason is a strong word, but not too strong, rather too weak, to characterise the situation in which the Senate is the eager, resourceful, indefatigable agent of interests as hostile to the American people as any invading army could be, and vastly more dangerous." In general terms, he referred to "the utter rottenness of the leaders of the Senate and the House" and to their "thievish legislation, preventing decent legislation, devising ways and means of making rottenest dishonesty look like patriotism."

Although such language appeared most vehement, even I was a sophisticated enough observer of the political stage to know that politicians allow their critics a voice as long as that voice does not become too personal. For their part, members of the press generally honour such a relationship in order to keep on a safe footing with representatives of the government who can furnish them with interesting stories and pregnant titbits of information. Phillips, therefore, must have surprised many a prominent figure with his complaints that the moneyed trusts had purchased control of the United States Senate and that the easily bought state legislatures should be replaced by the voting public as determiners of who should represent the people in that august body.

Since accusations of such a general nature are always being made by the discontented, I was greatly shocked at Phillips's personal attacks on specific members of the government. He called Senator Chauncey Depew of New York "the sly courtier-agent, with the greasy conscience and the greasy tongue and the greasy backbone and the greasy hinges of the knees." He described Millard Pankhurst Buchanan, the other New York senator, as an "in-law of the upper class whose marriage licence seemed instead a hunting permit that offered up the American people for sport." He said that Maryland's Arthur Pue Gorman had "absorbed and assimilated all the mysteries of the Senate—all its crafty, treacherous ways of smothering, of emasculating, of perverting legislation," while to Philander Chase Knox of Pennsylvania, Phillips wrote,

"America has meant, not the American people, but the men who exploit the labour and the capital of the American people of all classes, even of their own small class of the colossally rich." More than twenty senators received such treatment from Phillips. It was heady stuff, I thought, but was it grounds for murder?

As Phillips's writings had made eventful an otherwise uneventful voyage (if one's maiden journey to America can ever truly be regarded as uneventful), it seemed appropriate that I had imbued myself with Phillips's honest yet almost naive American voice; for when at last on that sunny afternoon I first saw the Statue of Liberty holding high her torch, I viewed that lamp as symbolising not only political freedom, but also the artistic freedom that had enabled this literary *provocateur* to criticise his own government. Indeed, that last day at sea, it was as if I were reading *The Treason of the Senate* not by sunlight at all but rather by the illuminating flame of that monument to freedom.

Soon, amid a great clatter of bells and sirens, the *Majesty* entered the Port of New York, released her families of immigrants to the customs authorities of Ellis Island, and with the help of a fleet of tugboats was pushed, cajoled, prodded, and coaxed up the Hudson River to berth just opposite, as my map revealed, the centre of Manhattan.

All large seaports, I should imagine, have much in common: the bustle of individuals on their own specific missions that, when taken in the aggregate, seem but a baffling hurly-burly: stevedores unloading cargoes of wooden crates and oversized tins and drums; porters pushing their precious loads of baggage to awaiting carriages and motor cars; passengers debarking into the arms of long-lost family. A babble of voices in diverse languages, a cacophony of whining engines and creaking steel–I could have been standing in Southampton or in Naples or in Marseilles–any great port city; but, in fact, I was in New York, and somehow I knew it felt different from being in those other places. There was an invigorating mixture of traffic, electricity, and excitement all presided over by those modern-day Babels of progress, architectural wonders that I could recognise myself from magazine illustrations I had seen in England: the sparkling Metropolitan Tower, the tallest building on earth (having just recently outclimbed the rival Singer), and the as-yet unfinished Woolworth, in the process of claiming the title for itself. Awed, bewildered, exhilarated–where else could I have been but in New York City, gateway to the New World?

Suddenly my eyes refocused. From the skyscrapers in the distance I turned my gaze to the throng before me and a hand-lettered sign about the size of a standard piece of writing paper. On it appeared my name. It was held by a well-dressed man in dark overcoat with astrakhan collar and cuffs and a black trilby. A few wrinkles suggested he must have been middle-aged, but his trim physique and rugged good looks belied his years. He was tall, had a sharp, angular jaw, and was sporting one of those high collars that Phillips himself had fancied so much. Indeed, he could have passed for the writer's brother.

"Dr. Watson?" he asked when I reached him. "Dr. John Watson?"

"Yes," I said, "I'm John Watson. But I'm afraid–"

"I'm Albert Beveridge, Doctor. *Senator* Albert Beveridge. *Former* senator, to be more accurate. But you can call me 'Bev.' I was Graham's closest friend, and Carolyn–that is, Mrs. Frevert–asked me to meet the *Majesty* personally and see that your were properly welcomed to New York. I travelled all the way from Indiana for the occasion. Mrs. Frevert decided to remain at home to oversee tonight's dinner. You *are* coming, of course. After all, I reckon you're the guest of honour."

Holmes, I knew, had sent a telegram to Mrs. Frevert with details of our change in plans and his decision to remain awhile longer in England, but that was no reason for the lady herself to be absent. Was I to interpret her failure to meet me as a lack of faith in Holmes's representative? And who was this former Senator Beveridge to take her place?

"I hope your trip was okay, Doctor," Beveridge went on. "I have a car waiting just down the walkway." Turning abruptly, he located a Negro porter in blue velveteen and issued him instructions. Despite the latter's greying hair and stooped shoulders, the man tipped his cap and proceeded to secure my baggage on a small wagon.

Followed by the porter who was steering my trunk, we elbowed our way through the crowds until we reached a great yellow motor car with a short, sombre young man in grey livery standing before it.

"This is my driver, Rollins," Beveridge said, "and this little machine," he added with obvious pride, "is a 1910 Packard 'Thirty.'"

Rollins nodded slightly, but his deep-set dark eyes and square jaw prevented any warmth from emanating. The great yellow motor car did not appeal to me. I make no apologies even now, many years after the advent of the automobile, of my preference for the horse and carriage. Perhaps less self-sufficient and more limited in range than contemporary self-propelled public transport, a hansom cab under the reins of the right driver could surpass any of today's horseless wonders. Besides, the drumbeat of hooves echoing down Baker Street on a dark, foggy night is for me the essence of London in the '90s, the scene of so many adventures I shared with Sherlock Holmes. Each of us, I think, adopts a comfortable and familiar era or place in which to plant ourselves; and from then on, that which disagrees with our memories–a new building here, a change in paint there–is forever jarring and anachronistic.

Breaking into my musings, Rollins barked at the porter, "George, put the trunk up top!"

As the older man struggled to tie the large box to the roof of the Packard, I said to Beveridge, "I've worked with Sherlock Holmes for more than twenty years, and yet I haven't the foggiest notion of how your man there deduced the name of the porter."

"Ah,"–Beveridge smiled–"You call all porters 'George'–after the ones who work in railroad stations. They're named for George Pullman, the man who invented the sleeping car."

I observed the old porter labouring under the gaze of the younger man. The former had seemed to wince when Rollins spoke. I thought it was owing to the chauffeur's tone, but now I realised it was the pejorative name. Not counting the ferocious pygmy who met his death that dark night on the Thames, the only Negro with whom I had any dealings was Steve Dixie, the bellicose boxer known as "Black Steve" of the old Spencer-John gang; no more threatening a ruffian would anyone care to meet. I had never before concerned myself with why a man of the coloured race might be so contentious; but after mere minutes on American soil, I seemed to be confronting the questions a mixed society raises.

"Get to know Rollins and the Packard, Doctor," Beveridge was saying, oblivious to my thoughts, "because I am going to make them available to you and Mr. Holmes. I'll be staying at my club on Vanderbilt Row, but Rollins will be waiting in front of your hotel whenever you need him; his aid should make your investigations run a lot smoother than if you have to depend on New York hacks."

Watching Rollins oversee the porter who was still bundling my trunk atop the automobile, I didn't need to be a detective of even an amateur variety to wonder for whom the chauffeur would be performing the greater service: for me and the start of our investigation or for Beveridge who now had in place a pair of eyes and ears that could record for his employer much that I, and later Holmes, might uncover. But such suspicions were easily eclipsed by more threatening concerns. After finally seating ourselves in the Packard, we rolled into the mainstream of motor traffic in that amazing cosmopolis—on the wrong side of the carriageway!

"Calm yourself, Doctor." Beveridge chuckled at my dismay. "You're forgetting that we drive on the opposite side of the street here in America. Believe me, with Rollins at the helm you have nothing to fear."

Before I could reply, the Packard abruptly halted with a short screech. We had barely escaped running into the vehicle in front of us.

In contrast to my own anxiety, Beveridge responded calmly, "You see, it's just as I told you, Rollins can drive with the best of them."

Trusting that Beveridge was correct and placing myself in the hands of Providence, I leaned back in the deep cushions and gazed out the window at the buildings standing tall in the waning sunlight. As much as I wanted to see the sights, however, Beveridge claimed my attention.

"Even on this side of the Atlantic, Doctor," he said, "we know of your exploits with Sherlock Holmes. Thanks to your own magnificent storytelling."

"They're not stories, you see—"

"Keep your shirt on, Doctor. No offence intended. I'm simply trying to make your acquaintance and explain how much I'm looking forward to meeting Sherlock Holmes."

I expected Beveridge to recount some adventure of Holmes that he particularly admired, but he suddenly became pensive and silent. After a minute or two and a deep breath, he said with resolve, "I'm fully prepared to help you get to the bottom of Graham's death, Doctor." He paused for another moment and then, to my amazement, began ticking off on his fingers a number of encounters he had planned for me: "Tonight at dinner, before we deposit you at your hotel, we'll see Carolyn and her husband. Tomorrow morning I've arranged a meeting for you with Senator Buchanan. On Saturday we're going to visit the former President of the United States in his home at Sagamore Hill, and on Monday we're travelling to Washington to meet some of my former colleagues in the Senate. I think that about covers it."

Despite his own enthusiasm, my suspicions were once more aroused. Who was this Beveridge to direct my enquiries? He'd already supplied me with a motor car and driver. At best, it was bad detective procedure to let a friend of the victim become too involved in an investigation; at worst, he might have his own sinister reasons for pointing me in certain directions or encumbering me with his chauffeur. Besides, I resented the idea of my interrogations being planned by an amateur like him.

"Just a moment," I said sharply. "Although I appreciate all your efforts, what made you decide that I would want to see those particular people?"

"Why, Mr. Holmes himself." Beveridge laughed. "In the telegram to Carolyn announcing his change in plans, he asked her to provide you with access to some of the principals in the sordid story. It was he, in fact, who proposed the trip to the Senate. I was the one who suggested Roosevelt, and Carolyn agreed. The president and Graham didn't get along well at the start, but later each came to respect the other. The point is that T.R. has a lot of insight into the minds of Washington people. If someone in Roosevelt's political circle wanted Graham removed, T.R. might offer us some leads."

I nodded, hoping to conceal my vexation. Holmes had, after all, given me an outline of what he wanted me to do—interview people close to Phillips but wait for the actual criminal investigation until he himself arrived. Now I was discovering that he didn't see fit even to allow me the privilege of choosing those I would interrogate. It was so typical of Holmes to send me across the ocean with no specific instructions only to find that behind my back he had arranged my itinerary in advance.

"If I may continue, Doctor," Beveridge said, "former Senator Buchanan was one of Graham's targets in *The Treason of the Senate.* He and his wife are leaving for England tomorrow afternoon, so we are fortunate to have the chance to see him at all. Most of the other senators you'll meet in Washington." Beveridge paused again and then, almost as an afterthought, added, "I sure hope that someone out of all those people can shed light on who really killed Graham."

Although the afternoon sun was fading quickly, I turned to study his face. "You doubt the official story too, then, Senator?" I asked. Somehow I could not call him "Bev." In fact, we were a funny pair: I could not utter his sobriquet; he, for some reason, would not speak my surname.

"I may have been defeated back in 1910, Doctor," he said, "but I'm still a politician. And, therefore, I'm always a bit sensitive about being too definitive too quickly. I'm used to keeping an open mind until all of the evidence is in." It wasn't so dark that I could not detect his broad smile or see his expression quickly turn serious again. "But Graham was my friend, you see, and I'd love to put my hands on the rats who had him killed. If there are any rats to catch, that is."

Street lamps framed our pathway as we travelled down a large thoroughfare. Night had fallen, but this city was anything but ready for sleep. "A beautiful sight," I murmured, and Beveridge nodded silently.

"Graham and I attended Asbury together," he said at last.

"Asbury University?" I asked, recalling the details in Holmes's biography of Phillips.

"In Greencastle, Indiana," Beveridge went on. "We're Hoosiers."

"Hoosiers?"

"People from Indiana," Beveridge explained. Then he told how Graham and he had befriended each other, how they used to philosophise about the strengths and weaknesses of man. As he talked, I continued staring at him: the handsome profile, the penetrating eyes, a man of strong opinions and quick responses, the political leader out to defend the weak. How had Phillips himself put it?–that "magnetic something which we try to fix– and fail–when we say 'charm.'" The "shrewd, easy-going good humor." It was, of course, Hampden Scarborough, the hero of Phillips's fiction, I was observing, and the mutual admiration that Beveridge described in their relationship merely underscored the point. Phillips had immortalised his friend in print, but Scarborough had gone on to become President while only Dame Fortune knew what was in store for the man sitting next to me.

At that moment the motor car made a turning into a smaller road.

"We're almost at Carolyn's apartment, Doctor," Beveridge said, "but before we get there, take a look out the window to your left."

I turned in the direction he had indicated; but because of the darkness and in spite of a few street lamps, all I could distinguish was some solitary trees and what looked like the railing of a long, high fence.

"Gramercy Park," Beveridge announced. "Where Graham was killed. The scene of the crime."

Four

DINNER WITH THE FREVERTS

"The first principle of a successful defense is complete frankness. Innocence that strives to conceal cannot loudly complain if it creates the impression of guilt."

–David Graham Phillips, *The Assassination of a Governor*

Although in her lodgings at 119 East Nineteenth Street, Mrs. Frevert looked much as she had in London, she seemed quite a different person; and despite my own fatigue following a week's travel, I knew my perceptions were not based simply on her cat. Still attired in her customary mourning, she had replaced her black lace fan with a white, long-haired feline. He was a large animal that must have weighed close to a stone, although to give him his due, much of his bulk was deceptive. The thick, rich coat with its collar-like mane contributed to his imposing image; but, in truth, if the cat had got drenched and his hair matted, I believe he would have looked a great deal more like a timid kitten than the leonine lord he appeared. Ruffle, for so he was named, spent much of his time in Mrs. Frevert's lap, and just as she had so animatedly waved her fan, she now stroked the cat. She began at the bridge of his nose and worked her way in one sinuous motion up between his eyes and then his ears, down his neck, over his back, and along the feathery tail that frequently curled like a question mark. Ruffle played no favourites, however. Walking slowly into whichever room people were inhabiting, he allowed himself to be picked up and stroked by anyone, eventually emitting a low purr which seemed to say that all was right with the world when all was not.

Mrs. Frevert still lived in the same flat she had shared with her brother in the wood-panelled, sky-lighted block known as the National Arts Club. The building, I learned later, is situated on part of the former estate of Samuel Tilden, the celebrated candidate for president in 1876 who received more votes than his opponent but, owing to some idiosyncrasy of the American political system, did not gain victory. Greeted by Mrs. Frevert and Ruffle at the door, Beveridge and I were directed immediately into a well-lit dining room where, already seated at one end of the long damask-covered table, was a fourth guest whom I correctly assumed to be Mrs. Frevert's husband. A quiet, retiring sort, incongruously dressed in a bright-green suit, he spoke very little at first, his drooping eyelids giving him an air of sadness that seemed to permeate his very being. Although he was balding, he directed whatever hair he could across his shining crown; and, as if to compensate for the bareness of his head, he sported a well-trimmed goatee on his chin.

"Dr. Watson, allow me to introduce you to my husband, Mr. Henry Frevert," our hostess said.

He was about to speak, but Mrs. Frevert continued, "Legally, we're still married even though Henry moved out some five years ago."

When Mr. Frevert rose, I could see that he was short. I extended my hand, which he shook meekly.

Mrs. Frevert let Ruffle leap to the floor, and we three joined her husband. The Freverts sat opposite each other, as did Beveridge and I. Hoping for morsels from our plates, Ruffle would slowly pad round the table, generally stopping and gazing up at whoever was talking. He liked the attention, electing to sit next to whichever of us was the cynosure at the moment.

We began our late-night repast with Norwegian anchovies and champagne, and that heady drink accompanied all of the courses. As the meal progressed, I continued noting the change in Mrs. Frevert. Where was the charming lady I had so admired in England? The dignified mourner I had met in my surgery seemed supplanted by a kind of harridan. What in Sussex had passed for commanding self-control, here in America—at least, in the presence of her husband—resulted in mere command. She directed him, spoke for him, even tried conducting his dinner for him.

"Finish your appetizer, Henry, so we can move on," she said.

"If you please, Carolyn," he said at last, "I've had enough. The anchovies are too salty."

"Oh, Henry, then why not have spoken up instead of accepting more? Honestly, Dr. Watson, if I've said it once, I've said it a thousand times: It's a good thing Henry wears loud clothes; otherwise, he'd never be heard." And at the joy in her well-worn pun, she allowed herself a girlish giggle.

Seeking to change the subject, I asked Mr. Frevert his occupation.

"Machines," his wife answered for him. "He does things with

machines—selling them and the like."

A silence descended, the men perhaps embarrassed by Mrs. Frevert's usurpation of her husband's authority. For some moments only the ring of silver on china could be heard as we ate our galantine of turkey. Then, as if drawing courage from Bacchus himself, Frevert drained his glass and cleared his throat. The white cat, who had been sitting next to his mistress with his paws tucked under his body, stood up, stretched to his full length, and ambled over to Frevert. As though this were his signal to speak, the little man said boldly, "So, Dr. Watson, you and Sherlock Holmes have come to believe in Carolyn's obsession!"

Uncertain if this last utterance was a declaration or a question that deserved an answer, I responded with a question of my own: "You, sir, I gather from the tone of your remark, do not?"

"Oh, Henry disagrees with me all the time, Dr. Watson," Mrs. Frevert explained. "He's not to be taken seriously."

Beveridge, who had remained quiet throughout the meal, exchanged glances with me. Ruffle looked at us both.

"Please, madam," Frevert said. "Permit me to speak for myself— at least on a matter so grave as this." Then, patting his lips with the white linen from his lap, he said succinctly, "Carolyn loved her brother so much that fuelling a conspiracy hypothesis is her personal way of keeping him alive."

I waited for more, but as he picked up his knife and fork and proceeded with his meal, I realised he had concluded his thoughts on the subject.

Beveridge, however, had not. With the arrival of a refreshingly American dessert of ice cream, apple pie, and coffee, he resumed the dubiety he had revealed earlier on the drive from the docks.

The cat, noting the change in speaker, strolled silently round the table to the senator's side and sat down next to him.

"Tell me, Doctor," Beveridge said after tasting his coffee, "just what *does* make you and Holmes believe in Carolyn's conspiracy theory?"

"Why, the seventh bullet, of course," I said. "Doesn't that fact trouble you?"

"Yes, Doctor, it does. But it can be explained away so obviously. Inaccurate witnesses, for example. After all, the police do have the ten-chambered murder weapon."

"The *putative* murder weapon," I corrected him.

"To be sure, Doctor, to be sure. But now that Graham is dead and buried–I'm sorry, Carolyn–we can never be certain about the precise number of bullets fired at him."

Was the senator backing away, I asked myself, from his earlier resolve to find out more about the mystery surrounding Phillips's death? Aloud, I enquired of him, "Then what makes *you* believe in Mrs. Frevert's story?"

"Doctor, I was a United States senator. I'm used to seeing powerful men at odds with one another. When I was younger, I worked on a farm. I had little money and had to make my own way. I guess you could call me a self-made man. I'm familiar with struggle, Doctor, and I believe that those who achieve success deserve to. The Law of the Jungle is also the law of the business world. Perhaps more surprising to those who are unfamiliar with it, the political arena is much the same. In politics, however, 'kill or be killed' is supposed to be figurative. But I tell you, Doctor, mention the name of David Graham Phillips on the Senate floor, and you will see murderous looks that are anything but figurative."

Not even Beveridge's boyish visage could contradict the

Machiavellian menace he was ascribing to the brethren of his own institution.

"*The Treason of the Senate* destroyed people, Doctor. Graham attacked over twenty members of our club, and for one reason or another some two-thirds of them are no longer in the Congress. There's even talk now of a Constitutional Amendment to allow the people at large to vote for their Senators rather than continuing to have our friendly state legislatures perform the honour. What's more, as much as I loved Graham, I realise he was working for Bill Hearst, who had his own eyes set on the New York State House and ultimately the presidency. Still does, for that matter. And as much as Graham liked to talk of patriotism and democracy, those *Treason* pieces were part of a cleverly constructed plan to provide a political platform for Hearst and to take out some of his rivals on the way. Oh, no, Doctor, one doesn't need an extra bullet to smell foul play; one need only look at the ugly faces of vengeful senators to comprehend that Graham's death could have been arranged by others. Your famous Shakespeare readily understood the compulsion to commit murder–if not for one's own survival, then for the benefit of the state. Remember Brutus."

Yet another reference to the murdered Caesar, I thought. Beveridge raised his coffee cup again as if to signal the end of his explanation. When he finished speaking, he narrowed his eyes, but I wasn't sure if this last had been caused by steam from the hot coffee or whether it was more like the focusing glare of the predator on the hunt. I had read enough of Phillips's fiction to know that, although he had written about political heroes like Hampden Scarborough, he had written about political killers as well; and both characterisations were sculpted from the people he had met in reality–people like Albert Beveridge and his theories about the Survival of the Fittest.

Once we had all finished our coffees, Mrs. Frevert rose, invited us to remain seated for postprandial cigars and port, swooped up Ruffle, and left the room. As much as I longed for the friendliness of a bed–even a hotel-room bed–I recognised that I had promised Holmes to find out as much as I could about these people. Thus, I postponed my departure a trifle longer. With the strong-willed Mrs. Frevert out of our presence, I could at least expect to learn more from her husband. I was well aware that the man whose tongue might be silenced by a domineering woman might have it loosened quickly with the help of a seductive liquor.

We each clipped a cigar that Mrs. Frevert had kindly provided and partook of the port. I wanted to keep my wits clear but knew that I would have to appear a willing drinking partner to create the camaraderie that would encourage revelation.

Beveridge leaned back in his chair and, forming his mouth into a tiny O, puffed a circular cloud of white cigar smoke over the table. Then, like a satisfied author completing a well-wrought sentence with a flourishing exclamation mark, he punctuated his effort by driving a remaining blast of smoke through the centre of the evanescent ring. From the casual manner in which he enjoyed his tobacco, it was clear that Beveridge had said all that he cared to for that evening on the subject of Phillips's demise. It was equally clear from the way Frevert would stare into his crystal snifter and then glance in my direction that he had not.

"Mr. Frevert," I encouraged, "I sense that you wish to say more than you have."

He looked up at me and then at Beveridge. "It's not easy for me to talk in front of Carolyn," he said. "Bev knows. She simply overpowers me. That's why I couldn't speak out against her brother's coming to live with us—first back in Cincinnati and then here in New York. Twelve years on and off the three of us were living together. Then finally I couldn't take it any more." Here he slapped the open palm of his hand down onto the table; a moment later he was carefully straightening the resultant ripple in the white cloth. "I never did know just what was going on between the two of them—if you know what I mean—but I had my suspicions."

Sherlock Holmes might have pretended not to be shocked by Mr. Frevert's innuendo, but I was not so competent an actor. I could not—*would* not—allow him to utter such an insinuation uncontested. I put down my glass and demanded an instant apology. "Mr. Frevert, how can you impugn the reputation of your gracious wife? Not to mention a dead man who can no longer defend his honour! And in front of Senator Beveridge!"

Frevert's droopy eyes opened wide at my outburst, but almost immediately they resumed their previous attitude. "I had no intention of shocking you, Dr. Watson, but you must understand that my wife and her brother were very, very close. Bev knows. Ask their sister Eva. She thought that Carolyn was keeping Graham from the rest of the family on purpose. They seldom made it to family gatherings, and till the day he died they were hardly ever apart. Even when they *were* separated, they corresponded daily. Why, they dressed up for dinner every night!"

"There's nothing outrageous about dressing for dinner," I maintained.

Frevert took another sip of his port as if to fortify himself. "Maybe not," he said, "but when brother and sister are drinking champagne every evening and then remaining together all the night, I think there's something terribly wrong."

During Frevert's and my entire exchange, Beveridge sat smoking his cigar. No doubt he had heard it all before.

"Oh, come, sir," I said, "I'm sure there's a plausible explanation."

"Of course. Of course. He was writing all night, they said, and she was sorting and arranging his files. Perfectly natural, they said."

"You disagree?"

"All I can tell you, Dr. Watson, is that I finally had to leave. We hadn't been living together as man and wife for quite a while anyway."

But a few hours ago I didn't know this man, and now I was learning his most intimate secrets.

"You'd never see Graham with a girl. Oh, he'd escort some pretty young lady to a fashionable *soirée* every so often—or take along his sister. But he was never really interested in the fairer sex. You're a doctor; you know what I mean."

Although neither homosexuality nor incest have ever elicited the tiniest intellectual curiosity on my part, I confess in these pages that I did know exactly what he meant.

"When they were young," he resumed, "Carolyn's mother didn't let Graham play with any other children for the longest time—and then finally she would only let him play with girls. Dr. Watson," he said, looking me in the eye, "we're men of the world. We understand such things."

"Maybe so, Mr. Frevert," I said rising from my seat, "but whatever one may understand does not require one to draw the sordid conclusions that you are suggesting."

I turned to Beveridge, who was in the act of putting out his cigar. It was obvious to him, as I hoped it was obvious to Mr.

Frevert, that our interview had ended and that I was quite ready to go to my hotel.

Frevert, however, would not be denied. He rose and caught my arm. Positioning himself very close to me, he said with a hushed voice, "Perhaps, as you say, Doctor, we don't know anything for sure. But I'll tell you this, as Beveridge there is my witness, that woman so loved her brother that if he ever seriously looked at another woman, why, I think Carolyn might have committed murder herself to prevent someone else–anyone else–from possessing him."

With that, he sat down, obviously talked out.

Indeed, we were all tired. Thus, with Frevert's charges still reverberating, Beveridge and I excused ourselves, bade good night to our hostess and her remaining guest, and left for the hotel.

So sleepy was I and inattentive to my surroundings that I scarcely appreciated the largesse of Mrs. Frevert, who had obviously spared no expense in securing rooms for Holmes and me. As my head hit the pillow, however, I was contemplating neither the immense room in which I was lodged nor the testered bed in which I was now ensconced, but rather the initial peculiarities I had discovered in a case containing much that was not as it appeared: a provocative woman who seemed so different at home, a youthful senator who seemed to possess the cynicism of older men, a quiet husband who had so much to say. What had Holmes once observed about the deadly souls who practised deception? They were like the purring cat when he sees prospective mice.

When I began contemplating the fluffed-up Ruffle so thin underneath his snow-white fur, I knew that I was in desperate need of rest.

Five

POLITICAL PERSONAGES

"As the world knows, the eternal verities are kept alive solely by the hypocrites who preach and profess them."

—David Graham Phillips, *Light-Fingered Gentry*

When Mrs. Frevert said that she would take care of our accommodations, the Waldorf-Astoria, like the R.M.S. *Majesty*, was certainly more than I had anticipated.* Rubbing elbows with "nobs," as the local aristocrats were known, was not beyond the purview of Holmes's investigations. Indeed, on more than one occasion he had come to the aid of members

---

* Author's note: Watson is, of course, referring to the first Waldorf-Astoria Hotel whose demolition began on October 1, 1929, in order to free the site for the construction of the Empire State Building. In yet another of the many ironies connected with this narrative, the engine of Lieutenant Colonel William Smith's airplane, which had crashed into the Empire State Building on a foggy morning in the summer of 1945, careened across Thirty-third Street and into the art studio of Henry Hering, a sculptor then at work on a bust of David Graham Phillips. Not only was the sculpture destroyed, but so were almost all of the existing photographs of Phillips from which Hering was working.

of some royal family or another, but sharing their way of life was a different matter. With servants available at the touch of a button and marble pillars and satin wall-hangings providing the backdrop, one might envisage oneself residing at a palace instead of a hotel. Nonetheless, amidst all the splendour, I was able to locate and bolt down a simple breakfast of rashers and eggs in the Men's Cafe. Not for me the posh Palm Garden restaurant, separated from the Cafe by only a glass wall, or the celebrated Peacock Alley, the lengthy corridor leading to the Garden, from whose cushioned chairs beneath whirling ceiling fans people could gawp at the affluent or renowned characters who frequented the sumptuous hostelry.

After hurrying down the tessellated walkway and through the grand doors swung wide by a commissionaire in a long burgundy coat and matching flat, short-billed military-style hat, I found Rollins and the Packard waiting on Fifth Avenue between Thirty-third and Thirty-fourth streets where the night before he had requested that I meet him. At the very least, he was dependable. Blocking a service entrance, the motor car was no doubt stationed illegally; but, as Rollins put it with the utmost grimness in those dark eyes, "When your boss used to be a U.S. senator, the coppers usually look the other way." What other perquisites accompanied the role of legislator? I wondered.

I must confess, however, that the true wonderment percolating within me centred not on Beveridge's activities or even on my upcoming interview with the former New York Senator Millard Pankhurst Buchanan but rather on my trip the following day to Sagamore Hill, a journey that at least for the next hour I had to put out of my mind. Despite the fact that tomorrow I would be travelling with Beveridge to visit a former president of the United States, I had to remind myself that my primary concern was still this morning's stop in Columbus Circle at the New York *American* building.

Beveridge had secured an appointment for me with Buchanan, one of the men vilified by Phillips for the senator's close ties with the railroad trust and his ruthless handling of those who opposed his financial dealings. After being denied re-nomination by the Democratic party, so Beveridge had explained, Buchanan had gone to work in offices at the *American* as a political adviser to William Randolph Hearst, its owner, who, despite some earlier electoral failures, still coveted the presidency. Since Hearst was responsible for hiring Phillips to write *The Treason of the Senate* in the first place, it was ironic—to say the least—to discover Buchanan employed by the architect of the latter's own downfall. That peculiarity was but one of many questions Holmes would want me to ask the senator.

Bequeathing to Rollins the job of finding a place to leave the motor car, I entered a building very much like the newspaper establishments of Fleet Street. Surrounded by the insect-like chatter of countless typewriting machines, I made my way through a maze of corridors and lifts to the office of the senator's secretary, a young man with receding dark hair, who, according to the sign in front of him, was named "Mr. Altamont." Rising to great me, he revealed a commanding height and wiry physique that put me in mind of the young Sherlock Holmes.

"Dr. Watson," he said rather coolly after I had introduced myself, "the senator is waiting for you, but he asked me to warn you in advance that he is on a very limited schedule. He sails this afternoon for England and is only in the office at all to conclude a few final matters before he leaves. In short, he doesn't have a great deal of time."

I nodded and followed. Passing through an imposing oak doorway above which hung a single, rather weatherbeaten horseshoe, curved toe downward, we entered a large, dark, wood-panelled chamber with fixtures of brass and furniture of leather. One wall of the room from floor to ceiling was devoted to shelves full of uniformly bound, blond-leather law books. So high did these shelves climb that to the left of the wall's centre stood a ladder attached to a brass rail just below the ceiling. The senator occupied a massive red-leather chair behind a partner's desk with ormolu fittings. He was a tall, bulky man with a leonine head of white hair. That the white mane curled so dramatically upward at the nape of his neck put me in mind once again of Ruffle the cat and his interrogative tail. Happily, however, the senator was much more communicative. Indeed, if the instructions for Altamont had been to act abrupt with me, there was nothing in his own attitude to suggest it.

"Dr. Watson," he said warmly, offering me a firm hand to shake and an unfaltering gaze to regard. Were I more of a cynic, I would surmise that he had mastered that strong greeting at a school of acting. Let it suffice to say that his studied sincerity put me in mind of the great Henry Irving. Holmes used to compliment my insights into people's characters. Cutting through the layers of Buchanan's political posturing was going to present a challenge.

The senator motioned for me to sit, and I took the place opposite him at the partner's desk. Clasping my hands together in the same way he did, I felt very much like his mirror image.

"You see, Doctor," he said, trying to establish the perimeters of the conversation without losing his friendly touch, "as I trust Mr. Altamont has explained, my wife and I are leaving for England this afternoon, so I don't have much time to dally here at the office. In fact, the only reason I agreed to your little visit when I heard what you wanted was to see this matter laid to rest once and for all. That damned Phillips cost me my senate seat! His scurrilous lies depicted me as some dupe of the exploiters of the people. Anarchist drivel! Why, I come *from* the people! I used to be a farm boy upstate myself. I get angry all over again thinking about the hell Phillips caused me."

It was clear that the longer Senator Buchanan talked about Phillips, the more emotional he became. His face had begun to take on a florid hue when Altamont knocked gently on the door. This interruption allowed Buchanan the opportunity to collect his thoughts.

"Come in," he said, and Altamont entered, followed by a tall but unimposing man with brown hair, close-set blue-grey eyes, and wearing a green-chequered suit. Until the secretary mentioned the man's name, I never would have taken him for the authoritative monarch he was.

"Senator Buchanan," Altamont said, "Mr. Hearst asked if he might be allowed to attend your meeting with Dr. Watson."

"Why, Bill, come on in," Buchanan said, introducing me to the famous publisher. Hearst seated himself in the chair by my side and neatly folded his hands in his lap.

"Dr. Watson," he said, "it's a pleasure to meet you. I've read every word you've written about Sherlock Holmes. Your plots are so clever that some people don't even believe he's real and ascribe his genius to you. That's quite a compliment to your writing. If you ever want to work for an American newspaper, you can count on getting a job right here. You could help sell a lot of copy."

I thanked him for his generosity and for one brief moment—the briefest of moments—wondered how it might be to live in New York. To be sure, Hearst had distracted me, but his presence had also lightened the atmosphere in the office. Even the senator seemed to feel more jovial.

"Have a cigar," Buchanan offered. Obviously, the appearance of his employer, despite their Christian-name relationship, slowed the senator's plans for an early departure. In fact, he was the only taker of his own offer. After cutting the end with a brass clipper that was hanging from a fob at his waistcoat, he lit a panatella. Hearst pocketed his, and I refused altogether.

"You're not a cigarette smoker, are you, Doctor?" Buchanan asked between deep draws of the tobacco.

"No," I replied, "it's just a bit early in the morning for me."

He nodded, apparently approving of my answer. "Phillips smoked cigarettes, you know. Never could get him to smoke like a man."

"Now, Millard," Hearst said, "times are changing. You can't keep holding on to your old-fashioned ideas. Phillips may have had some peculiar habits, but there's nothing unmanly about smoking cigarettes."

"Which raises an interesting question, gentlemen," I interjected, having found an opportunity to ask one of the queries that troubled me. "If you feel so strongly about Phillips, Senator Buchanan, why work for Mr. Hearst? In fact, shouldn't your quarrel really be with him and not with Phillips, who was just carrying out Mr. Hearst's request in attacking the Senate?"

Buchanan coughed, a loose, ropey cough which warned me, as a physician, that cigars were probably not his best medicine. "Why, I don't hold the chief responsible," he said. "Bill was just doin' what was necessary to try to get elected governor. I know that. Why, you might accuse somebody of wantin' to kill Bill Hearst here instead of just stoppin' with Phillips."

It was obvious that the nearer the senator came to talking about Phillips's death, the more his language lapsed into its familiar roots. Dropping his *g*'s was emblematic of how Buchanan's formal speech began to revert to the drawl of the impoverished background that Phillips had highlighted in illuminating the senator's rise from rural poverty to political power. According to Phillips, it was not a noble climb, and it included an expedient marriage.

"I beg your pardon," I said. "I didn't intend to accuse anyone of anything."

A silence ensued during which I watched the smoke of Buchanan's cigar hang in the thick air. Suddenly, the long ash at the end fell on to his desk, landing on a piece of paper. A moment later, a lick of yellow flame shot upward.

"Quick, Doctor!" the senator barked, as he tried to pat out the fire with his naked palm. "Water! On the shelf behind you."

I turned to see a jug of drinking water on a shelf just beyond the ladder to my left. I sprang to get it, leaning under the ladder to do so.

"Stop!" Buchanan bellowed. "Are you mad? Walking under a ladder?"

I sidestepped the ladder in question, fetched the water, and poured enough on the offending flame to extinguish it. Only then did I notice that Hearst had been sitting calmly during the entire episode. Indeed, he had not even unclasped his hands.

Buchanan was extinguishing the cigar as Hearst explained, "Mill may know his politics, Doctor, but like Phillips he has his oddities. The man is a superstitious rube."

"The horseshoe above the door?" I recalled.

"Exactly," Buchanan said, "open end up to prevent the luck from pouring out."

"Would you believe," Hearst said, "that he made me cancel a political speech two weeks ago just because it was scheduled to be given on Friday the thirteenth?"

Buchanan laid several sheets of blank paper over the puddle of water forming on his desk. Hearst chuckled, despite the smell of burnt paper lingering in the room. Then, becoming more serious, he returned to the subject at hand. "Phillips didn't want the *Treason* assignment to begin with. That's what's so funny about all this. He wanted someone else for the job. Said he was a novelist, not a journalist any more, when I asked him to take it on. If you want my opinion, it was his sister talking. Phillips said he couldn't be bothered. 'Get William Allen White to do it,' he said. I said, 'Name your price.' Phillips was that good. He said, 'You couldn't afford to pay me what I want.' 'Try me,' I said. And he did–although I think he was bluffing just to avoid the assignment. Still, I met his offer, and the rest is history. But, you know, I think that for the remainder of his life, he couldn't rid himself of the idea that he had written those articles to make a small fortune."

"Wrote lies, you mean," added Buchanan.

"Oh, he exaggerated a bit," Hearst agreed, "but name me one

good newspaperman who doesn't."

I was well aware of Mr. Hearst's views on what constituted responsible journalism. The sensationalist "yellow" press, which many people have come to regard as the true cause of America's war in Cuba with Spain, was generally believed to have been sired by the man sitting next to me. Indeed, by some he was known as "The Yellow Kid."

"Occasionally," Hearst added, "even I had to step in and tone down some of Phillips's charges. But in the main, they were accurate; our lawyers were always looking over his shoulder. And if the body politic forced Mr. Buchanan here to step down, why then, who am I to disagree? At the same time, I recognise his talents and political acumen. 'One man's meat is another man's poison,' I believe the saying goes. He might be through in the Senate, but that doesn't mean if I want to be president I still can't profit from the services of a good Democrat. Hell, I pay him enough. Every man has his price. In that way, I guess Millard here is just like Phillips." The explosion was the clamour of Buchanan's large chair falling over as he jumped to his feet.

"You've gone too far, Bill!" he shouted. "Don't go comparin' me to that good-for-nothin' nance!"

"Offer Dr. Watson a drink, Mill," Hearst said calmly. "And have one yourself." Buchanan righted his chair and then, opening a drawer on his side of the desk, produced a silver flask and three small cut-crystal glasses. Without saying a word, he poured an inch of the brown-coloured spirits into each glass; nodded at both Hearst and me; and then, tossing his head back, drank the entire contents of his glass in a single gulp.

Hearst imitated his example although I must confess that I was considerably more restrained.

When we had finished our potation, Buchanan said, "Bill, with your permission, although I'd like to continue this discussion, I do have to go. That ship won't wait."

"I know," Hearst said. "You've got to go to England to buy some more books."

"First editions," Buchanan corrected. "In Charing Cross Road," he explained to me as if his employer were beyond such knowledge.

Hearst chuckled. "I go to Europe and buy roomfuls of antiques; I guess *you* have more self-control."

"Pay me your income and see how much self-control I have," Buchanan replied, and both men broke into laughter.

As the interview had obviously reached its conclusion, I stood up and shook hands with both of them. Mr. Altamont directed me out of the building, and I soon emerged in the city's traffic to see where Rollins had moored the Packard. As I ambled, I thought again of Hearst's offer of employment. I looked at the mammoth edifices surrounding me, listened to the roar of afternoon motor cars that were so much noisier than their horse-drawn relatives. Would I really want to live here, I wondered, a stranger in a foreign land? Americans might think we shared a common language, but those of us who enjoy the precision of accurate expression can quite justifiably disagree. Besides, although I was indeed closing down my surgery, I was still a doctor. Could I find a home in American medicine? Could I enjoy my retirement in a place of so much bustle? And most importantly, could my ever-tolerant wife adjust to the fast pace of living that was so different from the domestic tranquillity of our red-brick home in Queen Anne

Street? To all of my questions, I found myself happily responding in the negative.

As it was never too soon to begin preparing the notes I would give to Holmes upon his arrival, I asked Rollins to recommend a quiet locale where I might review the information I had so far acquired. His choice, a small white bench not far from a reflecting pond in Central Park, was ideal. Just the opposite of the busy thoroughfares, the vast sprawl of lawn offered a serenity I would not have thought possible to find but a few minutes before. Like Londoners, New Yorkers seem to enjoy their parks, and it was refreshing to view children of all ages playing gaily in the distance.

I told Rollins to return for me in two hours' time and, after taking out notebook and pencil, sat down to begin my contemplations. The chauffeur, however, hadn't moved.

"In two hours' time," I repeated, but his surly expression indicated he was not about to leave.

"Senator Beveridge wants me to watch out for you," he said. "To be sure nothing happens to you."

"My man," I said, "what can possibly happen in the middle of these delightful grounds?"

Still he remained stoic.

Finally, we compromised. Rollins agreed to stand off in the distance to my right, close enough to keep watch, but far enough away not to disturb my thoughts or—for that matter—to oversee my notations. In fact, I was interrupted only once. A curious Alsatian lumbered up to sniff my bench, but I quickly sent him on his way.

Although I had detected nothing of a criminal nature after a day in New York, I had certainly found it evident that there was an abundance of persons who didn't much care for Mr. David

Graham Phillips; but did distaste lead to murder, I wondered, and if so, how did such a plan involve the now-deceased assassin, Fitzhugh Coyle Goldsborough?

I wrote in my notebook the first name to be considered. Frevert, it seemed to me, offered the greatest case for revenge in that Phillips had supplanted him as his wife's companion; but that triangular affair had been an issue years ago, and nothing lately appeared to have arisen that would have exacerbated Frevert's rage.

Buchanan, whose name I copied down next, was also a prime suspect. He obviously felt that Phillips had libelled him directly and had indirectly cost him his Senate seat; but the *Treason* articles were some five years old when Phillips was killed, and it hardly seemed plausible that Buchanan would plan a murder taking half a decade to perpetrate.

Even less plausible to me was Frevert's suggestion that his wife might be driven to jealousy by anyone or anything that could deprive her of her position of closeness with her brother—unless, of course, her brother was involved with persons unknown or activities unnamed that aroused in Mrs. Frevert some level of passion resulting in murder; but then it was Mrs. Frevert who had come to Holmes and me in the first place. Why would she have wanted to open an investigation that already had been closed by the police if the results of that new investigation might implicate her?

I could also not forget Beveridge, Phillips's old friend. Despite the suspicious behaviour of his chauffeur, who was still observing me from his post beneath a great tree some hundred feet away, I saw no reason whatsoever for suspecting the former senator. And yet there was such a jarring inconsistency between his outward insouciance and the nefarious secrecy he seemed so eager to attribute to his colleagues. When Beveridge described that ugly world just below the surface of reality, was he in fact describing his own divided self?

It was an interesting question to ponder, and so I glanced up—as people are wont to do when undertaking contemplative activities—and noted a quick movement at the bench about seventy-five feet down the footpath to my left. A bearded man in a dark suit appeared to be reading a book. I say "appeared" because in point of fact I believe he had been staring at me while I was engaged in writing, and only my abrupt change of position caused him to regard his own text so closely; but as he was holding the book in front of his face as well as sitting too far away, I could not get a really good look at him. Besides, I wasn't completely convinced of my suspicions in the first place.

Putting him out of my mind, therefore, I returned to my previous thoughts. In my notebook I completed the list of the four names I had been considering earlier and placed pluses after Frevert's and Buchanan's to represent my suspicions—however meagre. After Mrs. Frevert's and Beveridge's I marked minuses. Then I went back to each name and scrawled a question mark next to it. That symbol, I believed, best conveyed my thoughts about guilt. Hearst, I might add, seemed so far removed from the incident that I didn't think his name warranted noting at all. Why would a man of his prominence have any reason in the world to want Phillips out of the way? And yet, he did hire Buchanan, who felt just the opposite.

I also had to remember that Holmes was not only interested in criminal motivation. He wanted the sense of what a victim was like, of how a victim affected people around him; and that information, Holmes used to say, was what I was so valuable in collecting. On the few occasions that he complimented me, it was my selective powers he generally chose to praise, my sense of what was important. That he also accused me of seeing but failing to observe was why he had insisted on delaying any investigation of the murder scene or of actual witnesses until he could interrogate them himself. That I always seemed to acquiesce did not denote that I necessarily agreed; but because it was our way, I would continue to perform what I believe the American constabulary calls "legwork."

Once I signalled Rollins that I was ready to return to the hotel, I pocketed my notebook with care. Indeed, I looked twice at the ground beneath the seat upon which I had been resting to be certain nothing had fallen from my jacket. I had almost forgotten the mysterious stranger down the road. When I looked to see if he was still there, I saw only an empty bench.

Throughout my writings about the exploits of Sherlock Holmes—indeed, in these very pages—I have frequently resorted to the benefits of metaphor to emphasise the similarities between the detective's search for wrongdoers and the predator's quest for game. Implied in these parallel views of sleuth and hunter is a similarity of nerve, skill, perseverance, and intelligence. I had always regarded myself and Holmes as hunters. After all, had we not rid the world of that ferocious hound in the Grimpen Mire in Devonshire or that savage Andaman Islander and his poisoned darts or the deadly swamp adder trained by a mad doctor? Such temptations of fate were part of our job, however—professional responsibilities, not dramatic confrontations we actively sought out. In fact, I came to realise on that Saturday afternoon at

Sagamore Hill that, until I met Theodore Roosevelt, I had never truly been exposed to what hunting really involves. Holmes and I had our memories, a few small souvenirs, and a number of stories in print that recorded our safaris into the under-world; but we had no tangible trophies. Sitting in the North Room of the president's home and confronted by antlers that looked like trees or by the heads of silently screaming bison or by the pelts of big game cats, jaws frozen in the act of roaring, and then realising that the man with the surprisingly high-pitched voice before me had stalked and killed all of these creatures just because he wanted to, I must confess to being awestruck. A chronicler like myself who has always done his best to avoid encounters with danger could not compare with this rugged tracker who lived for such adventure. From behind the walrus moustaches, the golden *pince-nez* and the smiling yet clenched teeth, he greeted us in that reedy voice that detracted not at all from the *Übermensch* he was. Beveridge had warned me of the president's gruff demeanour, but he had also said that Roosevelt enjoyed perpetuating that portrait of himself.

"T.R. is okay; don't be intimidated by him," Beveridge had said in the train *en route* to Oyster Bay. "He told me that he's really looking forward to meeting you—despite his schedule. He just announced last month that he wants to be president again, you see, and he's going after the Republican nomination. It'll be tough, but if anyone can do it, he's the one."

Despite his good intentions, the more Beveridge tried to make Roosevelt seem ordinary, the more ill at ease I felt; and once I was actually confronted by the man, I realised that heeding the senator's advice to "take it easy" would require great fortitude.

Rollins had delivered Beveridge and me to the docks at the

foot of Thirty-fourth Street a few hours before. We had ferried across the East River and proceeded by train from the Long Island City depot to the station at Oyster Bay. There we had hired a wagon that transported us the three remaining miles up the hill to the Roosevelt house. It was a chilly March day, and the cold wind off the bay cut right through our clothing. The road followed the shoreline for a while, taking us past stately houses, many of which were characterised by the white columns that one usually associates with Southern plantations; but we were not in that region of the country, I had to remind myself, and Beveridge pointed out one house in which George Washington himself was reputed to have stayed.

Past an antique cemetery we began our slow, bouncing climb up the hill, looping our way back and forth like hikers trekking on switchbacks. Behind us lay the brown pastures and bare trees of winter; beyond them, the waters of the salt marshes, of Oyster Bay, and of Long Island Sound. I held on to my bowler as Beveridge laughed.

"This ride is downright smooth compared to the way it used to be," he said. "T.R. only had the road hard-surfaced last year. In his younger days, you know, he used to ride his bicycle all the way up."

The bicycle anecdote was but a minor example of bravura, and yet it further confirmed for me the idea that we were about to visit a legend. Such figures I could never imagine being involved in murders, let alone committing them. Holmes, on the other hand, suspected everyone until he was sure of who the real culprit was; but not even Sherlock Holmes, I believed, would have the temerity to implicate a former president of the United States in some kind of conspiracy against Phillips.

At the top of the hill the wagon made a left turn on to a straight road of about a hundred yards at the end of which stood the half-frame, half-brick Victorian house.

"Sagamore Hill," Beveridge announced with a nod in its direction. "T.R. built the place some twenty-five years ago. It was his summer White House, and it still looks pretty good."

Indeed it did. Angular gables and proud chimneys capped walls of yellow shingles and pink trim, all of which stood upon a reassuring brickwork foundation; but Sagamore Hill was more than just the "man's house" Roosevelt had ordered. It was also the eighty acres of woods and fields and gardens that surrounded the building and overlooked the bay. I'm sure it has been said before, but if one had never seen the entire panorama, it is precisely the picture a person would paint of the home of the Rough Rider himself. Yet it was also a picture that bespoke a kind of dignity far removed from the cowboy image we in England had construed of the president.

Once the wagon had pulled under the *porte-cochère*, we disembarked. A maid met us at the door and ushered us through the oak-panelled entry hall and into the North Room where Roosevelt, dressed in a suit of navy-blue wool, his waistcoat pulling the buttons at his ample girth, was waiting, arms akimbo. Beveridge's advice notwithstanding, I could feel my heartbeat quicken. It would not be a trifling matter to speak to *any* former president of the United States—let alone one whose masculinity caused males to envy and women to admire him wherever he was known. Surprisingly, however, Roosevelt began by reassuring me that he had enjoyed my published accounts of Sherlock Holmes's adventures, and I immediately began to be more comfortable.

"First-rate stories, Dr. Watson. Bully!" he said, hitting his open palm with his fist. "I've never missed a single one of your episodes. I'm sorry Holmes isn't here too. I'd enjoy the chance to discuss some old cases with him. I was police commissioner of New York City, after all. Same kind of work you and Holmes did—as amateurs, so to speak."

Why public police officials all had to sound the identical note when it came to their private rivals I never could understand, but hearing the same calumny from Roosevelt that we were so used to hearing from Inspector Lestrade (before he retired from Scotland Yard after some forty years of tenacious service) certainly made it easier to forget to whom I was speaking.

"I told Dr. Watson," Beveridge interceded, "that you might fill him in on some of the background relating to Phillips and the Senate."

"Of course, Bev, of course. Although what makes you want to go muddying still waters I can't understand. The police have laid the case to rest. I recognise that some people are never happy until they can show the errors in police work, but I know those men in New York, and I can assure you they didn't miss a trick."

I smiled, hoping he would get back to the subject of Phillips.

"I don't mind telling you," Roosevelt said, "that at first I didn't like that man. Sissified airs. Funny clothes. I heard that once he even wore a white suit to cover a coal miners' strike—"

"The only reporter the miners would talk to!" Beveridge interrupted.

"—but when he went after the Senate," Roosevelt continued as if Beveridge had not been present, "that was too much." The president shook his fist for emphasis and then repeated, "Too much! Why, there was a time I myself would have liked to see him out of the way."

"Quite" was all I could muster in response to such a confession, even though Roosevelt himself ignored the implication.

"'The Man with the Muckrake' I called him in a speech," Roosevelt said. "That was when he'd started those damn articles. I wanted to use his name, but I was advised against it. Damn foolish to hold back, I thought at the time. Still do. There you have it."

What "you had" I couldn't quite see, but I could clearly recognise that once Mr. Roosevelt had begun, he was hard to slow down.

"In the end I relented. I thought Phillips was just doing his job—even if it was for that son of a bitch Hearst. And I told Phillips so. I even invited him to the White House. Three times I invited him before he agreed. You know, I don't think he was too happy mingling with us bigwigs. But he came. Finally. I guess he could change his mind just the way I changed mine." Roosevelt paused for a moment; he seemed to be thinking. "I respect that in a man," he said once he resumed. "What's more, I'll tell you something else: the idea of letting people vote for the Senate themselves—damn good plan! I didn't think so at first; but, by God, I'm just about ready to support it in public."

"Do you think Taft will agree, Mr. President?" Beveridge asked.

"To torpedo me, he might. But it's going to take a lot more than that to get me out of this race." Roosevelt moved to the edge of his chair and leaned forward. I could feel his breath as he spoke softly to the two of us. "In fact, gentlemen, just between us—and, Bev, I'll have your head on this very wall with all the other dumb beasts if you blab it about—I'd be prepared to head a third party if it comes to stopping that big–"

"And I'd be right behind you, Mr. President," Beveridge agreed. "If the Republican party can't appreciate our virtues, then we should turn our attention to those who have a greater vision and understanding of what the American people desire."

As the conversation was taking a political turn whose precise implications I was far from comprehending, I cleared my throat to gain their attention.

"If I might, Mr. President," I interjected as forcefully as I dared, "could we return to Phillips and the Senate?"

"Sorry, Dr. Watson," the president said. "Politics always gets the best of me." He took a white handkerchief from his breast pocket and, after removing his *pince-nez*, frosted them with his breath, and began wiping the lenses vigorously. When they seemed clean and he had scrutinised them, he smiled approvingly and then mysteriously repeated the entire process. Only after the procedure had been completed this second time was he ready to resume.

"Dr. Watson," he said, "you just tell your friend Sherlock Holmes that Graham Phillips was one hated fellow. There were plenty of men on the Hill who would have loved to see Phillips dead. I can tell you that a lot of people down in Washington had the opportunity, the motive, and certainly the money. Don't get me wrong. I'm perfectly satisfied with the excellent job the police did. Goldsborough–and Goldsborough alone–was the assassin. But I will admit to you that, with all that bad feeling in the Senate towards Phillips, I can well understand why there are still suspicions surrounding the man's death."

Roosevelt seemed to have concluded, but then almost as an afterthought he added, "Goldsborough shot Phillips in Gramercy

Park, you know, not far from where I was born on East Twentieth Street. I know the neighbourhood well. I remember all those brownstones."

The former president stared off, as if he were reliving an earlier time, but then Beveridge explained that we were planning to visit the Senate on Monday, and Roosevelt became animated again. "Though I think you're making a mistake, Dr. Watson, who could resist helping Sherlock Holmes? Let me get you started properly. Bev, here, can slip you through the Capitol doors, but even if I'm not in Washington any more, my name can help get you into those smoke-filled rooms our reporters like to write so much about."

With that, he strode to his desk, extracted a piece of paper from the top drawer, and pulled a pen out of the most garish inkwell I had ever seen. It looked as though it had been fashioned from the bottom of a rhinoceros's foot, a provenance (later confirmed by Beveridge) so singular, I suspected, that not even one of those journalists to whom Roosevelt had just alluded could have invented such a detail. He signed his note with a flourish and handed it to me.

"This should stand you in good stead in Washington, Doctor. But I would be careful if I were you in New York. As I'm sure you know from your work with Scotland Yard, the police do not take kindly to people trying to overturn their completed investigations. Just a word to the wise."

Stifling a grunt, Theodore Roosevelt got to his feet, indicating that our audience had come to a close. With *pince-nez* reflecting brightly, he changed his tone. "I can't wait to read your report about this case, Dr. Watson," he chortled. "I want to see how I turn out." Then, extending a warm, soft hand, he clenched his teeth once more. "Good day," he said, and showed us to the door.

I was so exhilarated by our visit to Sagamore Hill that I almost did not espy the shadowy figure following Beveridge and me as we boarded the train at Oyster Bay, but at the last moment a dark suit amidst the less formally attired residents of Cove Neck caught my eye entering the carriage two cars behind us. The clothing in question was being worn by a bearded man–the same bearded man, I was almost certain, that I had seen in the park the day before. Such a happenstance was too coincidental to be anything less than planned. But to what purpose? I wondered. Why were Beveridge and I being followed?

The stranger, who had seemed to be doing his best to stay out of my sight on the train, also boarded our ferry for the return to Manhattan. Standing at the opposite end of the ship's railing, he continued peeking out at us from behind a newspaper; but even as Beveridge noted the man's peculiar attitude, the longer I observed, the more familiar he looked. In fact, I was beginning to believe that I could penetrate this disguise.

"I say, Doctor," Beveridge whispered, "have you seen that bearded fellow over there who seems to be watching us?"

"Have no fear, Senator," I said in my most commanding tone. "My good friend Sherlock Holmes is most fond of hiding behind childish masks and makeup when he rejoins me on a case. It's his flair for the dramatic. Pay no attention to that stranger."

Because Holmes was not due in New York this soon, I was especially delighted with my perspicacity; in fact, by the time Rollins, who had been waiting for us at the pier, deposited me back at the hotel, I was in fine fettle. Not even the delay caused by a suspicious puncture, a nail driven into the side of one of our tyres, dampened my spirits. To be sure, as we left the docks, I turned to look behind us to see if we were still being followed, but there were too many headlamps to tell with any certainty. Perhaps I should have been worried, but in reality I was quite pleased with myself for having outwitted my old friend. Whenever I recalled how he had so callously deceived me almost two decades before by re-appearing in the guise of an ageing bookseller when the entire world thought he had drowned three years earlier at the falls of Reichen-bach, I grew angry, and this anger fuelled my desire to pierce the duplicity of his innumerable disguises.

I looked behind me in vain, however, upon entering the hotel. I even traversed the grand lobby several times to ascertain if the mysterious bearded man was already inside. At last, seeing no sign of him, I was about to enter the lift when a young man in hotel livery marched past me shouting "Dr. Watson! Dr. John Watson! Message for Dr. John Watson!"

I turned round at the first call of my name and in the process did indeed catch a glimpse of the bearded man darting past the potted palms and into Peacock Alley. Obviously, I should have been more vexed by this shadow, but there was that familiarity about his figure that put me at my ease. Ordinarily, I might have longed for my revolver that was upstairs in my trunk, but I was too pleased with my own detecting to be concerned: the height, the agility, the disguise created by the hirsute mask, and an absent consulting detective. Not this time, Mr. Sherlock Holmes.

"Dr. John Watson!" the boy repeated.

Lost in my momentary reverie, I had forgotten to claim my message. Still pleased with my deductive powers, I picked the paper off the silver tray the lad was carrying, tipped him, and began to read.

Watson [the dispatch ran],

I await you upstairs in our rooms. Try to avoid bringing along that wretched man with the false beard.

It was signed:

Sherlock Holmes.

THE DIARY

"To think is to aspire, to think is to long for immortality, for infinite development upward and ever upward–for eternal life, eternal happiness, eternal love. These are the dreams of thought. And the tragedy is that they are but dreams."

–David Graham Phillips, *The Mother-Light*

No sooner had I stepped from the lift than I heard the familiar–albeit muffled–strains of a violin filling the hall. Despite my concern over the vexing identity of the man who had been following me–or perhaps because of it–never did I find that music so comforting, for I could tell in a moment by the distinctive bowing that Sherlock Holmes had indeed arrived from England.

"Holmes!" I cried in a burst of enthusiasm as I fairly bounded into the sitting room.

Standing before me in that familiar mouse-coloured dressing gown, violin at his chin, he nodded in reply but continued his fiddling until he reached what I had come to recognise as a crescendo. With a dramatic weaving and twisting that were as much a part of his musical repertoire as Paganini, he finished his performance with a spirited but—at least to my untrained ear—cacophonous flourish.

"Watson, my old friend," he said when he had concluded. "Pray forgive me for not greeting you sooner; but, with all due respect, I had to complete my homage to Sarasate. Ever since his death, his music has contained an even greater poignancy."

"But not, I think, as clearly attacked as I've heard before," I ventured.

"Bravo, Watson!" he exclaimed with his eyes twinkling. "I believe you're developing a bent for music. This instrument is most inferior in tone. I borrowed it from a busker near the Baker Street Underground Station. I wished to avoid taking my own to sea. A Stradivarius and salt water don't mix."

We both chuckled for a moment until I recalled his note and the stranger who had been following me. "The bearded man," I reminded him. "I thought he was you."

"Really, Watson. Now it is your turn to disappoint me. When did you ever know me to wear such a preposterous beard? Why, this fellow's hair is black, and his whiskers are a grizzled brown."

"Well, then, Holmes, how did you know he was following me?"

"Elementary, really. When I arrived not more than thirty minutes ago, I overheard our bearded friend asking the hall porter what your room number was."

"The puncture," I now remembered. "It provided him a significant head start."

"I imagined something of the sort," Holmes observed. "At any rate, as the hall porter replied that you were out, the bearded chap said that he would wait in the lobby and then proceeded to ensconce himself at the turning of a corridor. He could see who entered the hotel, but he himself could not be seen. Or so he thought. Since it was you he had enquired about in the first place, I merely assumed that you were to be the focus of his watch. Was I mistaken?"

"N-no," I spluttered, "but why did you not approach him or wait to warn me?"

"Really, Watson. The melodramatic note, I confess, was a product of my sense of the theatrical. But could any harm come to you in the crowded foyer of the most famous hotel in America? I'm sure our lookout will surface again, and judging from the carelessness of his positioning, I believe that we will encounter little difficulty in locating him when the time comes."

As he spoke, he walked to the sideboard and the bottle of wine that stood upon it. "Sherry?" he offered.

"To celebrate our reunion," I said. Accepting a glass, I sampled the slightly sweet liquid.

"A bit lighter than the usual, eh, Watson?" he said. "Actually, it's amontillado. Think of it as a tribute to Mr. Poe. We're in *his* territory now, and whatever I might think of M. Dupin's ratiocinations, I cannot fault his creator's taste in sherry."

"Speaking of 'his territory,'" I said, "what are you doing here? Aren't you still supposed to be in England?"

"Actually, old fellow, I ran into a bit of luck. Do take a seat and let me tell you what I have learned."

We sat down in the velvet chairs near a low round table in the centre of the room. An aura of discomfort often attached itself to Holmes when he found himself unaccompanied by his familiar books, friendly chemicals, and artful clutter. On this occasion, however, as if we were both in our old sitting room again, Holmes removed a briarwood pipe from a pocket of his dressing gown, filled the bowl with dark shag, lit the tobacco, and inhaled deeply. A moment later he emitted a great cloud of blue smoke that quickly filled the chamber with its familiar pungent aroma. Indeed, were we to shut our eyes, we might almost have been in the soft, well-worn armchairs of Baker Street once more.

"To begin with, Watson," Holmes said, "Goldsborough's sister and her husband returned to England the day after you sailed. They were a week early. It seems the official he had gone to visit in Rome was no longer there. Thanks to Mycroft, we were able to complete our interview in London last Saturday night, sparing me the trip to Nottingham. After arranging for a fellow apiarist to look after my bees, I left Southampton on Sunday; and, behold, I stand before you seven days later in New York City. The wonders of modern travel!"

"Well done, Holmes! And has what the Americans told you elucidated the case before us?"

"Let us remember, Watson, what we learned from brother Mycroft about Mr. Fitzhugh Coyle Goldsborough. Goldsborough, you will recall, had a great love for music in general and for the violin in particular."

I nodded in agreement.

"He studied with Josef Kasper in Washington for four years and with Jakob Gruen in Vienna for three. He played with orchestras in Pittsburgh and Georgetown."

"But what does any of that have to do with Phillips's murder?" I asked.

"Why, Watson, you surprise me! What better way to pursue

a motive than to understand the psyche of the putative killer? Goldsborough spent two years studying at Harvard College, for example. Does it seem reasonable for a man of the arts as well as the recipient of at least two years of university education to be so compelled by a fictional work of literature that it would lead him to murder?"

"That ridiculous vampire business again, eh, Holmes?"

"Indeed, but I am getting ahead of my story." Holmes pulled on his pipe and then crossed his right leg over his left. Looking quite comfortable, he seemed prepared to start from the beginning; in the interim I took the opportunity to finish my glass of sherry.

"Goldsborough's sister, Anne," Holmes resumed, "married William F. Stead, American Consul at Nottingham, on the twenty-fifth of February of last year at their family home in Maryland. Originally the marriage was to have taken place in a large church, but naturally the tragic ordeal of the previous month rendered such an ostentatious display inappropriate."

"Quite," I agreed. "The Goldsboroughs must then be a sensible family."

"Oh, yes, Watson. The father is a successful member of your own profession, an occupation that, as you know, is most remunerative on this side of the Atlantic. The family has wealthy connections in Maryland and Washington and proudly claims relationship to Admiral Goldsborough of the American Civil War."

I nodded approvingly. How, I wondered, could a family of such good breeding and military background spawn so insane a scion?

"Actually," Holmes said, "Mrs. Stead spoke very little to me. As she wanted to forget the entire wretched event, it was her husband who did most of the talking. Mr. Stead seems to have faith in our ability to restore the good name of his wife's family."

"Most admirable," I observed.

"In his diary–about which I'll have more to say later–Goldsborough wrote in the middle of October 1910, that he would be earning fifty dollars a week within ten weeks. Which means that he expected to be gaining a substantial income some time in early January of 1911. At that time he was living in a rented room at the rear of the top floor in the Rand School of Social Science on East Nineteenth Street at three dollars a week."

"Three dollars a week? A young man from so wealthy a family? Outrageous!"

"Stead explained how 'Goldie,' as he was known to his friends, had ventured out on his own to build his career. And without much success, I might add. For despite his musical accomplishments, Goldsborough was what the Americans term 'seedy.' He was, in fact, quite impoverished."

"But three dollars a week, Holmes–that's less than a pound!"

"It gets worse, old fellow. The Rand School is the home of Socialists."

"Outrageous!" I said again. To imagine that a person from such a family could contemplate anarchy when his own family had contributed so much to society seemed beyond comprehension.

"Be at ease on that point, Watson. Goldsborough was no Socialist. All the residents of the Rand School agreed on that."

"Then why move in with those wretched creatures?"

"Because, Watson, the Rand School faces the National Arts Club in which Phillips and his sister lived."

"Why, that is the very place where I dined Thursday last with Mrs. Frevert and the others. Little did I realise then that I was socialising across the road from the killer's rooms."

Holmes smiled at my surprise.

"But surely," I thought aloud, "Goldsborough must have been on Phillips's trail from the start if he went to the trouble to move in so close by."

"Perhaps. But within the month of Goldsborough's move to New York, the poorly dressed fellow was seen dining in a respectable Fifth Avenue restaurant with a well-dressed woman. Not much earlier, he also claimed that he was being followed. He even complained to the mayor, suggesting that the mayor's secretary had donned old clothing to disguise himself. It's all in his diary, as you shall see. Nothing came of these allegations, of course."

"But, Holmes, what does it all mean?" I asked.

"Possibly nothing, Watson. You know how I balk at speculation. But certainly the opportunity presented itself for Goldsborough to be influenced by someone who could attract him with money. We don't know for sure what he was supposed to do to earn it in January of last year, but we certainly know what he accomplished."

"But doesn't that still leave him as our assassin?"

"Perhaps. However, neither does it rule out a conspiracy, a hypothesis most consistent with Mrs. Frevert's suspicions. But come, Watson! You must see what I have procured from Mr. Stead's generosity."

Holmes walked quickly to the armoire, a majestic structure with a boiserie of floral design. From within it, he removed a small, mauve-coloured Gladstone bag. "The original photographs were not available," he explained, putting the Gladstone on the round table before us as I barely managed to move the sherry glasses out of danger, "but Stead furnished me copies of these reproductions of Goldsborough's diary. Given the point of view I expect the local police to have, I'm afraid that these are all that we will have access to."

Opening the bag, Sherlock Holmes produced a handful of photographs, each the size of a sheet of foolscap, the uppermost dominated by a bright rectangular image flecked with what appeared to be random inkblots and a handwriting of varying characteristics.

"Read," Holmes suggested. "Then we will discuss your conclusions."

I picked up the first sheet and examined it more closely. As I would discover in the case of each photograph, the bright rectangle was in fact a reproduction of a different page from Goldsborough's diary. The entries were spattered with ink, and the hand of the writer was shaky, rendering the script most difficult to comprehend, a condition also complicating the task of identifying the author. Unlike Holmes, I had scant knowledge of graphology, but even I knew that one could determine very little from the photograph of a word that had been drowned in a blot of ink. Nonetheless, I proceeded to decipher the entry before me, which I here reproduce exactly as it was written:

"June 11, 1910. Certain happenings recently led me to think it advisable to jot down data. I believe David Graham Phillips is trying to fake a case against me or do me serious bodily harm or both. Yesterday afternoon ... I was sitting in my window, when I noticed a pretty-looking woman seated in a second-storey window of the Art Society Building. This woman was about twenty years old or a little more, I should say, and had a large hat with flowers around it. She smiled over at me in a pointed manner, and on first catching sight of me lifted her hand and waved it. I could not decide whether this was an involuntary motion of interest on seeing me or was meant as a sign of encouragement for me to start flirting with her. I got rather the latter impression."

"Who can this mysterious woman be?" I asked. "Surely not Mrs. Frevert. This woman is much too young."

"Pray continue," Holmes instructed.

"A man was half in sight near the window. I think it was David Graham Phillips, but I am by no means sure. I looked steadily at this woman for a few moments, then glanced away just as the man came to the window to look out. I then kept my eyes away from that window as much as I could. The woman, however, continued for perhaps half an hour or three-quarters, enough, longer to sit there and take evident notice of me.

It occurred to me that when I flirted with her a claim of my having acted in an annoying way might have been circulated to my detriment. I must be careful of what plans this blackguard may have to injure me. The theory that he is seeking to do so rests on stronger evidence than the mere incident just described."

"This young woman," I persisted, "who can she be?"

"As usual, Watson, you seem to be taking an extraordinary interest in the fairer sex."

"An unjust charge, Holmes," I countered, informing him of Mrs. Frevert's possessive jealousy that I had learned about from her husband. "Hell has no fury like a woman scorned," I reminded him.

"Ever the romantic," Holmes quipped, "although I must confess that seldom have I heard you attribute to a woman the desire to murder. And yet you raise a significant point."

He was right, of course, and I thought he might wish to continue this discussion, but instead he motioned towards the photograph of the diary page and urged me to proceed.

"A few nights ago (I will try to get the exact date later) I found myself shadowed by a man who by fixed staring at me in an impertinent manner on the street and rattling the spoon in his coffee cup when he came in a tenement restaurant evidently wished to arouse me into beligerency [sic].

I turned back on this man two or three times, always apparently after he had left my trail, but caught him each time. Now, detectives would probably have sought to irritate me to provoke a scrap. This man's appearance was as follows. Slightly below medium height, pale projecting lower jaw, as of someone worried or careworn, face rather long, eyes brown, rather dark, and somehow a little small for a face so round. They were somewhat sunken. It looked like a good family likeness to Mr. Adamson, secretary to Mayor Gaynor, but his clothing was worn and second-hand looking. He looked distinctly downcast when he noticed my turning back on him the last time, just as if he realised all his troubles had been in vain. I give these facts for what they may be worth."

A provocative description, I thought, looking up from my reading once more. With a little imagination, it could put one in mind of the pallid, dark-eyed chauffeur furnished us by Senator Beveridge. Or was I unfairly linking everyone I had met in New York to the people in Goldsborough's diary? Blinking my eyes to reduce the strain, I returned to the crimped text before me.

"Called last night on Ph[illips]. They said he had gone to Pittsfield, Mass. If so my trouble has been in vain. ... Phillips' ignoring my last letter and twice excusing himself after it, is in itself a confession of guilt of a sort. A man who has done no wrong will listen to one who claims he has. Moreover, the tone of that letter shows my intentions to be as amicable as he would let them be."

The next photograph contained a shorter entry. It was dated four days later:

"June 15, 1910. Forgot to mention that I passed a man in Central Park on the 13th of June that looked very much like D.G. Phillips. He was with a girl and walking about toward Seventy-fifth Street. I wish I could have been introduced to him some time ago.

"A girl," I muttered. "Could this one have been Mrs. Frevert, or was she the same younger woman Goldsborough had described at Phillips's window?" Holmes made no response, however. He simply remained in that characteristic pose, eyes closed, drawing on his pipe.

The third photograph was almost devoid of writing. It contained but five words printed in capital letters: "*LOVE, CRIME, MONEY, SEX, ATHLETICS.*" Beneath the words were two small cartoon-like drawings of open umbrellas.

The fourth photograph was more provocative still. It reproduced the page Holmes had spoken of earlier in reference to Goldsborough's anticipated wealth.

"October 18, 1910. In ten weeks I will be earning $50 a week."

What followed next was nothing less than bizarre:

"Notes—Data for Vampire. Note: To create characters with real blood in their veins, beyond the powers of many writers. Much easier to take them from real life, to utilise their actual flesh and blood by the easy, distinguished, legalised, and lucrative method of literary vampirism. ... How to safeguard against being guilty of vampirism. ... Brotherly love the only safeguard. ... One could picture the vampire as a scoundrel, a trenchant pen perhaps, egotist, possessed of intense pride, keen sense of artistic value, but not that which moves the sun in the heavens and all the stars. Vengeance unjustifiable, wrong to use poisoned arrows on any enemy."

"But this is amazing, Holmes," I said. "All this supernatural fol-de-rol. Once you allayed the fears of poor Bob Ferguson in Sussex so many years ago, I never expected to be investigating vampires again. Where does it come from this time?"

In reply Holmes returned to the Gladstone and extracted a thin, grey volume, which he handed to me.

"You forget the book we discussed with Mrs. Frevert in England, Watson."

"*The House of the Vampire* by George Sylvestre Viereck," I read aloud from the cover.

"A novel that was quite the rage a few years ago," Holmes explained. "I found this copy at Hatchard's and perused it on board ship only yesterday. It recounts the tale of one Reginald Clarke, a patron of the arts who produced works of literature that captivated the entire artistic world. What no-one knew, of course, was that Mr. Clarke was feeding, if you will, off the intellect of a small entourage of *artistes* whose company he solicited. The more he fed, the more genius he gained, and the more his victims' minds were depleted. What's more, unlike Mr. Stoker's Dracula, Viereck's vampire is not defeated in the end."

"Utter claptrap!" I responded. "Who would be foolish enough to believe such a tale?"

"The novel was popular enough to have been followed by a theatrical production called *The Vampire*, which was based on the same theme. And if this diary can be construed as truth, an assumption I am not yet ready to grant, then we may conclude that Mr. Goldsborough was affected by it as well. Goldsborough seemed to believe that Phillips's literary skills were being sucked out of Goldsborough's very essence."

"Only a madman could be so persuaded, Holmes," I offered.

"Exactly, Watson. 'Persuaded' is *le mot juste*."

"Then we have our motive, demented as it is?"

"Perhaps," Holmes said. "And yet I also learned from Stead that Goldsborough had been demanding through the post that Phillips stop writing about Goldsborough's sister. It would appear that he was offended by the domineering role of the heroine in Phillips's novel, *The Fashionable Adventures of Joshua Craig*. Goldsborough was most protective. I am told that he got into arguments with his father for reprimanding his sister–they almost came to blows, in fact."

"Indeed! How extraordinary!"

"And yet not so extraordinary, my good fellow, when we recall the other pair of siblings connected with this case. Let us not forget that it was Phillips's closeness with his own sister, Mrs. Frevert, which brought her to England to seek our aid in the first place."

I was astounded at the implications of Holmes's observation. "Holmes," I said, "you seem to be drawing a very close parallel between the murderer and his victim."

Holmes smiled. "Yet another reason–albeit distastefully psychological, Watson–for Goldsborough's imagining himself to be Phillips."

"But if Goldsborough thought that he was really Phillips," I reasoned, "and if Goldsborough was also put off by how Phillips–

or should I say 'Goldsborough'—was treating his own sister, then Goldsborough must have been terribly upset with himself. Killing Phillips was like destroying his own alter ego; moreover, to his deranged way of thinking, he would have to kill himself to complete the grisly job."

"Quite a thorny problem, eh, Watson? No doubt worthy of the distinguished Dr. Freud."

Before I could answer, Holmes swept up the photographs and replaced them in the bag. He then proceeded to forage for something else within it, continuing to speak as he searched. "But let us not allow such complexities to cloud the actual history of this diary. It seems to have fallen from the assassin's pocket when he shot himself. It was then picked up by a citizen at the murder scene who presented it to an assistant district attorney who in turn claimed to have kept it locked in a safe for the rest of the night and most of the following day. Indeed, it was not relinquished to the coroner until late the next night. And, according to Mr. Stead, the coroner was most displeased. In point of fact, Watson—" and here Holmes looked up to emphasise the issue—"the coroner actually accused the assistant district attorney of holding back evidence."

"But why, Holmes? To alter the diary, do you suppose?"

"A moment," Holmes said, finally producing yet another photograph from the seemingly bottomless Gladstone. This reproduction depicted numerous bits of paper, each with variations of the name Fitzhugh Coyle Goldsborough written on it. The smallest pieces contained only the name itself; the larger pieces, his name written more than a dozen times around a common axis. There were also figures of stars and wheels, the lines and spokes respectively comprised of variations in Goldsborough's signature.

"Why would a man write his name so often?" I asked.

"Perhaps, Watson, we might ask why someone *else* might have the need to practise writing a single name so often."

"To perfect the handwriting?" I offered.

"Capital! Now, if we have the suggestion of a copied hand and certainly the time in which to do the copying–not to mention the clear case of a confused individual who up to this point was like the distraught King Lear, more sinned against than sinning–then I believe we can see the foundations of a conspiratorial plot. Couple these observations with Goldsborough's belief that he was being followed."

"But if the diary *was* altered, why not delete such incriminating evidence?"

"It is always easier to add than detract, Watson. Especially when Mr. Goldsborough obligingly left so much space unwritten upon. If pages had been deleted or cut, anyone would have noticed. But in restricting one's alterations to exaggerations of what people already know to be true, one can create the most extraordinary scenarios."

"Who would have believed it?" I asked.

"All is most circumstantial at this point, old fellow," Holmes cautioned. "But when a murder is more then a year old and the rail has grown cold, even the dearly departed Toby would have had a difficult time picking up the scent. Although I do not like to trifle with surmise, sometimes, like a Platonic shadow, it can reflect reality."

I leaned back in my chair, trying to take in the enormity of the crime at which Holmes was hinting.

"Come, Watson," he said with a smile. "Despite the lateness

of the hour, his grey eyes were keen and sharp. "You have been keeping notes on your own investigation, and I would like to see what you have been up to."

Sitting in Central Park, I had believed my observations quite important. Now, compared to the diary I had just been permitted to read, I thought my rambling naive and pedestrian. Nonetheless, after furnishing Holmes with a brief report on my memorable visit to Sagamore Hill, I handed over my notes. He in turn leaned back in his chair, relit his pipe, and proceeded to spend the rest of the evening learning as much as I knew about the principal characters in the drama. The electric light in the sitting room remained ablaze when I retired to bed.

Seven

Seven

POLICE PROCEDURAL

"It is one of the most curious and delightful fast of psychology that
anyone easily deceived at it than any other."

–David Graham Phillips, *Hayseed*

Greeting us with a grey face, Sunday, the twenty-ninth of
March, did not appear to be the ideal day for a stroll in the
park, but that was just what Sherlock Holmes had planned for
Mrs. Frevert and me that morning. It was time to visit in daylight
the scene of Phillip's murder. Thus, after we had partaken of an
early breakfast, Holmes and I located the omnipresent Rollins
in front of the hotel and instructed him to convey us to the
National Arts Club.

Dressed in a black fur coat to protect her from the cold,
Mrs. Frevert was waiting for us in front of the building. Holmes
consulted his watch with a quick smile. "There is nothing so
desirable–or rare–as a punctual woman, Watson," he observed as

we alighted from the automobile.

"Oh, Mr. Holmes," Carolyn Frevert said, "I'm so glad to see you again. Your very presence makes me feel as if we are getting closer to the truth."

My friend smiled and, pointing his ebony walking stick east, announced, "Let us begin."

What a bundled-up troupe we must have seemed to any of the few pedestrians that early Sunday hour who bothered to look our way–Mrs. Frevert in her heavy fur, I in my ulster, bowler, and scarf, Holmes in his well-worn inverness and ear-flapped travelling cap.

"Graham and I breakfasted a little later than usual on the day he was killed," Mrs. Frevert explained as we walked down Nineteenth Street. "He slept late following a long night of his work that very session. As it was, he didn't get to bed until seven in the morning. And it wasn't until one-thirty in the afternoon that he wrapped himself up in his overcoat and left for the Princeton Club to check his mail. He walked east on Nineteenth Street–just as we are doing–to get to Irving Place and then to the park."

"He walked on the north side?"

"Of course, Mr. Holmes. There would have been no point in his crossing over."

Holmes had stopped and was staring at the other side of the road. The object of his gaze was an old red-brick tenement house that faced the National Arts Club. "The Rand School of Social Science, Watson," he explained. "The lair of the assassin."

It was a nondescript place as drab as many of the other brownstones nearby. There was certainly nothing to distinguish it as the spawning ground of so heinous a crime as murder.

Just as suddenly as he had stopped, Holmes turned left and

began walking north on the west side of Irving Place where a few sparse trees lined the roadway. In the winter, when Phillips had been killed, they would have been sparser still. Although relying every so often on the support of his stick, Holmes could maintain quite a rapid pace; thus, it was apparent that the deliberateness of his gait resulted from a desire to view the scene with great care and not from any significant debilitation of his physical powers.

Despite Holmes's lingering attentiveness, it took but a few minutes to traverse the distance to the fenced enclosure known as Gramercy Park, which Irving Place itself actually abutted. In England, such an area would be called a "square," blocks of building surrounding a pleasantly rectangular plot of grass, offering the fortunate nearby residents who had access through its high, black and locked metal gates an oasis-like haven in which to rest and reflect.

Mrs. Frevert directed us to the left once we encountered the metal fencing. Our path took us along the pedestrian walkway that followed the turn of the railing and pointed us north once more. Through the black vertical bars we could observe the lawns and hedges and trees of the park, the same vista that Phillips himself would have seen scarcely more than a year earlier. Across the road to our left, stately houses marked our progress.

When we reached Twenty-first Street, the northern boundary of Gramercy Park, Mrs. Frevert halted and pointed a gloved finger towards the middle of the walkway. She seemed to be directing our attention to a location just before the entrance of Lexington Avenue, the northerly street that, like Irving Place to the south, terminated at the park. "Right there," Mrs. Frevert said, "across from number 155. That's where Graham was shot."

"A moment," Holmes said despite the importance of her pronouncement. With his stick he seemed to be stirring up some green leaves and white flower petals on the pavement near the rounded corner of the fencing. Quite suddenly, however, he began walking again, taking markedly long strides until he reached the spot Mrs. Frevert had indicated.

"Two of Graham's colleagues were leaving the Princeton Club at Twenty-first and Lexington over there"–again she pointed, this time at a red brownstone building with white woodworking– "when they saw a man leaning against the fence about half the distance between where we are now standing and the entrance to the Club. It was Goldsborough, of course. He walked up to Graham and shot him in the stomach. 'That'll do for you,' the cretin said, and then he quickly fired five more times." Here Mrs. Frevert bit her lip but, displaying the same kind of strength she had revealed in recounting the story to us in Sussex, continued bravely. "Graham swayed and grasped onto this iron fence for support until his friends carried him into the Princeton Club and an ambulance finally arrived."

"And Goldsborough?" Holmes asked.

"He shot himself in the head and died instantly," she said. "His body lay right there in the street untended for hours. It should have rotted in the gutter."

"Quite," Holmes offered. "But what did happen to it?"

"The police took it to the East Twenty-second Street Station."

"I see," he said softly.

Sherlock Holmes looked up and down the road and then regarded the brownstones with their garniture. Squinting, he eyed the thin trees that lined the walkway near where Phillips had fallen against the railing. With the ring of his footfalls the only sound we could hear, he marched to the precise spot of the murder and then, with arms folded, looked directly at the façade of the Princeton Club, which, behind short, thick bushes and a waist-high fence, seemed to stare defiantly back.

"That building has its own macabre story to tell," he observed.

Mrs. Frevert nodded, but I had not a clue to what they were referring.

"It used to be the home of Stanford White, Watson," Holmes explained, "the celebrated architect. He was shot and killed in 1906 by the husband of a woman whose company he had been keeping before she had married."

"Before she had married'!" I repeated. "By God, despite the beauty of this place, it would appear that murder is all around us."

"Remember the Garden of Eden, Dr. Watson," Mrs. Frevert said.

During this brief conversation, Holmes had not taken his eyes from the front of the Princeton Club. But now he slowly began to rotate his body to the right, allowing his gaze to encompass the entire panorama beginning with the building itself, then the adjacent roadway, and finally the tall limestone palazzo with its projecting balconies at the corner of Twenty-first Street and Lexington.

Suddenly what I recognised instantly as a pistol shot cracked the fragile stillness of the grey morning.

A tiny rain of sparkles accompanied the report as a projectile struck the rail of fencing not two feet from Holmes's head. I was aware of a quick movement in the bushes at the far corner of the Princeton Club, but Mrs. Frevert emitted a cry of fear, and it was only after the brief moments it took for her to regain her composure that I could focus my attention on what had happened.

By this time, I could barely hear the echo of running footsteps fading into silence.

Holmes, however, was already sprinting across the road in the direction of the gunshot, his walking stick still in hand.

"Watson!" he shouted back to me. "Look to the lady!"

The younger Holmes of our Baker Street days might have had some change of apprehending the culprit whoever it was; but age and retirement did little to enable Holmes's still-agile frame to keep pace with an obviously younger assailant.

I did my best to comfort Mrs. Frevert, all the while keeping a keen eye on Lexington Avenue, the road down which Holmes had disappeared. What would happen if my old friend actually succeeded in confronting his quarry I could only guess. To the best of my knowledge, he wasn't carrying a pistol. I for one had left mine in the hotel. Presumably, the armed gunman Holmes was pursuing could easily overpower a man accoutred with only a walking stick. Each passing minute rendered me more anxious about Holmes's welfare.

My nervousness, however, did little to prepare me for the ludicrous scene that soon transpired. Rounding the corner where I had last seen him and looking for all the world like a common villain came Sherlock Holmes in the company of two uniformed policemen. A third man, wearing a bowler, a khaki overcoat on his stocky frame, and who, judging by his familiarity with the other two, was obviously a policeman himself, carried Holmes's stick.

"You see," Holmes was saying as they all reached Mrs. Frevert and me, "here are my friends, just as I explained: Mrs. Carolyn Frevert and Dr. John Watson."

The detective pushed his bowler up at the front of the brim

so that the hat rested precariously on the back of his head. He eyed both me and Mrs. Frevert, rubbed his chin, and returned the walking stick to Sherlock Holmes.

"Okay," he said, "I guess you really are who you said you are. But you can't be too careful when you find somebody running down the street like that. I'm Detective Ryan. Detective Flannelly of the Central Office told me you'd be here in Gramercy Park nosing around and asking questions about a case he worked last year."

"The Phillips assassination," a ruffled Holmes muttered.

"Yeah, yeah, I know all about it," Ryan said. "I got a call from the D.A. himself. And he got a call from Sagamore Hill. There ain't too much that escapes us, you know."

Detective Ryan offered us perfunctory sympathies for being shot at and then, noting the cold, recommended that we return to Mrs. Frevert's flat since it was close by. He talked all the way back to Nineteenth Street, complaining about the rising rate of crime in the neighbourhood and suggesting that we were probably just another set of victims, no doubt the unlucky targets of some armed thief who had nothing whatsoever to do with the Phillips case. Only a slightly upturned curl of the lips revealed Holmes's impatience; it was an expression I had seen numerous times in our many frustrating encounters with Lestrade. I knew Holmes would not be looking forward to any further confrontations with Lestrade's American "cousin."

No such opportunity immediately presented itself, however, for as soon as we had restored Mrs. Frevert to her lodgings and removed our own heavy coats, a loud pounding on the door made it rattle on its highes. The resounding rap sent the white cat, who had just arrived to greet us, leaping to the tall, stand-up writing desk of dark mahogany in the corner of the room. Detective Ryan outran the maid to discover the cause of the disturbance.

It was an out-of-breath Senator Beveridge who confronted us all in the doorway.

"What's happened?" he asked between gasps. "Is everyone all right? Carolyn told me last night of your plans to visit the park. But when I arrived to join you, the grounds were nearly deserted. Some stranger told me about hearing a gunshot."

"Everyone's fine, Senator," replied the detective, who obviously knew Beveridge. I could see Sherlock Holmes surveying the latecomer as the latter entered the sitting room. Was he the person Holmes had been chasing down Lexington Avenue? I wondered, as I introduced my old friend to the man who claimed a similar affection for Phillips.

"How is it that you're so winded, Senator?" Ryan then asked.

"My chauffeur is working for Mr. Holmes here in New York," Beveridge explained. "I had to run all the way from the park."

"And where might the car be?" Ryan asked.

"It's parked down the street," Mrs. Frevert offered. "It's beyond the building, so we didn't pass it when we walked by."

"Any idea who might want to take a shot at you, Mr. Holmes?" Beveridge asked.

I was about to describe the man with the false beard when Holmes interrupted me. "No-one in particular," he said, "although I do have a few general suspicions. It's quite obvious that someone does not want to see this investigation proceed."

Holmes turned to Mrs. Frevert, who was in the process of lifting Ruffle from the desk. His solemn tone, however, caused her to put down the cat and face my friend directly.

"Mrs. Frevert," he said slowly, "I believe there can be no doubt now that a conspiracy existed to kill your brother. I believe that it is still at work, as we have witnessed today, to prevent its exposure. Having ascertained that much–or rather, having that much ascertained for us this morning at the risk of our very lives–I hope we can also establish just who it was that must have persuaded Goldsborough to shoot Phillips so publicly. For I am now convinced that another assailant must have stood close by– in all probability, just where our unknown marksman fired from today. Otherwise, Goldsborough could have shot Phillips here on Nineteenth Street. There are many good vantage points. From a window in the Rand School, for example. Instead, he waited until Phillips made himself an easy target for the crossfire of two gunmen. A steady hand with a revolver could easily have fired that elusive seventh bullet."

"But no witnesses saw anyone else with a gun," Beveridge said.

"When witnesses see an assailant actually shooting someone, they don't generally look round for others to blame. They concentrate strictly on the person with the weapon. Hence, a second assassin can make his escape while the witnesses are preoccupied with the first."

Detective Ryan punctuated Holmes's explanation with a derisive laugh. "I've listened to all this quietly, Mr. Holmes, for despite our outward gruffness, we members of the New York Police Department do spend some time reading, and the adventures of the Sherlock Holmes, as told so entertainingly by Dr. Watson, have earned you a great deal of respect. But here in New York we deal with dangerous brutes, not the tea-and-crumpet variety of criminals you're used to in England. And we don't go in for theorising when speculation isn't needed."

"What about Jack the Ripper?" my patriotic duty forced me to ask. "He was as beastly as any killer in the world."

"What about him?" Ryan retorted. "Scotland Yard never caught the man, did they? Nor did you, Dr. Watson, if I'm not mistaken." The detective then turned to Holmes. "If you're so smart, Mr. Sherlock Holmes, explain how these conspirators would be able to convince their pigeon to give himself up or—as in the case of Goldsborough—to shoot himself to death before a captive audience in Gramercy Park?"

"That's the genius of it, Ryan," Holmes said. "It all hinged on finding a person angry and deranged enough to follow a plan. Perhaps a form of hypnosis was employed or a strong drug—to convince the assassin that, for the greatest glory, suicide would be his crowning achievement."

"Commissioner Roosevelt warned us, Mr. Holmes, that you'd be snooping into long-buried matters," Ryan said. "But I don't think even a former president of these United States could imagine the story you have concocted. Hypnosis—what a laugh!"

I expected Ryan to leave at that point; instead, however, he opened his brown coat and produced from it a folded, yellowing envelope. "Still," he said, "we were told to co-operate with you from very high sources—which is the only reason I would ever consent to letting you see our file on the murder of David Graham Phillips."

He handed the envelope to Holmes, who motioned for me to join him in perusing its contents.

"Use my brother's desk, gentlemen," Mrs. Frevert suggested, indicating the writing desk. Its gently sloping top currently occupied by the Sphinx-like Ruffle whose front paws were tucked under his chest, the desk looked much like a draughtsman's table.

"*I* could never write at such a contraption," I observed.

"Actually, Doctor," Mrs. Frevert explained, "you might be interested to know that Graham used it for reasons of health. He feared an appendicitis from stooping over, and he thought the 'old black pulpit'–as he called it–could prevent that from happening. In fact, that desk over there travelled with him around the world."

"Remarkable" was all I could bring myself to respond.

In the meantime, after sending Ruffle on his way, Holmes had splayed across the desktop in question the contents of the envelope Ryan had given him and bade me join in their scrutiny. Upon examination, the pages proved to be the official police report including the testimony of the witnesses who had observed the sad affair. In brief, the file added nothing more than a few new names to what we'd already learned. Newton James and Frank Davis were the two members of the Princeton Club who had witnessed the shooting. The former was a broker; the latter, a mining engineer. They were some hundred feet away, and both agreed that they had heard six reports when Phillips was shot. They said nothing of another gunman (although, of course, their attention was directed at giving immediate aid to Phillips), not to mention the ghastly coda of Goldsborough's own self-immolation. Jacob Jacoby, a florist in the neighbourhood, who happened to be walking past, joined James and Davis in helping Phillips into the Princeton Club where they all waited until the ambulance arrived. The coroner reported six wounds including those in the chest and bowels. The police report identified a ten-chamber revolver and a dead assassin, killed by a single bullet from the same pistol. There was no mention of Algernon Lee. He was the witness Mrs. Frevert had told us about who had called the gun a "six-shooter," the vernacular appelation that, if accurate, rendered impossible the total of seven wounds, including the fatal blast to Goldsborough's head.

"And how do you explain the omission of any reference to a six-chambered revolver?" Holmes asked the detective.

Ryan removed the bowler from his head and began fingering the hat's inner band. "It don't bother me, Mr. Holmes. Six bullets. Seven bullets. Maybe the doctors counted where a bullet entered and exited as two entrances. Who knows? We got the killer–that's all that matters."

"Perhaps," said Holmes as he returned the report to the detective who was now preparing to leave.

No sooner had the door closed on the three police officers than Holmes said to me, "The police may not have any use for Mr. Algernon Lee, Watson, but you and I are going to pay him a visit. His address is, after all, just across the road. And once we speak to him, I think a visit to Bellevue Hospital might be in order."

We paid our respects to Mrs. Frevert, who snatched up Ruffle to prevent him from bolting through the open door. Then, after making final plans with Beveridge for our meeting in the nation's capital early the following day, we left the National Arts Club and traversed the simple roadway separating so much more than mere brick buildings.

If the late Karl Marx had wanted to illustrate what he regarded as the basis for class struggle, he could not have found a better study in contrasts than these two residences: 119 East Nineteenth Street, the opulent home of Phillips on one side of the street; 112

East Nineteenth Street, the modest brownstone of his assassin on the other. The latter was not rundown by any means, but it certainly lacked the plush fittings and fixtures of the building across the way. To those myopic experts on wrongdoing who, in seeking to blame the origins of crime on the influence of evil neighbourhoods, can seemingly ignore the differences that exist directly opposite each other, I might easily say "Let them come to East Nineteenth Street!"

Algernon Lee was the secretary of the Rand Club, a society of New York Socialists. Although I offer no sympathy to any of that ilk who preach the downfall of an economic system that has brought justice and civilisation to most of the world, I must confess to having found Mr. Lee a most affable gentleman. Balding and bespectacled, he looked like a public school headmaster. What's more, he seemed most pleased to help us shed light on a mystery that, as he put it, had never been satisfactorily resolved.

"Understand, Mr. Holmes," he said in his office of papers and books wedged into every possible recess, "I never actually saw Goldsborough's pistol."

"Then what makes you so positive that it had six chambers?" I asked. "I believe you described it as a 'six-shooter.'"

"That's correct, Dr. Watson. I used that term because it was the one I heard the police say over and over. I am not familiar with firearms as a rule, and I couldn't possibly be expected to make up such an expression."

"Just when did you hear them talk about the pistol?" Holmes asked.

Lee removed his round spectacles to rub his eyes. In the process, he seemed to be remembering. "The night of the killing," he said after repositioning the glasses, "the police swarmed all over this place. Two assistant District Attorneys, Ruben and Strong, led the investigation, but uniformed officers were stationed throughout the building. Goldsborough lived in the back. He was merely renting the room, you see. He had no political or social ties with our organisation whatsoever. But the agents of the corporate state must be thorough in their investigations of those who threaten the status quo, and as a result they interviewed most everyone who lives here. George Kirkpatrick lived next to Goldsborough, but even George didn't have much to say about him. Oh, Goldsborough used to complain about being followed or not being appreciated or not having enough money–although on that score he kept reminding us that he would soon be getting some. But no-one could have possibly guessed that he would kill anybody."

"The pistol, Mr. Lee," Holmes reminded him, "the pistol."

"Ah, yes. Please, forgive me. I have a tendency to digress. I was sitting in my office making some notes for a lecture I was scheduled to give. Two police detectives–I don't know their names–were talking in the hallway just beyond my door. One said that Goldsborough had used a 'six-shooter,' and the other laughed and said, 'Who did he think he was, Wild Bill Hickok?'"

"If that is the case, Mr. Lee," I asked, "then why would the press say the gun held ten bullets?"

"A good question, Dr. Watson," Lee replied. "I'm only reporting what I heard, but one of my associates has suggested that to protect their own class, the capitalists wanted to fix the blame for Phillips's death on a single gunman. Since a six-shooter couldn't fire seven bullets, the police–or the people who control the police–would have to concoct a weapon that could have done all the damage itself. Ergo, the ten-chambered revolver. Mind you, this is pure conjecture, but it is indeed a plausible theory, don't you think?"

As he asked this question, he raised his head so that the light from the overhead lamp reflected in his glasses and concealed his eyes.

Since it was obvious that the query required no answer and since it was equally obvious that its implications would remain unspoken, Holmes thanked Algernon Lee for his time and got up to leave. I rose to join him; but just before we reached the door, Lee stopped us.

Surprisingly, it was I he addressed. "If you ever write up this story, Dr. Watson," he said, "Please do one thing: please be so kind as to impress upon your readers that–guilty or innocent– Fitzhugh Coyle Goldsborough was never one of us. He was never a Socialist. Good Lord, he was one of the Goldsboroughs of Maryland. Need I say any more?"

A brief drive brought us to the large blocks of buildings overlooking the East River that comprise Bellevue Hospital. White sea birds circled above us in the grey sky to the accompaniment of mighty blasts from the sirens of nearby ships. Not even the confines of a hospital could deaden the sounds from life on the river. We had little time for philosophising, however; we were hoping to meet a number of doctors who had been involved with Phillips after he had been attacked.

In addition to Phillips's personal physician, Dr. Eugene Fuller, who had been called to the scene of the shooting, we wished to speak to the team of surgeons–Drs. Donovan, Moses, Wilds, and Dugan–who had examined Phillips's wounds at the hospital. It was Dr. Wilds, we had been told by Mrs. Frevert, who had accompanied the stricken author in the ambulance. But most of all, we wanted to converse with Dr. John H. Walker and Dr. I.W. Hotchkiss, the two men who had actually performed the surgery on Phillips.

In fact, we spoke to none of them. Rather, an imperious nurse with heavy jowls referred us to Dr. Milton Farraday, the hospital's director. He had apparently made it very clear to his staff that all questions concerning the Phillips assassination should be addressed to him.

"I'm a very busy man, Mr. Holmes," Dr. Farraday said. He had agreed to speak with us on the run, as it were, pausing in the corridor amidst the clang of metal or glass containers jarred by the nurses who were carrying them from room to room. Robed in a floor-length white coat, he was a tall, hirsute man with a single eyebrow line giving intensity to a demeanour undermined by what is commonly referred to as a wandering eye, an orb not synchronised with its fellow.

"I must concern myself with the health of those still living," Dr. Farraday said, fixing an eye on Holmes, "not waste my time– or allow any members of my staff to waste theirs–by dredging up some year-old murder case that no-one cares about." Then he turned that eye on me. "Certainly, Dr. Watson, as a medical man, you can understand my position."

I muttered something in response that, I trust, sounded sympathetic without denigrating the importance of conferring with the examining doctors. Nonetheless, he refused our request, agreeing only to consult his files on Phillips to answer whatever questions we would put to him as long as they were brief. So brief did he intend his remarks to be, in fact, that he obdurately refused to return to his office, requiring instead an officious nurse to bring him the appropriate hospital records right there in the corridor.

"Please, keep it short," he reminded us, glancing at his watch and then nervously scanning the passageway. He seemed to be searching for eavesdroppers.

"A single question, Dr. Farraday," Holmes said. "How do you explain seven bullet wounds in Mr. Phillips and Mr. Goldsborough caused by a revolver with only six chambers?"

"Oh, that is your line of enquiry, is it?" Farraday said. Exhaling deeply, he seemed to relax a bit. "See the police then. Don't talk to me. The nature of the weapon is not the hospital's concern."

"We've already done so, Doctor. They've told us nothing new."

"Look, Mr. Holmes, that shooting was over a year ago. My memory is hazy. Phillips was brought in here, as I recall, one afternoon and died late the following night. We spent all that time trying to revive him. All kinds of people wandered in and out of his room, important people."

"Of course, Doctor, but after he died—when you had the time to do a thorough examination of his body—did you find the tracks of five or of six bullets?"

Dr. Farraday consulted his notes. Then he looked up and began to recite, "One bullet entered the right side of Phillips's chest between the first and second ribs, perforating the right lung and exiting the back under the left shoulder. The examining team considered this wound to be the most serious. The second bullet passed through the right side of the abdomen, exiting from the left side, barely missing the intestine. The third bullet passed through his left thigh; the fourth and fifth bullets passed through his upper right thigh, the fifth lodging itself in his hip from where it was later extracted, the only bullet that had actually remained in his body. The sixth bullet passed through his left forearm between the elbow and his wrist. Six bullets, twelve perforations."

"But there should have been only eleven," Holmes reminded him, "if one bullet remained in his body."

"Hmmm," Farraday intoned. He stared for a moment at the sheet before him. "You're right, of course. I never noticed that discrepancy before. But what's the point? It does nothing to shed light on the nature of the gun."

"True," Holmes said, "but it certainly serves to raise questions about the credibility of the medical report."

"What's the difference, Mr. Holmes?" a more humble Dr. Farraday asked. "Six bullets. Seven bullets. Eleven or twelve perforations. The man can't be brought back to life. Nor can his assassin be further punished. Now, if you'll excuse me?" And with that he walked briskly down the hall, making an immediate right turn into the nearest corridor that would remove him from our line of vision.

"Curious, Watson," Holmes said as we remained standing in the middle of the hospital hallway. "Six bullets. Seven bullets."

"Exactly what Detective Ryan said, eh, Holmes?"

"Precisely, old fellow," he mused with a dry laugh. "Quite a coincidence. But come. We must return to the hotel and ready ourselves for the night-train to Washington."

By the time we left Bellevue, the already grey afternoon had begun to darken. Rollins deposited us at the Waldorf, where Holmes and I filled two small valises with the accoutrements we would need for our brief journey to the nation's capital and then rejoined the chauffeur who motored us to the Pennsylvania Station.

Eight

THE SENATE

"The real 'unruly classes' are those 'respectabilities' with 'pulls,' and these governmental officers who are 'pulled; they violate the laws; they purchase or enact or enforce unjust legislation; they abuse the confidence and the tolerant good nature of the people; they misuse the machinery of justice."

–David Graham Phillips, *The Reign of Gilt*

"Well, Watson," Sherlock Holmes asked me as we emerged from the long concourse, "what do you make of Union Station? It is but five years old."

We had just disembarked from our railway carriage in Washington, D.C.; and despite the natural excitement engendered by our locale, I must admit to having felt tired. The journey by train that had begun late Sunday night in New York and that had terminated early Monday morning at the virtual seat of the American government had fatigued me.

Grasping the back of one of the numerous wooden benches,

I gazed upwards at the cavernous Main Hall in which we now found ourselves.

"It is remarkably large," I responded unimaginatively, feeling dwarfed below lofty arches of coffered ceiling and airy skylighting. Encircling the vast room on a sort of abbreviated mezzanine a few yards above our heads stood some fifty centurions of stone, each at stoic attention behind a massive shield.

"It rather reminds one of Ancient Rome," I added, hoping to give a better account of my powers of observation.

"Capital, Watson! In spite of your exposure to the New World, your sense of history has remained intact. Constantinian arches. Pompeian traceries. Indomitable legionnaires. Indeed, the whole structure is said to be modelled after the Roman Baths of Caracalla."

He allowed me no time to relish my architectural acumen, however. "Onward, old fellow," he prodded. "We have an appointment with Beveridge to keep."

Holmes and I emerged into a grey, damp morning. Beneath the mammoth statuary depicting Prometheus and Thales, Ceres and Archimedes, and Freedom and Imagination that peered over the three curving portals of the railway station, we edged through the crowd to Massachusetts Avenue, the street immediately before us, taking care not to slip on the wet pavement. "The District of Columbia, Watson," Holmes said, waving his ebony stick as if it were a brush and he a landscape artist painting the broadest of canvases. "The capital of America designed by a Frenchman. A city of ironies—like the country itself."

Holmes's energy seemed boundless. A restless night in a train would tire most men his age as it certainly had wearied me, but not Sherlock Holmes! Ever the enthusiastic cicerone, he pointed out in the distance to the right the obelisk that is the Washington Monument and, closer to us, the massive columnar white buildings that put me in mind of the imposing and stolid edifices of Whitehall. So zealous was he that my own drowsiness began to fade, and I soon experienced the rush of excitement that being in a world centre generates. To be sure, the youthful capital that surrounded us lacked the grandeur and the majesty of London, the hub of empire, but this emerging metropolis, so dramatic a representation of the democratic ideal, seemed poised to herald the arrival of a new and mighty power which, like the city itself, would rise in stature, set to take her place of importance on the world's stage.

"Regard," Holmes said, aiming his stick down Delaware Avenue, the tree-lined road that rolled out directly before us and at whose end, framed by red oak trees, stood the magnificent white-domed Capitol.

"Beautiful," I murmured. "Who would think that such a grand edifice could be the home of the despicable corruption documented by Phillips?"

"Yes," Holmes agreed. "Or in whose rotunda the bodies of three presidents–all murdered within some thirty-five years of one another–would lie in state. Lincoln, Garfield, McKinley."

As I contemplated his macabre litany, he asked, "Do you see the statue at the top?"

I could barely distinguish a figure high above.

"Freedom Triumphant," Holmes explained. "A fitting piece, don't you think? It was cast in bronze by slaves."

In light of his previous observation, I assumed he was once more being ironic.

"The sculpture was done by Thomas Crawford," Holmes continued. "One hand holds a wreath; the other rests on a sword. Do you know, Watson, that although she's wearing a feathered headdress, she reminds me of the statue of Justice atop the Old Bailey."

"The dome makes me think of the cupola of St. Paul's," I observed.

Here Holmes smiled. "May good acts in both temples," he intoned with mock solemnity, "lead their inhabitants to heaven. But lest we become too pious, Watson," he added, his eyes twinkling, "let us not forget how the late Mark Twain described the inhabitants of this so-called holy place: 'the only distinctively native American criminal class."

We both laughed and, lightened by our levity, undertook the short walk across Massachusetts Avenue to Delaware at whose terminus, as I noted previously, stood the Capitol. To its right, I might add, began the recently laid out greensward known as the National Mall. Would that we had had the opportunity to visit the provocative museums bordering the verdant grounds, enticements such as the castle-like, red-sandstone Smithsonian Institution– "Built with money bequeathed by the scientist James Smithson. An Englishman, Watson," Holmes said with not a little patriotic pride–but since we were shortly to see Beveridge, we had no time for adopting the guise of tourists.

Our destination, however, was not yet to be the Capitol, but rather the newly completed Senate Office Building just down the road on our left. Holmes had arranged its northwest entrance, the corner closest to Union Station, to be the site of our meeting with Beveridge, who, having left New York with Rollins in the motor car immediately following our mutual encounter with Detective Ryan in Mrs. Frevert's flat, was due to have arrived in Washington late the previous day. Beveridge had eagerly offered to convey *us* as well, but Holmes had desired the opportunity to speculate and theorise unobserved by principals in the case.

When we reached our rendezvous point in the marbled foyer, there was no sign of the former senator. Holmes consulted his pocket watch and, fearing any unnecessary loss of time, concluded that we should begin our enquiries at once. Armed with the letter of introduction that Roosevelt had given me, therefore, we soon found ourselves in front of a tall, dark door bearing a circular emblem about a foot in diameter that contained an American Indian holding a bow and down-turned arrow. Below the insignia, which proved to be the seal of the Commonwealth of Massachusetts, was a nameplate proclaiming the office of the most prominent personage on Holmes's listing of senators charged by Phillips in his article: the senior senator from the aforementioned state, Republican Henry Cabot Lodge.

"'Vain' and 'self-centred,' Phillips called him," Holmes reminded me before we entered.

"But isn't he quite respectable, Holmes?" Even had I not recently read Phillips's review of the man, I would have recognised the famous family names.

Holmes extracted a small notebook from inside his coat pocket. "Aristocratic pretence, Watson," he said, referring to his notations on Lodge. "Phillips called the family's reputation undeserved; he claimed it was based on the slave trade."

"My word," I murmured.

"Yes," Holmes agreed, and then read aloud what he had

previously copied from *The Treason of the Senate.* "A scurvy lot they are with their smirking and cringing and voluble palaver about God and patriotism.' Strong poison, eh, old fellow?" Holmes asked as he placed his hand on the shining brass knob of Lodge's office door.

"Wait!" commanded a stentorian voice, and we both immediately turned to see Senator Beveridge running at full gallop down the corridor. Hair askew, too winded and distracted even for cordial greetings, he looked very little like the heroic Hampden Scarborough of Phillips's novels. It also occurred to me that he was beginning to make a habit of arriving on the scene at the last moment.

"I've already scheduled appointments for you, Mr. Holmes," he said after finally catching his breath, "and Lodge's office isn't on the list. In fact, he's set to give a speech on the Senate floor momentarily, so he isn't even here. All the senators I've arranged for you to see know exactly when you're expected and when you'll be leaving."

"But surprise is just the point, Senator," Holmes explained in exasperation. "Surely you recognise that the best witnesses are those that are taken off guard–who haven't had the opportunity to fabricate responses."

"Perhaps you're correct, Mr. Holmes, but that's not the way it's done around the United States Senate. Think of us as a club with our own set of standards. I may no longer be a senator, but I shall always retain my membership and therefore be obliged to abide by the rules."

With a steady gaze that told us he was not to be denied, Beveridge extended his arm to indicate the direction we were to take, and Holmes and I followed; only the white knuckles of my friend's hand on the walking stick suggested just how much this concession frustrated him.

Undaunted, Beveridge led us down the corridor, and we soon found ourselves in front of a doorway exactly like that which we had almost been able to enter, only this one belonged to Massachusetts's junior senator. The name on the plate read "Senator Winthrop Murray Crane."

Once within the large waiting room, Beveridge reminded Senator Crane's secretary, a Mr. Knowland, about the nature of our business, and the short young man in the dark suit, after knocking only once, escorted us into an adjacent office where the senator was seated at a shiny mahogany desk. Crane rose, shook our hands warmly, and introduced himself, his quiet voice expressing less enthusiasm than did his firm grip. A receding widow's peak highlighted his balding crown, and drooping moustaches concealed the entire length of his upper lip so that it was hard to determine whether he was smiling or sombre.

"I've agreed to talk with you, gentlemen," he began, "because both Senator Beveridge and President Roosevelt have asked me to." It was apparent, I realised, that Theodore Roosevelt must have been in very close contact with all his friends linked in some way to the author of *The Treason of the Senate.* "But," Crane went on in a decidedly serious tone, "the subject you wish to know about—David Graham Phillips—is still most displeasing. He called me an 'enemy of the country,' gentlemen, and I don't deserve that sort of treatment. If a man differs with me, that's fine. But to call me 'a treacherous servant' in print—as that blackguard did—without offering me equal space to rebut is sheer cowardice. It's been six years, and I still haven't forgotten. Many of us here on the Hill haven't forgotten."

"Then you were not saddened, I take it, by the news of Phillips's death?" Holmes asked.

"Gracious me," Senator Crane said, eyebrows arching like those of a mild-mannered vicar not wishing to offend his flock, "No-one could be happy to hear of anyone's death. But I will admit to having felt some relief when he was killed; at least I wouldn't have to read his insults any more."

"Of course," Holmes murmured. He paused for a moment, conveying the sense that his next question had not in fact been composed well in advance. Then he asked, "Have you any suggestion, Senator, as to who might have put Goldsborough up to the deed?"

In spite of the moustaches, at this question Crane's grin radiated confidence. "As far as I know, Mr. Holmes," he said slowly, "Goldsborough acted alone. But go talk to Van den Acker. He's always had some screwball notion about the assassination."

"Van den Acker?" I asked, having forgotten a name I obviously should have recognised.

"The former senator from New Jersey, Watson," Holmes reminded me. "Another of Phillips's targets."

As our conversation turned to pleasantries and it became apparent that we could extract nothing more from Crane about Phillips, we expressed our appreciation to the senator and followed Beveridge out of Crane's office and down a flight of curving stairs into what appeared to be the basement. With no purpose that I could fathom, Beveridge led us through a long, dark corridor lined at the ceiling with inelegantly exposed water pipes. Much to my amazement, however, I soon discovered down there in the bowels of the building an open, four-wheel, eight-seat vehicle awaiting our arrival; for (so Beveridge explained) there existed beneath the Senate Office Building a special subway system connecting the block to the Capitol itself. Indeed, following a ride of not more than a minute through a dimly lit, curving tunnel, the self-propelled Studebaker coach deposited us at our destination.

Brushing ourselves off from our brief but dusty journey, we now followed Beveridge up into the Capitol itself. Although entering from its lower level neatly allowed us to avoid the crowded rotunda, we also—unhappily, so the former senator informed us—missed its celebrated Trumbull paintings of the American Revolution. I thought it might be most amusing to view the conflict from the colonists' side; but Beveridge continued on his course across a multi-hued floor of yellow, blue, and terracotta tiles, up a marble staircase, past some uniformed guards who nodded in recognition at our escort, and through a doorway where we ultimately found ourselves standing in the visitors' gallery of the Senate chamber.

Because it was still early and the balcony was nearly devoid of people, we had little difficulty finding seats. Anyone who has ever attended a trial at the Old Bailey will certainly appreciate our coign of vantage—in this case, overlooking a large hall about twice as wide as it was deep. Arranged in four semi-circular, concentric rows were wooden desks that faced a multi-tiered rostrum set against the front wall. Despite the fact that business was obviously being conducted, the Senate floor was nearly empty.

"I know that Julius Caesar was murdered in the Roman Senate," I whispered to Holmes, "but it's hard to believe that so much of the mischief Phillips documented could occur in so vacant a hall."

Holmes nodded. "Perhaps that is *why* it occurred," he replied in a low voice, but then put a finger to his lips to indicate silence. It was obvious as he leaned forward that he wanted to hear the current speaker on the Senate floor, a tall, soft-spoken man with a neatly trimmed Vandyke who, with right hand clasped to a well-tailored lapel, was just concluding his remarks. From the little I could distinguish, the latter seemed to be cautioning his few colleagues present against closer relationships with the Kaiser and Germany. His peroration was greeted with only a sprinkling of applause from the gallery; still, he turned sharply to exit the chamber before this sign of appreciation had ended.

We too left, following Beveridge downstairs to the corridor in which Henry Cabot Lodge was awaiting us, for it was indeed he who had been addressing the small assemblage. From the distance, his aloof demeanour and measured speech had put me in mind of an Oxford don; on closer inspection, his piercing gaze and pointed beard reminded me more of Mephistopheles than Faust.

"I will admit to you, Mr. Holmes," he said when my friend asked him about Phillips, "that he hurt me deeply. I could tolerate the barbs aimed at me, you understand, but those directed at my family I couldn't abide."

"Quite," Holmes said.

"As a rule, I don't speak ill of people—however common," Lodge said, his eyelids fluttering. "Ask anyone, Mr. Holmes."

"Like Senator Van den Acker?" Holmes queried.

Ignoring the question, Lodge said, "But the man who shot David Graham Phillips laid to rest a great source of personal irritation for me."

I was impressed with Lodge's candour.

"I understand," Holmes said simply. Then, changing topics, he asked, "Did you perchance know the assassin's family, Senator? I should imagine that the Goldsboroughs and the Lodges must frequent the same social circles."

Lodge shook his head. "Excluding the perpetrator of this evil deed, Mr. Holmes, I have heard only the most well-deserved accolades bestowed upon the family. But, alas, no, I have never had the pleasure of meeting them."

It might have been my imagination, but it seemed to me that following Holmes's last question, Senator Lodge began to grow anxious. Perhaps he was merely warm when he mopped his brow with a linen handkerchief, but he did all too quickly fish out of his waistcoat pocket a great gold hunter, which he popped open to consult.

"I really must be going, I'm afraid," he said. "At any moment I'm expecting the bell to announce a vote. I'm terribly sorry about what happened to Phillips; but, you see, that is the risk one runs when one goes in for character assassination."

"Are you condoning murder then, Senator?"

"Mr. Holmes!" Beveridge exploded. "You go too far!"

"Relax, Bev," Lodge cautioned, laying a hand on Beveridge's arm. To Holmes he said, "I merely mean that rankling the wrong people can end up being costly. Phillips should have stuck to his novels. Many critics thought them quite good. He should have stayed with real fiction instead of what he tried to pass off as Truth." Lodge then clapped his hands. "Gentlemen," he repeated, "I must run." And with that, he walked briskly down the long corridor and beyond our view.

I was about to comment on Lodge's implied threat when, with a surreptitious shake of his head, Holmes gestured for me to remain silent. For his part, an annoyed Albert Beveridge ushered us out of the building.

"Please, Mr. Holmes," he said once we reached the open air, "try not to insult these men. They are my friends, after all, and I am the one responsible for bringing you here."

Holmes grunted a noncommittal reply.

It was by now late morning, and bright sunlight had cut its way through the thick clouds. From the steps of the Capitol, Beveridge pointed out the Mall just across the road; our journey was to the Botanic Gardens at its centre. Once within the luxuriant grounds, we followed a footpath amidst the swaying greens until we reached a large pool up from which rose an impressive exhibition of statuary.

"The celebrated Fountain of Light and Water, gentlemen," Beveridge announced.

Holmes and I inspected the Classical and Renaissance forms. Painted to look like bronze, three cast-iron nereids more than ten feet tall supported with their gracefully up-stretched arms the large basin rimmed with light fittings that crowned the display. Rivulets of water cascaded from atop the affair down to the base where reptilian sea creatures were endlessly spitting out their own streams of water.

"Water and light," Holmes mused prophetically, "one so prominent in this drama, the other so meagre." Then he said to Beveridge, "The fountain was designed by Bartholdi, if I'm not mistaken—the creator of your Statue of Liberty."

"Quite right, Mr. Holmes," Beveridge responded. "Just because our meetings are of a serious nature doesn't mean that our surroundings have to be." He then pointed in the direction of two darkly clad men who looked uncomfortable seated so stiffly in the bright sunshine on a stone bench but a few paces past the fountain.

Beveridge was obviously right about the benefits of being outdoors, however. Sounding much more lighthearted than he had with Lodge just moments earlier, he presented us to the strangers almost gaily. "Mr. Holmes, Dr. Watson," he said, "allow me to introduce you both to Senators Bailey and Stone from Texas and Missouri. I thought it best to isolate the Democrats!"

This last seemed a joke since, despite their apparent formality, the Democrats in question laughed right along with Beveridge. "Good thinkin', Bev," the senator identified as Bailey drawled, "especially when you pick so gorgeous a day to do the isolatin'. In fact, we were just talkin' about the cherry trees Mrs. Taft helped plant here last Friday."

"A gift from Japan," Beveridge explained to us. "When they finally bloom, all Washington will look like a spring bouquet."

Unfortunately, however, the promise of the season did not guarantee the success of our enquiries, for neither Bailey nor Stone had anything more to contribute to the story of Phillips's demise than had Crane or Lodge earlier.

Our subsequent meeting with Republican Senator Shelby Cullom of Illinois was particularly frustrating since our rendezvous took place in the seclusion of the Spring Grotto just west of the Capitol. We had taken the few steps down into the red-brick, triangular hideaway that enclosed a much smaller and simpler fountain than Bartholdi's, and with our voices protected by its reassuring gurgle and our conspicuousness shielded by the ferns and moss-clad stones beyond the grilled oval ports, we hoped for some news of the Phillips case that warranted our isolation. But Cullom, like the two Republicans with whom we later lunched in the Senate dining room—Knute Nelson from Minnesota and Boies Penrose from Pennsylvania—had little to add beyond his irritation with Phillips. Indeed, the highlight of our meal in the Capitol was not any information relevant to Phillips that we gleaned from the senators but rather the delectable Senate Bean Soup that they had recommended as the starter for our repast.

"The secret is using Michigan pea beans," Senator Nelson confided in hushed tones.

In point of fact, each of the seven senators we met that day (not to mention former Senator Buchanan on Friday last) offered little variation from what Senator Crane had initially told us in the morning—that he was relieved not to have to read Phillips's lies any longer, but that no-one should rejoice at the death of any other human being, and that Van den Acker seemed to be the person with whom to converse on the theory of conspiracies.

"Tell me," Holmes asked Beveridge after we had finished our interviews, "how do you account for the uniformity in the responses of so many of your colleagues?"

Beveridge considered for a moment, a crease furrowing his usually unruffled brow. Then he said, "I believe you'll find, Mr. Holmes, that professional politicians learn to deal with certain topics in similar ways. Take higher taxes. It's an issue that generally evokes a disagreeable reaction. What politician is going to say he's *for* them? But, as we all know, it's very easy to state a policy and then not support what you've said because of pragmatic considerations. The same is also true about death. No politician would ever want to be overheard applauding the demise of a fellow countryman—especially that of a prominent or formidable opponent like Graham. Hence, the similar answers."

"Death and taxes, eh, Senator?" Holmes mused. "I believe it was your statesman Benjamin Franklin who observed that no two events are more certain."

"You know your American history, Mr. Holmes; I'll give you that. But I'm not so sure you understand our politics. You seem to disagree with my explanation. Do you have another idea?"

"Only the obvious one," Holmes countered. "That all these men have discussed in advance precisely what they were going to tell us."

We left Senator Beveridge shaking his head in the corridor.

As Holmes and I were not planning to depart for New York until the next morning, we took rooms in the stately Hotel Washington just across the road from the Treasury and the White House. Fortunately, we saw nothing of President Taft during our stay because I am certain that if we had, Holmes would surely have asked him just how the chief executive himself was connected to the Great Phillips Murder Mystery!

Empty-handed—or so it seemed to me—we made the journey back to New York early the next day. Despite my own feelings of frustration, Holmes looked remarkably contented sunk in the softness of his green-velvet cushions adjacent to the door that gave access to the corridor, a carriage configuration typical of the American railway. His silence prompted my gaze at the luxuriant countryside skipping past. We had the compartment to ourselves, and both of us might have enjoyed the view afforded by a window seat, but Holmes seemed quite willing to forgo the pleasure. Indeed, as the train banked slowly at bends in the roadway, he seemed especially pleased to stare vacantly in the opposite direction.

"How can you be so calm, Holmes?" I finally asked. "This trip has been a waste of time! We saw fewer than half of the senators described by Phillips because the rest are out of office, and the seven with whom we did speak answered in unison like a Greek chorus."

Until my last remark, Holmes had been watching the empty passageway without expression. Smiling now, he turned to me. "One can only be disappointed, old fellow, when one has great expectations. I never thought that we would learn much from this little venture. But still it had to be done. Remember our enquiries so many years ago concerning the poisoned razor strop. As in that ingenious case, it has been necessary for me to sense firsthand the resentment and loathing so many of these men must have felt towards the victim."

"But surely, Holmes, you can see that in this instance there are too many suspects. Counting all those politicians–not to mention the Freverts and even Beveridge–"

"Don't forget Roosevelt," he added with another grin.

"Really, Holmes!" I cried. "Can't you be serious?"

"An open mind, Watson, can be the best conduit through a closed case. I suspect everyone until the culprit is known."

"But so many people were so greatly troubled by Phillips's behaviour at one time or another."

"On the contrary, Watson," Holmes said, "I think you're overestimating the bleakness of this affair. Phillips charged the Senate in 1906; he was killed five years later. That is a long period during which to harbour a grudge. I would cautiously suggest that we might direct our attentions to someone who had a grievance against Phillips only just prior to Phillips's death, someone who only recently might have undergone an experience that could have triggered a murderous hatred of the writer."

"Amazing, Holmes. You do bring order out of chaos."

"You know my methods, Watson. In order to eliminate the impossible, you must first become acquainted with all the characters in the drama. That is why I am so surprised to hear you say that you think our journey to Washington was fruitless. Discovering the prevalence of so much animosity regardless of who was actually to blame is one of two reasons I feel we must be making progress towards understanding what really happened in Gramercy Park."

"But how can we possibly survey so personal an investigation of so many people?"

"Tut, tut, Watson," he chided. "The pages of any old local newspaper would suffice for a start. What sort of person did Phillips hurt the most with his journalistic attacks?"

"Why, members of the Senate."

"Exactly. But what would wound a politician even more than poor notices in the press?"

"A political defeat?" I offered.

"Right again! And so we turn to the election closest to the date of Phillips's murder to see if any of the targets of Phillips's sharpened pen were voted out in November 1910, but a few short months before he was killed."

"Beveridge!" I ejaculated. "I thought as much. I never have trusted him—or that chauffeur of his. The bearded man who was following me was always in the proximity of Rollins; maybe they were exchanging messages. And a sinister-looking man like

Rollins could very well fit the description of the ill-clad vagabond Goldsborough wrote about in his dairy." It all made sense to me, everything except the motive. "But what I can't understand is why politics would be more important to Beveridge than his lasting friendship with Phillips."

"Why indeed, Watson," Holmes said with a wry smile. "As usual, you have constructed an excellent argument, but I am afraid that you have neglected to note a key ingredient of the case against the assassin."

"And what might that be?" I asked, hoping my clipped words conveyed my irritation at being corrected.

The train whistle hooted, and Holmes waited for it to cease before he answered.

"Are we not operating under the premise, old fellow, that the suspect in question was one of those attacked by Phillips in *The Treason of the Senate?*"

"Exactly!" I said.

"Then, Watson, you forget: It is true that Beveridge was Phillips's best friend, and it is also true that Beveridge was defeated in 1910, but Beveridge never became a victim of Phillips's pen. He was not a target of the articles."

Holmes was right, of course. I had forgotten.

"Then who *was* both a target and also recently defeated, Holmes?" I asked. "How many are there?"

"Just two, Watson, just two. And while I don't say these two are our only suspects, I do suggest that they represent a beginning. One is Millard Pankhurst Buchanan, Democrat of New York, whose acquaintance you have already made."

"A most melodramatic fellow he is," I said. "And the other?"

"The other is Peter Van den Acker, the Republican from New Jersey about whom we have heard some tantalising remarks. Indeed, since I have learned from your most thorough notes that Senator Buchanan has gone abroad, I suggest that, before too much more time elapses, we pay a visit to former Senator Van den Acker. He lives, I have been told, in Morristown. It's about twenty miles from the Hudson River."

"But you mentioned *two* reasons that you believe we are making so much progress, and you have told me only one. What is the second?" I asked.

"Only the fact that someone cares enough to have had us followed, Watson," he explained as calmly as he could over the clatter of the train on the rails. "Your friend with the false beard has been standing at the far end of the corridor since we left Washington. I caught sight of him as we boarded in Union Station."

"That miscreant? Here on this train?" Unable to see up the passageway from my seat near the window on the swaying carriage, I rather cumbersomely tried leaning across Holmes to view our pursuer; my friend, however, stayed me with his hand.

"He's not there any longer, Watson. He propped himself in a distant corner, but I've been watching his reflection in the window opposite. As soon as we began to approach New York, he moved away. He could be anywhere on the train. And without his beard–and aided, no doubt, by a change of coats–we might never recognise him. He could even be off the train by now, in light of how slowly it has been taking these curves. But have no fear. One day we'll catch up with him and find out what his game is."

Since this fellow might have been the same assailant who had shot at Holmes in Gramercy Park, the fact that he had vanished provided some comfort until the train finally rolled into the Pennsylvania Station.

Before Rollins had left with Beveridge for New York on the previous day, Holmes had asked the chauffeur to meet our train. That was how it came to pass that Rollins was waiting for us at the station when we arrived in New York. Unbeknownst to me, however, Holmes had also been busy sending telegrams while we were in Washington—probably when I had been tardy in dressing. I was unaware, therefore, that Holmes had asked the chauffeur in advance to stop at the Princeton Club after leaving the station or that Holmes had asked Newton James and Frank Davis, the two members of the Club who had rushed to the aid of the mortally stricken Phillips, to meet us there.

Although it retained much of its charm, the house that once had belonged to Stanford White had lost most of its luxuriant trappings after his murder in 1906, the same year in which *The Treason of the Senate* was published. We could see one of his massive black marble fireplaces that, Ozymandiaslike, seemed to lord over what once had been. But, we learned from the porter, just as one of the carved wooden lions that guarded the premises and the first-floor baroque ceiling had both been purchased for over three thousand dollars by the ubiquitous Mr. Hearst, so the other treasures of Stanford White had long since been sold before Princeton alumni began to occupy his celebrated home.

Two young men were waiting for us in the foyer when we arrived. One was talking animatedly while the other sat and nodded in silence. Both wore dark-blue suits of serge, both had short brown hair, and both turned out to be tall. After introducing himself to the pair, Holmes said to the talkative one, "In your own words, Mr. James, what happened when Mr. Phillips was shot?"

"Just a moment, Holmes," I interrupted. "We know their names from the police report, but how could you possibly distinguish the identity of one from the other?"

Holmes smiled, and I might even have detected a wink in the direction of the "twins." "The police report quotes Mr. James extensively as do the newspaper cuttings. From Mr. Davis, we hear very little. When we encounter the young men in question and discover one to be orating and the other to be listening, it takes not too much deductive reasoning, old chap, to conclude that the speaker of the two is Mr. James." Holmes then turned to the gentleman in question and repeated his query.

"As I told the police over a year ago, Mr. Holmes," James said, "Frank and I ran over to Phillips as soon as we saw him wounded."

"Start at the beginning, if you would be so kind," Holmes said.

His eyebrows pinched together, James looked pensive for a moment, and then he began to tell his story. "Davis and I had just come out of the club where we had been lunching when the shooting took place. We saw Phillips coming in the direction of the club, as we knew was his custom about that time of day."

"You knew it was he?"

"Oh, yes. We recognised him because of his tall, spare figure and his black alpine, rather crumpled hat. We did not pay much attention to him or to the other people in the street until suddenly we heard the quick explosions of the automatic revolver. The six shots which hit Phillips were fired so quickly that, when we looked to see what the trouble was, Phillips was swaying against the fence opposite 115 supported by Jacoby–"

"The florist?"

"Yes, that's right. Goldsborough was standing at the edge of the kerb. As we started to run toward him, Goldsborough raised the revolver to his temple and shot himself, his body falling into the gutter, where it lay until the club servants went out and lifted it up to the sidewalk and covered it with a sheet until it could be carried to the police station on a patrol wagon."

"Did Phillips say anything to you?" Holmes asked.

For the first time in the narrative, it was Davis who spoke. "I'll never forget that afternoon: 'For God's sake,' Phillips cried, 'get me into a building. Get a doctor!'"

"Then," James continued, "I rather foolishly pointed at Goldsborough's body and asked Phillips if he knew him."

"And?" Holmes asked. His voice was hushed.

"He just said, 'I don't know.' Then we helped Jacoby carry him into the first-floor entrance of the Club and got one of the bellboys to call for an ambulance. They stretched him out on a settee in the foyer where, I'm sorry to say, a lot of other chaps stood around and gawked."

"Did you do nothing for him?" I asked.

"Of course we did, Dr. Watson. Someone tried to stop the bleeding."

Davis, who seemed to be the repository of Phillips's words, added, "Phillips himself cried out, 'I've been shot. I am suffering. Can't you do something? Have you sent for an ambulance?'"

"He complained of pain in his left arm and in his stomach," James continued.

"I shouldn't wonder," I said, "a man who'd been shot six times."

"Then he asked us to call his personal physician, Dr. Fuller, over on Lexington Avenue. In fact, Fuller arrived at the same time

159

as the ambulance and rode in it to the hospital. That about covers it, I think."

"Nothing else?" Holmes asked.

Davis and James exchanged glances. Davis shook his head.

"Then I have one more point to ask you about, gentlemen," Holmes said, "after which we'll take up no more of your time. Did you get a close view of that automatic revolver?"

"The six-shooter problem, eh, Mr. Holmes?" James asked. His smile suggested he enjoyed divining the point of the question. "Alas, no. I am only aware of what the police have said—that the gun could fire up to ten bullets, but I believe I speak for Mr. Davis as well when I say that neither one of us could identify the specific weapon."

Davis nodded his agreement, and, concluding we could gain no additional information from the pair, we offered our thanks and walked out into Twenty-first Street.

"Come with me, Watson," Holmes ordered, and I proceeded to walk beside him as he crossed the road, travelling west along the northern fencing of the park. Since this path was clearly not in the direction of the motor car, I wondered where we might be heading. Suddenly, some ten yards before we arrived at the turning, he stopped and pointed his stick at a makeshift, green-canvas tent that had been erected against the park railing as it turned south at the end of the grounds. Surrounding the tent as well as being enclosed by it were bright bursts of spring flowers arrayed in various bouquets to attract the eye of passers-by. A sweet fragrance hung in the air.

"Surely, Holmes," I said, "this is not the time to be buying nosegays."

"Behold, Watson—the establishment of Mr. Jacob Jacoby, florist,"

Holmes said in reply. "At the moment of the shooting, he happened to be near enough to Phillips to catch him as he fell against the fence."

"But how could you be so certain of the location of this stall?" I asked. "It was most decidedly not here on our previous tour of the park."

"Once again, Watson, you have seen but failed to observe."

Stung by Holmes's objurgation, however mild, I did now recall his cursory glances at the pavement when we stood at this same spot with Mrs. Frevert. What is more, Holmes knew that I recollected the incident.

"Yes, Watson," he said, "I observed the remnants of the flower stall when we visited the scene Sunday last. Gardenias–and their petals–are not to be found growing wild at this time of year."

As usual, it all seemed so obvious when the explanation was before me; but I had no more time to consider the matter, for we were now approaching the flower vendor himself.

Mr. Jacoby greeted us by removing the small, flat cap from his head. He was a short, egg-shaped man of middle age. Despite his threadbare black coat, his beard was neatly trimmed, and he presented us with so broad a grin that his eyes seemed to disappear behind his red cheeks.

"Gentlemen," he said amiably while replacing the cap on his head, "chrysanthemums for your lapels, or, maybe, roses for your ladies?" He spoke in the guttural tones of what I assumed to be an Eastern European accent.

"We'll each take a white chrysanthemum," my friend said; but as Jacoby was handing them to us, Holmes added, "perhaps like the ones you used to sell to David Graham Phillips, Mr. Jacoby."

The utterance of Phillips's name caused the smile to drop from the flower vendor's face.

"What do you want from me?" he asked. "My name, I see, you know already. How?"

"I am Sherlock Holmes, Mr. Jacoby, and I have read the official police files. I know that you were right next to Phillips when he was shot. I now want to know what you witnessed and what you can tell me about the gun you must have seen Goldsborough holding."

Jacoby removed his cap again and ran stubby fingers through his thin strands of brown hair. Apparently confronting some inner dilemma, he hesitated a moment or two. Then he began slowly. "Mr. Phillips–" he was able to say, but was immediately interrupted by a metallic clacking.

Glancing up the sidewalk, we all saw a muscular policeman in a tight-fitting, dark uniform running his cudgel horizontally against the rails of the fence as he slowly advanced towards us some twenty feet away.

"Come, sir, surely–" Holmes encouraged, but whatever Jacoby had been about to say, the little man now straightened up and spoke as if repeating a text he had memorised well in advance.

"I have been advised," he announced, "both by the police and by the District Attorney to remain silent."

I do not know if the officer was merely making his daily rounds or if he had been watching the flower stall or whether the police had been keeping an eye on Holmes and me, but it was clear from Mr. Jacoby's rigid stare and shaking fingers that the wretched man believed that it was for him the policeman had been sent.

"I have nothing to say to you!" he shrieked at us. "Now go!"

"Let me at least pay for the flowers," Holmes said.

"No, take them!" he pleaded. "Please."

Observing the agitated state of the little flower vendor and that people around us were beginning to stare, Holmes nodded in my direction; and after he dropped a few coins onto the counter, we walked off down the pavement, smiling first at the policeman, and then making our way back to Rollins at the other end of the park.

"What do you think of our witnesses?" I asked Sherlock Holmes as we entered the Waldorf-Astoria. "A pair of identical twins and one man too frightened to talk."

"In point of fact, Watson, none of them said anything they had not already told the reporter from *The New York Times.*"

"At least we still have Van den Acker to interview," I reminded him.

"Yes," he mused, "Van den Acker."

We stopped at the front desk to enquire after messages, but a ginger-haired hall porter whom we had not seen before failed to turn round at our arrival. Only after Holmes rapped smartly on the counter with his walking stick did the pale young man jump to attention. Checking our pigeonhole, he found two pieces of correspondence. To me, he handed a folded sheet of notepaper with my name on the front, but when he read what was printed on the cover of the envelope addressed to Holmes, he faced my friend with a wide grin.

"You're Sherlock Holmes, sir?" he asked.

Here in America, Holmes seemed particularly surprised by references to his fame. He merely nodded in response.

The hall porter gaped at my companion. "The *real* Sherlock Holmes?" he asked. "From England?"

Holmes nodded again. "It is I," he confessed, extending his

hand to receive the correspondence.

Before Holmes could take possession of the envelope, however, the young man looked both ways as if to avoid detection and then brought from beneath the counter a small leather-bound book that appeared to be always at the ready. After handing my friend a pen, he opened the book to a blank page. "Could I please have your signature, Mr. Gillette? I saw your performance as Sherlock Holmes right here in New York a couple of years ago."

"I'm afraid–" said Holmes.

"Please," he importuned, holding the book under Holmes's nose while his own fair cheeks and forehead turned a self-conscious pink. "Address it, if you would be so kind, to Miles Kennedy. That's me."

Fearing the envelope might be held hostage, Holmes agreed and signed the blank page. Young Mr. Kennedy scrutinised the autograph for a few moments and then said, "You really remain in character, Mr. Gillette. Even the name you sign is 'Sherlock Holmes.'"

Message secured, Holmes ushered me away from the desk.

"My friend Gillette again," he whispered, "the actor who sent me the calabash. His portrayal of me on the stage must have been quite convincing. Fancy that! I thought that being depicted in the cinematograph was tiresome enough, but now I see that I shall have to contend with stage actors as well. I am afraid, Watson, that all this is but the logical outgrowth of your melodramatic accounts of some rather mundane cases."[*]

"Really, Holmes," I said, "there are others who might be

---

[*] Author's note: By the end of 1911, at least nine silent films concerning the adventures of Sherlock Holmes had been produced. For further information on Holmes and the cinema, see David Stuart Davies, *Holmes of the Movies: The Screen Career of Sherlock Holmes* (New York: Bramhall House, 1978).

flattered to have so faithful a biographer." I then proceeded to unfold the paper addressed to me. To my surprise, it was from William Randolph Hearst, a reminder that, if I so desired, he was still prepared to make me a handsome offer to write for his newspaper–a very handsome offer indeed. Wondering how this proposition compared to the one with which Hearst had convinced Phillips to write *The Treason of the Senate*, I said, "You see, Holmes–"

But Sherlock Holmes was no longer at my side. He had stopped a few paces behind me to read the message he himself had received.

"It's from Senator Van den Acker," he explained. "He wants to talk with me as soon as possible."

"What? Now?"

"It would appear so, Watson. He says he lives alone and has given the servants the night off to ensure our privacy. 'It can't wait till tomorrow,' Holmes read. "He refers to a message sent to him from someone we talked with in Washington."

"But who, Holmes?"

"That's what we must find out from Mr. Van den Acker. What's more, Watson, one does not need Scotland Yard to detect that this envelope containing the message has been opened and amateurishly resealed. Just look at how easily the flap came up. It is obvious that someone else knows where we will be going tonight. Take along your pistol, old friend. I have the feeling that our presence here has finally set in motion such activities as will lead to a break in this case."

Mr. Hearst's inducement remained attractive, and I could well understand how the publisher had lured Phillips himself away from writing fiction to take on the Senate. But tonight–like so many nights in years gone by–the game was afoot, and no pecuniary offer of any size could make me vacate my position in the hunt alongside the tenacious figure of Mr. Sherlock Holmes. It was indeed like old times.

Nine

A Visit to Van den Acker's

"A great financier ... must build up a system–he must find lieutenants with the necessary coolness, courage and cunning ... to efface completely the trail between him and them, whether or not they succeed in covering the roundabout and faint trail between themselves and the tools that nominally commit the crime."

–David Graham Phillips, *The Deluge*

The address in the message from Van den Acker led us thirty miles to the west into historic and fashionable Morristown. New Jersey is another state, to be sure, but the trip was a manageable if tedious journey first by ferry across the Hudson, then by railway through the countryside, and finally by cab to the former senator's imposing residence. By the time we reached our destination on that cool spring night, complete darkness had descended. Only one lone light cast its glow through a window onto the flagstone footpath winding round the left side of the building. Holmes strode quickly up the brick walkway leading to the front door and twice lifted the knocker, a large brass American eagle, letting it fall each time with a resounding clang.

There was no response.

Holmes tried twisting the doorknob, but it would not turn, and the door itself would not open when he pushed.

"Come on, Watson," he said. "Around to the side where the light is shining. And keep your pistol ready."

Patting my coat pocket to see that my revolver was still there, I had no time at all in which to think. I followed Holmes, who surprised me with his agility by fairly bounding over a small hedge, an obstacle that I could get past only by pushing through a break in its clutching branches. Once on the other side, however, I immediately found myself on the flags that led in the direction of the light we had seen earlier.

When I caught up with him, Holmes was transferring his walking stick from his right hand to his left and withdrawing his pistol from within the folds of his inverness; I did likewise, pointing my Eley's No. 2 upwards as I inched along behind him. With our backs pressed against the outer wall just before the window, we sidled towards the single source of illumination like a pair of cracksmen. Holmes peered cautiously round the edge of the double-hung sash window and then, moving to his left, bade me join him. We both looked in at the brightly lit room as if we were viewing a stage set under the blaze of spotlights.

As much as I should like to expunge it from my memory, I shall forever recall the grisly sight that greeted us that March night. At first glance, the study, for it was that chamber into which we were staring, seemed undisturbed. Countless leather-bound tomes stood at attention in the shelves that surrounded most of the room, and embers from a recent fire glowed red hot in the grate. Opposite the brick hearth stood a cherrywood desk upon which lay a single open book, its pages fluttering gently in a semi-circular arc.

After witnessing the spectacle at the centre of the room, however, one could not for a moment longer regard the scene as placid; for seated in a tall, black chair of cracked leather, his upper body folded over the top of the desk, his bloodied head glistening red like a sparkling ruby that reflected the light from the hearth, were the remains of him who must have been in life Senator Peter Van den Acker. A small bullet hole was apparent in his right temple; the left side of his head was a gaping hole of bone and tissue, much of the matter being thrown on the rear wall to his left. What appeared to be a six-chambered revolver lay on the floor just inches from where his right hand hung down.

"Follow me," Holmes said, proceeding to push upwards the bottom window sash, which was open now but half an inch.

With not a little difficulty, we created enough of a crawl space to enable us to help each other scramble through the window, experiencing, if the truth be told, much less ease than we used to enjoy in our younger days. Once inside, it didn't require my many years of knowledge as a doctor to recognise that the man before us was dead. Nonetheless, I felt for the pulse.

Unable to find one, I shook my head. "Suicide," I concluded aloud.

"Apparently," Holmes said, "yet ..."

We both replaced our pistols, and then Holmes immediately began that ritual of pacing, peering, studying a death scene from every conceivable angle. In addition to the corpse and the desk, neither of which he actually touched, he scrutinised with the aid of his lens the mahogany table that stood behind the desk. Blood had spattered most of the area to the rear of the body's left side, including the wall, which was covered in light blue-and-ivory patterned paper, and two large-framed oil paintings depicting what appeared to be outdated frigates in full sail.

I knew enough not to distract Holmes in such intense activity, but when, by looking up, he signalled he was finished, I suggested that we should ring the police. There was a telephone next to the corpse.

"Yes," he said abstractedly. Then he added, "But first, Watson, observe the book." Not handling directly the slim, claret-coloured volume that was lying open on the desk, he employed the tapered end of the ebony walking stick to flip its pages. In spite of the book's proximity to the dead man, it appeared remarkably free of blood. Its title, *The House of the Vampire*, stood out ominously in bold, black letters.

"The book Goldsborough had read," I remembered.

"The book we were to *believe* he had read, Watson," Holmes corrected. After riffling through the opening pages with the aid of his stick, he turned back to the flyleaf. "Note the inscription," he directed.

I leaned closer to my friend to read the finely penned handwriting on the inside cover. "Dear Senator," it read. "Herein are more chills for your collection." It was signed by the author, George Sylvestre Viereck.

"Holmes!" I cried, pointing at the deceased. "The case is settled then. We see before us what's left of the mastermind of the Phillips assasination."

"Really, Watson?"

"Of course," I said. "Van den Acker wanted to confess,

summoned you, then became frightened and took his own life. After all, each of the senators we met in Washington linked him to a conspiracy."

"Perhaps," he said, "but I wonder if …"

Whatever Holmes had in mind, to me he seemed to be complicating the issue.

"Holmes," I said impatiently, "postpone your idle speculation; let us ring the police."

"A moment, Watson," he murmured. "Why did you say suicide?"

"It's perfectly obvious," I said, eager now to show him my own powers of detection. Enumerating my data like a zealous science professor explaining an experiment to a slow class, I rushed into my presentation: "The gun lies near his right hand; there are gunpowder burns surrounding the hole in his right temple and in his right palm; and since the small watch with the leather strap he is wearing on his left wrist indicates that he is right-handed, one can easily surmise that the unfortunate Senator Van den Acker held the pistol in his right hand, pointed the barrel slightly rearward at his right temple, and proceeded to blow off the back left side of his skull."

"And where is the bullet—or what is left of it?" Holmes asked.

After scrutinising the wall for a moment, I pointed to a jagged little hole near one of the seascapes. "There!" I said, feeling pleased with myself.

"Yes, Watson, that's true. But you haven't gone far enough, old fellow. You haven't asked why a patch of wallpaper to the right of that picture is brighter than the rest of the wall."

I looked again, admittedly having paid little attention to the paper itself.

"Behold," he said, again using his walking stick, this time to lift away from the wall the painting to our right, which, I now could plainly see, was suspended from the picture rail by means of two fine wires extending upwards to a rosette-like hook that saved as their apex at the wall's juncture with the ceiling.

With his free hand, he pointed to a second splintery hole that was apparent behind the painting to the immediate right of where the left edge of the burnished frame had been hanging. "Just as I expected, Watson," he said. His eyes shone keen and triumphant at the same time. "Van den Acker was shot first at close range, the bullet implanting itself to the right of the picture, here." He punctuated the point with a rap of his knuckle on the wall next to this new bullet hole he had just revealed to me. "The assailant then placed the gun in the dead man's hand and fired again at the corpse's head, resulting in the powder burns, the wound that masked the first one, and that other hole in the wall which we both had identified earlier. It was mere child's play to stand on that table and move the hook a few inches to the left, thereby allowing the painting to conceal the additional aperture on the left but revealing the telltale bright patch on the right. Our suspect was a tall man, by the way. He had to be to reach the hook. And I'm sure you'll find that his left boot has a nail askew; you can see where it scratched the varnish on the tabletop. Two bullet holes and a moved picture can mean only, of course, that Senator Van den Acker was in fact murdered."

But Holmes didn't have time to relish his deductive powers, for no sooner had he completed his last statement than the slam of the front door could be heard reverberating throughout the empty house.

"Blast!" Holmes ejaculated, letting the painting swing back against the wall, "I am indeed getting old, Watson. Whoever that was must have heard everything we said. Quick, man!" And withdrawing his pistol, he ran through the corridor to the front door.

"But the police!" I cried.

"No time!" he shouted in response. "You ring! But let them discover that second bullet hole on their own. And for God's sake, don't tell them who you are!"

Holmes was out of the door before I could pick up the telephone receiver; fortunately, he did not need to remind me that I should hold the instrument with a handkerchief in order to leave no incriminating fingerprints.

It seemed an eternity until the operator who had responded connected me with the local police. I quickly reported the horrible deed, gave the address but not my name, and rang off. A moment later, following Holmes's trail, I withdrew my revolver from my coat pocket for the second time that night, left the house through the front door, and plunged down a dark road to the right where I had heard the diminishing echo of footfalls. I continued my pursuit for some hundred yards but, owing to my age and my old war wound, soon began to tire.

Almost immediately, Holmes was at my side. Bracing his stick against my chest, he whispered, "Be on your guard, old fellow. The footsteps stopped abruptly. No doubt he is stalking us now; we know too much, it would appear."

A street lamp down the road, too far away to do us much good, cast a dim glow in our direction. It was at least bright enough for us to determine that we were standing in front of a long, high, tree-lined, wrought-iron railing, not unlike that which circumscribed

Gramercy Park. This fence, however, was interrupted every ten feet for as far as we could discern by rectangular brick columns some eight feet tall. These columns supported two horizontal bars that in turn supported numerous vertical rods, each of which was topped by an individually mounted and sharply pointed *fleur-de-lis*.

Holmes and I stood back to back perusing the roadway, both of us attempting to distinguish any movement in the darkness beyond.

"The police should be here momentarily," I whispered.

"Our friend must suspect that too, Watson," he whispered in return, "so we may assume he will act quickly–if he has a pistol besides the one that is still lying on Van den Acker's desk."

Just then the whine of motor cars echoed up the road, their headlamps sweeping the neighbouring houses and trees as the police came round a turning; but though the flashes of light scarcely illuminated the blackness for more than an instant, I thought I could distinguish atop one of the brick columns the towering frame of the bearded stranger who had been so determinedly following us.

Whatever the villain's nefarious intentions, the arrival of the police had obviously prevented him from carrying them out, for as we were wondering what his next move was to be, his vaguely familiar and distinctly defiant voice rent the darkness: "I have no weapon now, Mr. Sherlock Holmes, but I will the next time when the law won't be around to save you ..."

I heard the scrape of his boots as he must have been turning to flee. Suddenly leaves rustled, we heard cloth tearing, the fence shook, and an agonising howl arose that prickled the very hairs on the back of my neck. In a moment, all was still again.

Striking a Vesta, Holmes revealed a most ghastly tableau. It was indeed the grizzled man who had been so doggedly pursuing us. With strips of his black cape still fluttering from the gnarled tree branch in which the cloth had so obviously become entangled, the wretched man lay where his misdirected leap had propelled him, facedown, arms extended earthward as if trying to embrace what fate would never let him reach, his mangled and bloody body impaled on a phalanx of miniature spears, the deadly *fleurs-de-lis* atop the wrought-iron fence.

There was no way to save the unfortunate devil, but—horrible as it is to describe even now years later—he seemed to make a final attempt at extricating himself, writhing in awful agony, his scarlet hands grasping at the rails just below his chest. My effort would be futile, I knew, but the medical man that I am forced me to his aid. Even as I took a step forward, however, all movement ceased.

"There's nothing to be done for him," Holmes said, holding me back.

I stared in disbelief at the contorted face of the dead man just a yard from my own. "But who is he, Holmes?"

"Who indeed, Watson?" Holmes echoed, as he slowly peeled away the false beard.

"Altamont!" I gasped as the countenance I now fully recognised appeared before me.

"Yes, Watson," Holmes said, "the personal secretary of former Senator Millard Pankhurst Buchanan." Suddenly he bent over. "Hullo," he murmured more to himself than to me, "what have we here?"

On the ground below the body, apparently having fallen from Altamont's hand, lay a crumpled envelope. Looking over Holmes's shoulder as he smoothed the cover flat, I could easily see before the flame of his match extinguished that my friend's name was written across the front.

"Open it, Holmes. It is addressed to you," I said. As I spoke, I could see lights going on in the darkened windows at Van den Acker's. "Hurry!" I cautioned. "The police have already entered the house."

"Yes, Watson, I see." Holding the envelope, he said quickly, "This is no doubt the message that Van den Acker had intended to give to me. And as such, I have no compunction about claiming it."

Holmes unsealed the flap, lit a second match, and discovered yet another smaller envelope inside. This one, which had been sent through the post to Van den Acker's address, bore the imprimatur of the United States Senate. Holmes opened this envelope as well and, seeing no letter inside, shook it so that, like a white moth, out fluttered a small, square piece of faded paper obviously cut from a newspaper.

Holmes struck another match, and as it flared, the two of us read what turned out to be a brief entry from the society column of the *Washington Post*.

"Eyebrows were raised last night at the reception following a benefit concert of Beethoven's Ninth Symphony at Continental Hall. Lame-duck Senator Millard P. Buchanan left his party, including his elegantly gowned wife, in order to engage in an animated and heated discussion in the foyer of the hall with musician Fitzhugh Coyle Goldsborough of the distinguished Maryland family. That Senator Buchanan was dressed in formal attire and Mr. Goldsborough was accoutered less suitably made their conversation all the more noticeable."

"But what does it mean, Holmes?" I asked. "Why is this article so important?"

Reflected in the light of the dying match flame, Holmes's eyes looked more piercing than ever. "It is the missing link, Watson. This cutting ties Goldsborough and Buchanan together. Continental Hall is in Washington, and the 'lame-duck' reference places their meeting after the 1910 election. Something that we said on our trip to the capital must have prompted one of the senators into sending Van den Acker this article to give to us; they all knew we were coming to see him. Whoever posted it really isn't important, but that Altamont was undoubtedly the culprit who intercepted Van den Acker's message to us certainly is. Or was."

Holmes and I had no time to ponder this revelation, however, for shouting voices and streaks of light told us that the police were beginning to search the grounds surrounding Van den Acker's house.

"Let us be off, old friend," Holmes said, scooping up the article and the envelopes. "I don't fancy spending the rest of this night explaining to the local constabulary what we were doing at the site of two mysterious deaths. You and I have more important matters to discuss."

We took our leave of the scene at a rapid gait, but I could not help noticing the head of a small nail protruding from the heel of the dead man's left boot.

As luck would have it, we were able to hail a taxi whose tired driver was on his way home for the night. The promise of a substantial gratuity ultimately convinced him to take us all the way to the ferry.

"You were not surprised to discover Altamont, were you, Holmes?" I asked once we had settled back for the ride.

"No, Watson. What we had discovered on Van den Acker's

desk had prepared me in advance."

"That book, Holmes! The one about the vampire."

"Bravo, Watson. The 'Dear Senator' inscription, you see—it was not addressed to Van den Acker, as we were intended to believe."

"But surely you can't be certain of that, Holmes."

"There's the matter of the blood on the book, Watson."

"But there was no blood on the book."

"Precisely, old fellow. Because the book was placed on Van den Acker's desk *after* he was shot."

Slowly I was beginning to understand.

"The police," I said, feeling a sudden burst of sympathy for the Morristown authorities. "Shouldn't we be telling them?"

Holmes smiled. "Let them conjure their own explanations of tonight's events," he said. "If they assume that Van den Acker's death is a suicide, then Altamont's body may also prove to be a puzzle to them. The longer it takes the authorities to connect the deaths with Senator Buchanan, the more time we will have to try to find him ourselves. I fear that if our suspicions were made known in New York, they might find their way to Buchanan in England before we do."

"But a man of his prominence is not going to give himself away on the basis of our circumstantial evidence or unsubstantiated theories," I said.

"Of course not," Holmes countered. "That is why we're going to pay a visit to the Senator's home in New York as quickly as we can."

The lights of the dock soon appeared before us, and it was just a matter of minutes before we began the late journey back to Manhattan and our hotel.

"Although today is April Fool's day, Watson, the local police are not as shortsighted as we had expected," Sherlock Holmes said to me at breakfast the next morning. "See for yourself," he added, handing me the copy of the *New York Times* that had accompanied his coffee.

"Former Senator Found Murdered at Home," the headline trumpeted. I continued reading aloud:

"Former Senator Peter Van den Acker was discovered murdered at his home in Morristown, New Jersey, last night. The police believe that the killer was attempting to rob the house and shot Mr. Van den Acker when the thief entered the study. The body of the man police believe to be the intruder was found a few houses away. He had been horribly killed by falling on top of a sharp rail fence while trying to make good his escape. The police speculate that in his haste to flee, the murderer lost his footing and fell to his death. The suspect carried no papers, and thus the police are at a loss as to his identity."

"A little time gained, eh, Watson?" Holmes said. "But to take advantage of it, we must be off."

On that damp overcast morning, Rollins (looking much less suspicious now that our enquiries were pointing in a different direction) drove us to the east side of Central Park. On Fifth Avenue near Ninetieth Street the soaring turrets of the Buchanan home took their places alongside the lofty pinnacles and minarets of the sumptuous palaces of their neighbours. Rising as they did out of that dank grey fog, however, those towers and chimney pots looked more like tombstones in a forgotten graveyard than architectural hallmarks of America's aristocracy.

I was reminded by Holmes that, according to Phillips's writings, the Buchanan mansion, like so many others of the Senator's treasures, had originally belonged to his wife, Mrs. Elise Bradford Buchanan, the only living offspring of Tyler Bradford. Her father had traced both his ancestry and his money back to the second son of a duke whose title had been created in the seventeenth century by a monarch said to have been his natural father. Despite its ostentatious air, the house did indeed convey a regal sense of power and strength in its massive design.

Having instructed Rollins to remain some distance away, at exactly 10:00 Sherlock Holmes rang the bell at the absent senator's red front door.

"Good morning," Holmes brightly addressed Buchanan's butler, a greying man with thick black eyebrows and small tufts of dark hair protruding from his ears. He had a forward stoop that gave him the appearance of being ready to depart when in fact he was solidly rooted to the ground. "I represent Bondy and Company," Holmes announced, "booksellers of Charing Cross, London." (How quickly he could assume a role never failed to amaze me. As I have stated on numerous occasions elsewhere, the stage lost a great actor when Sherlock Holmes took up the detection of crime.) "I know that your employer is abroad with his wife," Holmes proceeded. "It is thanks to that gracious lady that we are here. Mrs. Buchanan has instructed our company to send its sales representatives—myself, Josiah Wink, and my associate, Cecil Thoroughgood—to peruse Mr. Buchanan's library in hopes of settling on a suitable first edition as a surprise gift for, for—" (At this point Holmes withdrew the small notebook from inside his coat pocket and appeared to be searching for a misplaced occasion.)

"The Senator's birthday, sir?"

"Yes, yes," Holmes said, "just so."

"Mrs. Buchanan," the butler droned, "left no such word with me, sir."

"Apparently it was a decision she reached in London. I myself only received the telegram from my home office to come here this very morning."

"Really, sir." The butler stood immobile.

"Come, my man," Holmes said, "you may join us in our perusal. We seek to view only the library. Certainly you would not wish to thwart Mrs. Buchanan's plans for a surprise."

The butler remained stationary.

"C'mon, mate," Holmes finally drawled with a winsome grin, "give a bloke the chance to earn 'is salary."

Ever so slowly a perceptible grin began to creep across the old man's visage. He hesitated, finally turned, and, listing in the direction he was about to lead us, proceeded through the entry hall, and made a left turn to two highly polished doors of burled walnut both of which he quietly slid to either side. Before us stood the library, a large room with a bow window that overlooked the verdant gardens behind the Buchanan mansion.

Ignoring the vista as well as the musty smell of a book-filled room that had not been recently ventilated, Holmes began his search. That the volumes were arranged by genre made our hunt considerably easier. In the poetry section, we saw such familiar works as those by Browning, Wordsworth, and Coleridge— although from their pristine condition, I was forced to conclude that the good Senator and his wife read from those volumes infrequently, if at all.

Against the northern wall, framing the window, we found Buchanan's fiction library. The works of Mark Twain were there along with what appeared to be a complete set of Dickens. Ironically, the political novels of David Graham Phillips also had a place on the senator's shelves. Against the right side of the north wall we discovered a subdivision within the fiction collection, books dealing with the fantastic. Remembering Buchanan's concern with superstition, I was not unduly surprised by the discovery, but Holmes drew closer to scan the titles.

The only sound was that of the butler's heavy breathing behind us.

"I say, Thoroughgood," Holmes said at last, "here is an interesting collection: Mary Shelley's *Frankenstein*, Stevenson's *Dr. Jekyll and Mr. Hyde*, Goethe's *Faust*, Poe's *Tales of Terror*, Walpole's *Castle of Otranto*, Charles Gould's *Mythical Monsters*, Maturin's *Melmoth the Wanderer*, Lewis's *The Monk,* Jane Austen's *Northanger Abbey*, H.G. Wells's *The Invisible Man* and *The Island of Dr. Moreau*."

On the neighbouring shelf were occult books of an even more specific nature. I saw two copies of Bram Stoker's *Dracula*, Pierre Carmouche's *Le Vampire*, Dr. John Polidor's *The Vampyre*, Thomas Preskett Prest's *Varney the Vampire*, and–rather surprisingly since we had previously assumed that it was the volume we had discovered at Van den Acker's–Viereck's *The House of the Vampire*. If the case against Buchanan depended so greatly on that book at Van den Acker's being his, perhaps our rush to condemn him was premature. Holmes, however, appeared unruffled by the discovery.

"May I?" he asked the butler, indicating the books he wanted to examine.

The older man shrugged his assent, and Holmes began by withdrawing the two copies of *Dracula* from their positions and opening each in turn to its title page. After riffling their pages, he replaced both of them and, rubbing his chin, proceeded to inspect the books by Polidor and Prest. Only then did he reach for the claret-coloured work by Viereck, which he examined as he had the others.

As Holmes did so, the butler observed, "That's strange. I thought the senator had given that very book to his secretary, Mr. Altamont, just before the senator's departure."

So many books, I thought. How could this old fellow account for which ones were given out?

A few moments later Holmes returned the volume he was inspecting to its place on the shelf and, with a slight nod of his head, indicated to me it was time to retire.

"The Senator seems to be lacking in Poe," Holmes observed with mock gravity. Once again, I noted that macabre American author with whom my friend had some passing if not totally appreciative familiarity.

We thanked the butler, telling him that we would convey our purchasing suggestions to Mrs. Buchanan abroad without ever revealing how we had gained access to the Senator's library. The butler could thus rest assured that his master would have a most satisfying birthday due in great part to the perspicacity of a loyal but anonymous servant.

Sherlock Holmes said nothing as we walked back to Rollins and the Packard. In spite of my own anxieties, I could tell by my friend's smug grin that he had got the information he had been looking for.

"But Holmes," I said once we were seated in the security of the closed passenger compartment, "I myself observed the copy of the Viereck book on Buchanan's shelf. It should have been missing if his was the volume we saw on Van den Acker's desk."

"My dear Watson," Holmes said, "the man is a collector of rare books. That is why I was checking at the front of each copy. The two *Draculas*, for example–one was a Constable and Company first edition; the other, an American first from Doubleday. The rest I looked at were also first editions."

"Including *The House of the Vampire?*" I asked.

"That all depends on which copy you mean, Watson," he said with a smirk.

"But surely I saw only a single volume, Holmes."

"Back at Buchanan's–yes, that is so, and it was not a first. But the book on Van den Acker's desk, old fellow–don't forget it. Remember, the butler said that Buchanan had given it to Altamont."

"Then it *was* Altamont who was behind these murders?"

"Not *behind* them, Watson, although he played prominent roles in both. He certainly must have planted the book at Van den Acker's, and that book, I am convinced, is the linchpin of this investigation. It was a first edition, you see, and I have no doubt that the 'Senator' of the inscription was *not* Van den Acker, as we were supposed to believe, but rather the culprit who ordered it left at the scene of Van den Acker's murder–the honourable former senator from New York, Millard Pankhurst Buchanan."

"But how can you be so certain that Altamont wasn't acting on his own–perhaps out of some demented loyalty to his employer?"

"Because, Watson, Altamont would not have the capability to affect so many men of power and authority. He never could have orchestrated the unanimity we witnessed in Washington among all those senators."

"Then you think Buchanan's our man, Holmes?"

"Yes, I believe he is, old fellow. That is why we must return to England as soon as we can to confront this deadly betrayer of the public trust."

Holmes leaned forward to communicate with the driver. "Rollins!" he fairly shouted. "To the Waldorf! And quickly, man!"

Ten

Confrontation

"The much-talked-of difference between those born to wealth and power and those who rise to it from obscurity resolves itself to little more than the difference between those born mad and those who go insane."

–David Graham Phillips, *The Price She Paid*

Much of the next twenty-four hours remains an ambiguity. Holmes and I booked passage on the first available ship to England, the White Star Line's *Olympic*, leaving the following day. Mrs. Frevert, whom Holmes rang only to tell that the mystery of her brother's death was taking us back to London, insisted on seeing us off and commandeered not only Rollins and the Packard but also Beveridge himself in her efforts to facilitate our departure. And so it was that the day after our visit to Buchanan's library, Holmes and I and our luggage, along with Mrs. Frevert and Beveridge, made our way through the crowds as quickly as we could to the vast lengths of Pier 59. Just the previous year,

Beveridge explained, the dock had been extended an additional ninety feet out into the Hudson to accommodate the large ships of the White Star Line.

"What a pity," I lamented "that we never visited the Statue of Liberty. It's so typically American, after all."

"Oh," Beveridge replied, "with your trip to Washington and your stay in New York, Doctor, I think you've experienced the essence of what this country is made of."

"How true, Senator," Holmes said, as he shook Beveridge's hand in farewell, "how very true."

Not long after I had positioned myself at the rail of the great ship, a veritable fleet of twelve tugboats, like courtiers round a queen, struggled for position in helping the mighty vessel ease away from port. Beneath a bright and, I hoped, prophetic sunny sky, I stood waving my good-byes to Mrs. Frevert, to Beveridge, and to the chauffeur Rollins (whom I could easily make out in the distance thanks to his proximity to the yellow motor car). As I took in for the last time that celebrated skyline of New York, I realised I was also saying farewell to America–not to mention the seductive offer of employment made to me by Hearst. What would Mrs. Watson have done if instead of returning to England, I had telegraphed her to join me in New York?

For his part, Sherlock Holmes was already fiddling away in our cabin somewhere beneath the four massive funnels of the *Olympic.*

The week of travel passed slowly, especially for my companion. Like the trap that falls upon a jungle cat before the animal can spring, the confines of the ocean liner ringed Holmes in. He paced back and forth in our cabin; he played his violin in our cabin; he read more of Phillips in our cabin.

"Why pretend that I have freedom, Watson?" he said when I suggested that he stroll along the open promenade deck. "A means for ensnaring a villain is my goal, not deluding myself into thinking that, despite the tennis courts and bathing pools, I'm not aboard a ship."

His foul temper lasted the entire seven days of the voyage. I could only breathe a sigh of comfort when I contemplated the good fortune that had prevented us from sailing together in the opposite direction. I had foolishly believed that age might temper Holmes's easily sparked sense of frustration, but his restlessness that week proved me wrong. Indeed, before we reached my house in Queen Anne Street, I was even doubting the wisdom of having invited him to reside with me while my wife was still away.

Once we arrived in London, however, Holmes's calmer nature prevailed, and with a week still remaining of Mrs. Watson's stay with her aunt in the Midlands, I felt more than ready to share my abode with my old friend. Reassured that we could continue our investigation undisturbed for a while longer at our Queen Anne Street headquarters, Holmes wanted no time lost in implementing whatever strategy to lure our prey he had conjured during the past week at sea.

Our first task was locating Senator Buchanan. To that end, Holmes contacted our old friend Wiggins, one of the former young street Arabs whose acquaintance I had made in Holmes's and my initial case together, which I called "A Study in Scarlet." The nominal leader of the Baker Street Irregulars, for so the boys were known, Wiggins had aided Holmes on many an occasion. It was, however, Holmes's aid to Wiggins that proved more fortunate in the long run. A number of years earlier Holmes had secured the lad a position as bootboy for a great family, and Holmes and I beamed with pride as we watched the boy justify our faith in him, moving up to footman and then to valet through years of loyal service to his employers. Now in his early forties, the baby-faced man with the shock of black hair and toothful smile had been appointed butler to a small but influential household in Belgravia.

"Yes, indeed, Mr. Holmes," Wiggins said the afternoon of our return to London. "It should be no problem at all to locate this Senator Buchanan. Those who make the rounds of our finest homes are well known to us in service. A few discreet questions to the right addresses should yield results in no time at all."

True to his word and former Baker Street reputation, Wiggins reported back to us within the hour that Buchanan and his wife were currently residing at the nearby Langham Hotel. It was an obvious choice: the grand Langham not only suited the rich (the King of Bohemia had stayed there while visiting Holmes), but seemed to appeal to Americans in particular; the establishment claimed Mark Twain as one of its most famous guests. Since the hotel was just round the corner from Queen Anne Street in Portland Place, we proceeded to undertake the brief walk that very night. Unfortunately, however, we discovered at the desk that the senator and his wife were attending a performance of *Don Giovanni* at Covent Garden, whose opera season had only just commenced, so Holmes was forced to leave a note for Buchanan, informing him of our urgent desire to meet.

"We shall return at midnight," he announced to the sombre, moustachioed hall porter behind the desk. To me, he said with a smile, "Come, Watson, it is time to sample again the familiar taste of English cooking. I believe that roast beef at Simpson's would not be out of place while we await the completion of Senator Buchanan's enviable encounter with Mozart."

At the stroke of midnight we reappeared at the Langham. Seated in plush velvet chairs in the lobby, we awaited the appearance of Buchanan. Despite the lateness of the hour, the hotel was alive with pedestrian traffic. Visitors to London who wanted to squeeze vitality from every waking moment rushed in and out of the hotel as if the garish electric light were sunshine and it was the middle of the afternoon.

Three-quarters of an hour later, Senator Buchanan in evening dress and his wife in an elegant white-brocade gown and matching white fur entered the foyer. They were accompanied by another formally attired couple: a dark, extremely young woman and a much older man, distinguished by his thick moustaches as well as his considerable height.

"Colonel John Jacob Astor and his wife," Holmes explained, "the owners of the New York hotel in which we so recently luxuriated. Forced by the scandal of the difference in their ages to honeymoon abroad–Egypt, I believe."

"A beautiful young woman," I observed, "and judging from her radiance and marital status, undoubtedly pregnant."

"Watson, Watson"–Holmes sighed–"ever the romantic. You couple the science of medicine to the science of deduction then rely on intuition."

I had no time to react to what I chose to accept as a compliment–although I am not certain that it was so intended–for the hall porter was just then offering the senator the note Holmes had written and nodding in our direction.

Buchanan perused the paper, excused himself to the Astors, and whispered something to his wife whose raised eyebrows seemed to signal a sense of alarm. Bidding them all good night, he made his way in our direction through the assemblage of hotel guests. Since I had met him before, I introduced the senator to Sherlock Holmes, and then we all adjourned to a small round table in the corner of the large hall. Only after Buchanan insisted on ordering a brandy and soda for each of us could Holmes begin.

"You know of Altamont's death?" Holmes asked. "And Van den Acker's?"

"Yes, poor souls," Buchanan said. "I read about Van den Acker. And Altamont seems to have been a thief of some sort. Or so I was told by the Embassy. Was he not killed in a freakish robbery attempt?"

"That's what the New Jersey authorities are maintaining, Senator," Holmes said, "but I have another hypothesis."

Buchanan leaned back in his chair, studied the drink in the cut-crystal glass, and asked, "Just what might that be, Mr. Holmes?"

"I believe, Senator, that Altamont intercepted a message from Peter Van den Acker to me about an incriminating dispatch he had received from Washington. I further believe that as a result of Van den Acker's attempt to contact me and the suspicions he had of what really happened to David Graham Phillips, Altamont went to Van den Acker's house and brutally killed him, attempting to make the murder appear a suicide. I also believe that Altamont planted your copy of Viereck's *The House of the Vampire* at the scene of the crime so it would seem that Van den Acker had been the one who'd given that book to Goldsborough, the very book that helped ignite in Goldsborough's twisted mind the desire to kill Phillips."

"Indeed," Buchanan said softly once my friend had finished. The Senator's expression had changed not at all throughout Holmes's indictment. In the same soft voice Buchanan asked, "Now why would Altamont want to do all that, Mr. Holmes?"

"Because, Senator, he was working for you, and you were becoming frightened that Mrs. Frevert's desire to re-open the enquiry into her brother's death would ultimately implicate you."

Buchanan sipped his drink again; neither Holmes nor I had touched ours.

"There were many people," Buchanan said, "let alone senators, who wanted to see Phillips dead. Why pick on me, sir?"

I had heard stories about the ability of American legislators to remain so calm during their heated debates that they could refer to their contemned rivals as "The Honourable" or "Most Distinguished Gentleman." Now I was witnessing just such a performance firsthand, the volatile Buchanan appearing as civil as if he were conducting a harmless *tête-à-tête*. Instead, he was being accused of murder.

"Allow me to explain," Holmes said. "As much as I detest conjecture, the trail of this case was quite cold, and thus I had to rely on surmise as well as on the historical record. There were only two senators with a sufficiently compelling motive to have killed Phillips in January of 1911–the two who had lost their attempts at re-election the previous November thanks in great measure to Phillips's writings. One of those two senators is dead. You, of course, are the other.

"I assume that your hatred for Phillips had been growing ever since you first read the article he'd written about you in *The Treason of the Senate*. After meeting Goldsborough at a concert or some other cultural event and discovering his fascination with Phillips, you must have dangled the promise of money in front of him even before you actually decided to murder Phillips. You perceived that Goldsborough was an impressionable young man, suffering no doubt from what Dr. Freud might term paranoia. You cultivated his neurosis, twisting his interest in Phillips to a kind of repulsion. It must have been you who convinced him that his own sister was portrayed in that novel by Phillips and that Phillips himself was drawing the very identity out of Goldsborough's body.

"I further believe that after the November election, with the help of Viereck's book and those claims about vampires–not to mention the pledge of more money to come in January after he had done the villainous deed–you persisted in prodding the poor wretch to destroy the cause of his anguish. I think you aided Goldsborough in finding rooms across from Phillips's flat and had your man Altamont follow him to be certain the murder was completed successfully. I believe that Altamont–or you–forged Goldsborough's diary, and that no doubt it was Altamont who, hiding behind the shrubbery just as he attempted to do when he obviously followed us to Gramercy Park, fired that extra bullet into Phillips's guts to assure himself of Phillips's death. I imagine that in all probability he was even prepared to finish off Goldsborough if the poor soul hadn't done it himself."

"An interesting tale, Mr. Holmes," Buchanan said. He still sounded as controlled as he had at the start of our interview, although I thought I detected a slight jerk of the hand holding the glass at Holmes's utterance of the word "guts."

"Maybe," the Senator continued, "in a fit of madness Altamont believed Phillips had harmed me and deserved to be dispatched.

Or maybe he mistakenly thought I did order Phillips killed, just as you suggest, and believed he was protecting me. Or maybe, unbeknownst to myself, he was under the secret employ of any one of the dozen other senators who, I tell you in the strictest confidence, were more than happy to see Phillips dead. But even if all that you ascribe to Altamont is true, I see no link to myself."

"What about your copy of the Viereck book found at Van den Acker's murder?"

"So I loaned it to Altamont. I can't be responsible for what he did with it. No, Mr. Holmes, I'm afraid you will have to do better than that."

Buchanan put down his glass. At the same time Sherlock Holmes reached inside his jacket and produced his small notebook. From between its well-worn pages, he extracted the newspaper cutting we had discovered with Altamont's body. Holmes slid the small piece of paper across the shiny tabletop.

Buchanan perused the story about himself and Goldsborough; but, as collected as ever, he simply slid the paper back to Holmes. "Would you gentlemen care for a cigar?" he asked innocently.

Holmes and I both replied in the negative.

Buchanan shrugged. "Just as well. Three on a match always brings bad luck." Then beginning to rise, he said, "But now you'll have to excuse me, gentlemen; I've kept my wife waiting long enough. As far as I'm concerned, this interview is concluded." With that, he turned and strode from the room.

"What now, Holmes?" I asked. "He totally ignored the newspaper cutting." My companion, however, was still looking at the lengthy corridor through which Buchanan had left. Holmes's steely eyes narrowed, and he put his fingers together like steeples as he so often did when he was engaged in thought.

When he finally did speak again, it was not to answer my question, but rather to ask one of his own. "Did you note his decided emphasis on the culpability of other senators, Watson?"

"Now that you mention it, Holmes, he did suggest that Altamont might have been working for others. Why, to hear Buchanan state the case, a great number of senators would have enjoyed some sort of revenge against Phillips. But what about his failure to react to the story in the *Post*?"

"Not important, old fellow. What *is* significant is that he seemed to be laying the groundwork for a collective guilt of some sort." Holmes reached for the brandy and soda that Buchanan had originally offered.

"You don't suppose," I asked, "that we're talking about more than one culprit, do you?"

Sherlock Holmes sampled the drink. Observing the light in the room as it danced through the facets of the crystal he was holding, he said slowly, "Murder is a strange act, my friend. Sometimes it is a very private affair, and other times it is a deed that can be sparked only by the inducement of others. But come," he concluded, setting the glass on the table, "let us return to your home and ponder this matter further."

We walked quickly back to Queen Anne Street. Holmes may well indeed have pondered the case further that night; I, on the other hand, was too heavily burdened with the necessity of sleep to ponder anything deeper than the softness of my pillow.

I slept late the following day only to be greeted by a wet April morning whose darkness had no doubt aided the powers of Morpheus. Holmes had already gone about his adventures by the time I entered the morning room. A note upon the table announced that he planned to return before tea after a day in the haberdasheries of Oxford and Regent Streets—to what end I could not begin to imagine.

I spent the ensuing afternoon writing a letter to my wife in which, veiling the unfinished business upon which Holmes and I were embarking, I described my adventures in New York City. I did my best, as in fact I have attempted throughout this narrative, to minimise the lighthearted aspects of my stay there. After all, in spite of her aversion to sea travel, Mrs. Watson had always been curious about the States, so there was no point in attaching a sense of holiday to a trip that under the circumstances certainly did not warrant such an appellation.

A few ticks past four, Polly showed Holmes into the sitting room. I was about to ask him what he had been doing all afternoon when he raised a finger to his lips.

"In good time, Watson," he cautioned me, and then announced to Polly, "Show them in!"

Whatever I was expecting, it certainly was not a procession of some ten young lads little older than twelve or thirteen each dressed in the velveteen livery of the establishments that employed them. With their brass buttons shining, they marched into the room like an occupying army except that, in carrying the assorted parcels Holmes had obviously purchased on his outing, they looked no more menacing than a junior chorus line from some modern-dress production of *The Yeoman of the Guard.* One half expected them to break into song!

Pointing to a nearby table, Holmes instructed the boys to set down their burden, and then with the snap of his fingers he ordered the brigade to follow him out the door. Awaiting Holmes's return, I could easily see that the packages bore the names of various shops from Bond Street, the Strand, and St. James's Street as well as those thoroughfares he'd named in his earlier note to me. Of their contents and purpose, however, I had not a clue.

"Holmes!" I cried when he re-entered the sitting room, "I know that members of the fairer sex often rely on shopping excursions to relieve a troubled mind, but I never expected you to fall victim to such a passion."

"Steady, old fellow," Holmes said with a wink. "Let us have our tea, and afterwards I shall make all clear."

I rang for Polly to bring us the tray, while Holmes removed the parcels to the bedroom I had made available for him. He partook of the tea and cucumber sandwiches with great enthusiasm; I, on the other hand, was distracted, trying unsuccessfully to fathom just how he intended to ensnare Buchanan.

After finishing yet a second cup of tea, Holmes finally retired to his bedroom only to pop out a moment later to survey the chamber he had just vacated. His eye came to rest on the chesterfield of blue velvet upon which I was then sitting. "Perfect!" he exclaimed, and, snatching up the flattest of the cushions leaning against the arm, returned with it into the privacy of his room.

For well over half an hour I could hear him moving back and forth behind the door. Presumably he was dressing, but what costume he was preparing and for what reason he needed the cushion I could not guess.

"Are you ready, Watson?" he cried at last. Only after I answered in a bewildered affirmative did he make his entrance into the sitting room.

I knew Sherlock Holmes to be a wizard of subterfuge; indeed, I knew that at one time he had at least five retreats throughout London where he could don his various disguises; and yet I never ceased to marvel at his singular ability to conceal his own identity with a minimum of greasepaint. It was in creating the total effect that he excelled, the conception, as it were, of a completely different person from his own self—not an imitation of another personage, but another person entirely.

Thus did David Graham Phillips stand before me. The flowery silk-faced suit, I later learned, was from Shingleton's; the white linen shirt, from Sampson and Company; the pearl-button boots, from James Taylor and Son of nearby Paddington Street.

"Since chrysanthemums are out of season," he explained, "I had to settle for this carnation, which I confess to having plucked from your neighbour's window box; I had no time to track down hothouse flowers. This extraordinarily ridiculous collar I purchased from a shop in Tottenham Court Road after a most challenging search." His newly darkened hair was parted in the middle. He had applied a small amount of putty to broaden his nose. He had slightly increased his girth with the aid of the small cushion, and he was somehow able to replace his own angular movements with the more fluid motions of the younger Phillips.

"Amazing, Holmes!" I said in astonishment as he walked to the cheval mirror.

"Not so bad, really, Watson," he concurred as he admired himself in the looking glass. "Especially when you consider I haven't seen my subject in well over ten years. For inspiration, I had to rely on that portrait from my file—not to mention my own memory."

Scrutinising himself in the mirror, Holmes checked that his nose was firmly planted and then pressed both his palms against his ribs–or rather against the flat cushion–to ascertain that his foundations were equally secure.

"In light of the reflection you cast, Holmes," I quipped, "you're at least one David Graham Phillips that isn't a vampire."

"Right you are, Watson, but this is no time for joking. There's game to be hunted tonight if I'm not mistaken. Mr. Buchanan may have spent much of his life amongst the high society of New York and Washington; but in his heart he is just a poor farm lad who, as you yourself have already observed, is still full of the superstitions and fears with which he grew up, weaknesses we can well hope to exploit thoroughly. Let's be off!"

"But where to, Holmes? You've yet to tell me."

"To the Royal Larder, man! Down the road from Buchanan's hotel. Where else?"

Where else indeed? I wondered.

Despite Holmes's enthusiasm, however, our pace was immediately hampered by the unseasonably thick yellow fog we confronted as soon as we walked out of my front door. Indeed, it was only because we knew the way and because the distance to be traversed was so short that we dared make the journey at all. I could scarcely see my hand before my eyes.

Holding on to the wrought-iron railing on our left that was illuminated by the beams from the fanlight above the door, we felt our way down the four steps to the pavement, then turned left, and began our short trek eastward. The lights along the roadway spilled an eerie golden glow on the ground, and the long row of fencing kept us travelling in a straight line.

"How can we be sure that Buchanan will even be there?" I asked. To have made such an effort only to miss our man seemed pointless indeed.

"Because, Watson, I took the liberty of sending the senator a duplicitous telegram while I was on my travels this afternoon. I asked him to meet me in the Royal Larder at seven-fifteen."

Alert to the low rumble of whatever traffic braved the carriageway on such a night, we gingerly stepped off the kerb and crossed Wimpole Street.

Approaching Harley Street a few minutes later, I resumed my questioning. "The Royal Larder was Phillips's favourite public house, was it not, Holmes?"

I sensed more than saw the Phillips mask smile at me. "Yes, indeed, Watson. A bit of poetic justice, I should think. But more to the point: The room is dark; it will be difficult to see. Not much different from this blasted fog! My disguise should be most effective under such conditions. I told Buchanan he would recognise me by my black hat, and I signed the message 'A friend of Altamont.' That should lure him. You, of course, will have to hide yourself, for if he should lay eyes on you, we are undone."

The heavy mist continued to embrace us as we groped our way to the right into Chandos Street and then left into Portland Place, but the few intermittent breaks in the fog's density allowed me to marvel at the change in Holmes's gait. Gone was the walking stick. Normally, he would take long strides that made him sway slightly as his body's centre of gravity shifted from his left side to his right, but in this guise of Phillips he moved more ponderously and appeared more precisely upright.

A few minutes before the hour, we passed the Langham.

I remember having the feeling we were being watched from a window above us, and when I looked up through a break in the fog I was momentarily startled by a menacing countenance of narrow eyes, flared nostrils, and pointed teeth.

"A hotel gargoyle, Watson," Holmes reassured me, and we continued on in our measured pace.

We reached the Royal Larder at seven o'clock. It is a poorly lit, highly polished West End establishment full of oak furniture, brass fixtures, a cacophony of singing, and numerous persons aspiring to the upper class. We elbowed our way to opposite ends of the room, Holmes coming to rest at a small, square table in a corner; I, in a chair at the far end of the bar. As soon as he was seated, Holmes struck a match and lit a cigarette, purposely adding great clouds to the shadowy haze already hanging in layers like piles of folded, grey blankets. I then saw him dip into a large side pocket of his flowery jacket and produce what at first glance appeared to be a crumpled ball of black paper.

As I watched him unfold his bundle, however, I realised that he had within his grasp a small, black Alpine hat not unlike that which Phillips himself had been wearing the day he had been murdered. Slowly Holmes placed it upon his head, adjusting its abbreviated brim so that it came down to the bridge of his puttied nose. He then took a pull on the cigarette, inclined his head to smell the white carnation in his lapel, and turned his eyes to the door that communicated with the outside.

A pint of dark ale was my only companion as I gazed along with Holmes at the newcomers who entered: a raucous ginger-haired woman, two American men in formal dress, and two women with painted faces and swelling expanses of *décolletage* whose vocation

I should prefer not to mention.

Despite Holmes's expectations, we could not, of course, be certain that Buchanan would keep the appointment; and by the time I had begun my second tankard, I was beginning to doubt that he would. He was already a half hour late, and though it was foggy he had only a short distance to walk from his hotel. How many glasses would I have to drink before the man arrived? I wondered. I began to think about the lengthy nights Sherlock Holmes and I had spent together in previous cases so long ago, waiting for equally mysterious events to unfold: the dramatic arrival of Colonel Sebastian Moran and his airgun in that empty house in Baker Street or the emergence of the deadly swamp adder down the bell pull from Dr. Grimesby Roylott's dummy ventilator. Tonight, however, the wait was not as long.

At eight o'clock Senator Buchanan appeared. As he surveyed the room, no doubt seeking a distinctive black hat, I placed my hand over my brows and turned my head away to conceal my own identity. Making his way between the two women who had arrived before him, he did not notice Holmes at first; but just as one of them giggled and asked the distinguished-looking gentleman with the thick white hair what was undoubtedly an impertinent question, he laid his eyes on the shadow wearing the Alpine hat seated at the rear of the public house—Sherlock Holmes or, rather, the replication of David Graham Phillips.

(I could see the looks of frustration on the women's faces as Buchanan ignored them; but since Buchanan's back was to me, I have relied on Holmes's subsequent account of the meeting to complete this part of the narrative.)

Buchanan's mouth dropped open as he began to recognise

the ostentatious figure before him. Oblivious to the charms of the hectoring women at either side, he stumbled rather than walked towards Holmes's table. Stopping two or three feet in front of the spectre who continued to exhale smoke heaven-ward but now much less voluminously, Buchanan whispered, "You're dead. Everybody knows it." As if to reaffirm the fact, he repeated, "You're dead."

Standing motionless, Buchanan continued to stare.

Others in the room began to stare as well. They, however, were looking not at the dandified gentleman seated at the table, but at the transfixed senator, frozen in front of Holmes like Macbeth before the ghost of Banquo.

From my own position, I could see a macabre grin begin to cross Holmes's face.

"Don't smile at me!" Buchanan snarled, his voice beginning to increase in volume. "Don't say *I* did it. They all wanted someone to do it. Don't blame me if I was the only one with enough guts."

Suddenly Holmes jumped to his feet and pointed his index finger accusingly at Buchanan.

"No!" the Senator screamed as more heads throughout the room turned in his direction. "Leave me alone!" he cried as he took two small steps backward. Then he turned quickly and, after knocking over a chair, ran through the doorway and out into the fog that seemed to suck him up.

Holmes and I both sprang for the door, but before we could reach it the two women who had accosted Buchanan snaked their arms around our own.

"'Ere, now, luv," the one next to me said, "wot's your 'urry?"

"There's two of you, and there's two of us," the other said with a lascivious wink.

Once we were able to extricate ourselves and escape into the fog, Buchanan was nowhere to be seen. A murky halo of light from the front of the Langham beckoned, but when we enquired at the desk and even interrogated people in the lobby, it became clear to us that the senator had not set foot in the hotel since his departure for the public house.

London is a large city, and for that reason one may rightly deduce that–fog or no fog–it is easy to lose oneself. Such an axiom, of course, applies much more readily to an unknown soul than to a person of fame or notoriety.

"He won't get far, Watson," Holmes assured me. "It's difficult to travel in weather like this. Besides, too many people know the celebrated Mr. Buchanan. Tonight we can notify our old friend Stanley Hopkins at the Yard to keep an eye open for his whereabouts. Hopkins has just been made a Chief Inspector and should be able to help us. But as it will be impossible to find Buchanan ourselves in this fog, let us begin early tomorrow morning making enquiries within the American community. A former United States senator should not be too hard to track down."

Eleven

∽

PURSUIT

"What a world of twaddle it is! If men and women could only learn to build their ideals on the firm foundation—the only foundation—of the practical instead of upon the quicksand of lies and pretenses, wouldn't the tower climb less shakily, if more slowly, toward the stars?"

—David Graham Phillips, *The Husband's Story*

"Quick, Watson! We've not a moment to lose!"

Thus was I roughly roused from a sound sleep on the morning of Friday, April 10, by Sherlock Holmes.

"Quick, man!" he repeated. "I have only my own sluggishness to blame. Get dressed! We're off to Waterloo!"

Still drowsy from our escapades of the night before, I donned my clothes as rapidly as I could, for Holmes had already secured a hansom, which was waiting just beyond my front door. Not until we were securely seated inside did I dare ask him what had transpired.

Impatiently drumming his long fingers on the arm of the seat, he explained the events of the morning. Holmes had returned to the Langham to ask about Buchanan. Although the senator had still not come back and his distraught wife had no knowledge of his whereabouts, Holmes encountered the Buchanan's companions of two nights previous, Colonel and Mrs. Astor, who were in the process of leaving the hotel. The Astors, it turned out, were departing for America on that very day; and, after impatiently enduring great praise from them once my friend had made known his identity, Holmes learned that Buchanan had in fact enquired the night before as to when the Astors were leaving England. It seems that Buchanan, aware in advance of his friends' theatre plans, had been able to make his way through the fog to the playhouse in Drury Lane where they were in attendance. During the interval in a most agitated state—indeed, to Astor, looking as if he'd seen a ghost—the senator expressed his intent to leave the country as soon as possible.

"I don't jolly well blame him," I interjected.

Astor, Holmes continued, had informed Buchanan that he was sailing today and suggested that, although the ship was no doubt fully booked, some arrangements could certainly be made for a man of the senator's importance.

"In short, Watson, unless we arrive in Southampton by midday—that is, in less than two hours—Mr. Buchanan will be on his way to America. I myself only returned just now to collect my revolver."

"But can't we telegraph ahead for the police to detain him?" I asked.

"On what evidence, old fellow? That he bolted my performance as David Graham Phillips? Such a reaction might simply be regarded as a theatre critic's entirely appropriate review. That he met Goldsborough at a concert? The authorities would justifiably laugh. No, my friend, unless we can extract a full confession from the senator, I am afraid that he will return to America where there is no great desire to unravel a case which the police in New York have already labelled 'closed.'"

We arrived at Waterloo Station a few minutes before ten. Holmes hurriedly purchased two first-class tickets for the boat-train to Southampton but was cautioned by the clerk that the train was probably on its way by now. We rushed into the great hall and, thanks to the sunshine filtering through the glass roof, immediately located platform 12, the home of the White Star boat-train. Unfortunately, it was more than half the station away. Worse, at that very moment, off in the distance, we could see the green flag go up and hear the blare of the warning whistle. Before we had a chance to move—though God knows that even if we had, neither one of us could have run fast enough to catch it—we watched the railway carriages pull out of the station, gathering speed with every passing moment. We could see the unusually long and crowded parade of first-class coaches with their dark-blue broadcloth and gold-braided furnishings; but of Buchanan we saw nothing.

"Well, Holmes—" I began dejectedly, but to my surprise he was no longer at my side. He was instead springing up the stairs towards the doors through which we had previously entered.

By the time I caught up to him outside the station, he'd already squeezed his way through gangs of people, slipped between the arriving hansoms and motor cars at the kerb, and hailed a taxi, a black Renault, which was now idling in the roadway. "My man," he was saying to the driver as I puffed up to his side, "get us to Southampton before midday, and it'll be worth your while."

"'Ere," the driver sniffled, dragging a sleeve across his florid and bulbous nose, "are you serious, guv'nor?" He was wearing a dark ulster with the collar turned up and, despite the relative warmth of the morning, a red-tartan scarf draped round his neck. It was only too obvious that he was suffering from a cold.

Holmes threw several large coins on to the seat beside the fellow whose avaricious grin exposed a missing front tooth. Nonetheless, he seemed hesitant. "I-I'm not sure—" he began.

"Not sure?" Holmes repeated. "Not sure? Make up your mind then! Be quick, man! We've no time to waste haggling!"

I could not help thinking how rapidly Rollins would have had the yellow Packard on the move. Finally, after drawing his sleeve once more across his red nose, the driver said decisively, "'Op in!"

Our departure was anything but speedy, however. The heavy traffic approaching the station in the Waterloo Road prevented the quick start we had hoped for. Indeed, only when the soot-begrimed buildings of London gave way to the less cramped cottages of the countryside did Holmes lean back in his seat. Outwardly he appeared calm; only the resumption of his finger-drumming, this time on the black leather cushion between us, gave witness to his inner turmoil. For a quarter of an hour, Holmes and I said nothing.

Searching to break the silence as we rumbled along, I observed at last, "The boat-train seemed excessively crowded today. Quite a number of first-class carriages."

"A new ship, Watson," Holmes said tersely. "Lots of rich, Americans who want to be part of history."

"But how do we know that Buchanan is going to America at

all?" I asked, trying to distract him from worrying about that over which he had no control. "Many ships bound for America call at nearby cities before braving the Atlantic. Mine stopped at Cherbourg."

"Capital, Watson!" Holmes said, seeming to brighten. "Your esoteric knowledge never ceases to amaze me. Buchanan's boat does indeed stop at Cherbourg and then at Queenstown, but I'm sure we have nothing to fear from his jumping ship. Buchanan has too much at stake in America—his connections with Hearst for one, his wife's family for another—which means, of course, his fortune for a third. Besides, remember how many people might be implicated if it can be shown that Phillips's murder had been concealed. Why, such a scandal could reach all the way to a former Chief Executive. And Roosevelt is, after all, seeking to regain the presidency this year."

"To Beveridge and me, he even mentioned a third party."

"You see, Watson. Which is why Mr. Buchanan is on his way home—where he believes he will be safe. I think we can be sure of that."

Having come this far only to lose him seemed unfair. Yet we still had a chance, I knew, despite my antipathy to the motor car. As little as I wanted to admit it, this Renault, prototype of twentieth-century scientific knowledge, would enable us to get our man, a myopic wrongdoer relying on old-fashioned steam to outrun us—or so I tried to convince myself—and once the familiar brick buildings heralded our approach to Woking, I did feel more at ease, for soon we would be at Basingstoke and starting the long final stretch downward toward the sea.

Indeed, once we began descending, the landscape seemed to

race past even faster; and, noting the squat tower of Winchester Cathedral in the distance, Holmes consulted his pocket-watch, from whose chain dangled the gold sovereign given to him by Irene Adler for witnessing her wedding.

"Eleven-fifteen, Watson. There's still time."

As we motored into the city itself, however, the Renault slowed its pace, and Holmes and I exchanged distressed glances.

"Petrol!" the driver snuffled.

"What?" Holmes demanded, hitting the seat with his fist in raging disbelief.

"Petrol, guv. We can't continue without it. I tried to warn you earlier, but you seemed in such a hurry." Once more he wiped his nose on his sleeve.

The next valuable minutes were spent searching for a garage at which to purchase fuel. There were no further displays of temper, but I had never seen Holmes so furious. He simply sat. Only when we were back on the roadway did he even look at his watch again, and then he hissed from between clenched teeth, "It's doubtful now, Watson."

Hurtling down the uneven carriageway, we sped past horse-drawn wagons whose drivers were forced to pull their conveyances to the side of the road to prevent their animals from bolting at the roar of our machine. When at last we discerned the Itchen, Holmes edged to the front of his seat. When we saw the houses marking the outskirts of Southampton, he again looked at his watch; it was now 11:45; but even as he checked the time, we clearly heard the sharp blast of sirens announcing the ship's imminent departure.

Beyond the low buildings before us, we could see the four great funnels towering above her decks; but much closer at hand, we also observed a great congestion of motor cars and hansoms blocking our way. The Renault was forced to stop again.

Holmes tossed more money on the front seat and swung open the door. Immediately we were struck by the roar of cheering throngs. "Wait here!" Holmes commanded the driver; to me he cried, "Hurry, Watson!"

A second siren blast, however, told us that we were too late.

Even if the grand ship had not started to move just then, the thick wall of humanity on the White Star Dock would have prevented our reaching Berth 44 and the mountainous steamer whose dark bows loomed so high above us. Hundreds–no, thousands–of people had come to see her off. They crowded the thoroughfares; they filled the decks of neighbouring boats. Amidst the din of shouting and clamouring and from behind a chequered field of waving black hats and fluttering white handkerchiefs, all Holmes and I could do was stand by and watch, relegated from our role of missionaries of justice to one of mere spectators.

We could actually distinguish the Blue Peter being run up the fore yardarm in addition to the houseflag, a red swallowtail pennon with the famous white star at its centre, already hanging from the main mast; and the red, white, and blue of the French Tricolour dangling from her foremast since her immediate port of call was Cherbourg. We could easily have counted the white lifeboats suspended from their davits above the sundeck that ran fully two-thirds of the ship's great length. There were people on the quay who ran alongside her for a while, the band of gold that girdled her paralleling the extended pier below.

"If I have anything to say about it," Holmes said in exasperation, "awaiting Buchanan in New York at the end of his week's voyage will be a telegram to detain him signed by Chief Inspector Hopkins of the C.I.D. With references to the second bullet hole at Van den Acker's, the first edition of the Viereck book planted at the murder scene, and the *Post* story on Buchanan and Goldsborough, we can at least hope that such a message will present a significant legal obstacle for the senator until more facts about Altamont's criminal connection to Buchanan are revealed."

"I hope you're right, Holmes," I said. "But Hopkins won't be easily convinced to send such a wire."

"A little bit more time to build the case is all I need."

"I hope you're right," I repeated, watching with resignation as our quarry fled from English soil.

In the same instant, a choir of triple-valved whistles drowned out the cheering populace.

"The tugs of the Red Funnel Line," Holmes observed as he pointed to the small boats manoeuvring the ship down the River Test. "It would appear that even the gods are against us, eh, Watson?"

Only after reading the names of the little boats did I perceive his meaning: *Neptune* and *Vulcan* took the lead, followed by *Ajax*, *Hector*, and *Hercules*.

Just then, however, pandemonium erupted. Amidst a rapid series of explosive reports, the crowd surged towards the railing of the quay.

"Watson!" Holmes shouted. "That ship has snapped her ropes! She's heading straight for Buchanan's! The day may yet be ours."

The *New York*, a smaller steamship moored nearby in Berth 38 of the Test Quay, had indeed wrenched free. The water displaced by the larger ship that was passing had forced the former to bob and then to break the bonds to a third ship to which she herself was tied in tandem. As a result, after sending her thick cables arcing high into the blue sky, the *New York* began to swing out her stern, closing the distance between herself and Buchanan's ship steaming by.

The spectators pressed forward, silent now in anxious anticipation. My heart too was racing since for all the world a collision between the two ships seemed imminent. It was, I feared, the *Camperdown* and the *Victoria* all over again.

"God knows, I wish no harm to the innocent," Holmes said, "but even the most minor contact would require a return to port for inspection."

In the briefest of moments that it took for the scenario to unfold, however, the tugboat *Vulcan* was hooking her thick ropes around the *New York*'s stern and slowing her down. The larger ship also co-operated, ponderously reversing her direction. With the help of the remaining tugs, the *New York* was towed around Dock Head where she slid safely into an Itchen berth.

Although disaster had been avoided by mere inches, Holmes shook his fist in the air.

"Blast!" he ejaculated. "Nothing short of blind luck prevented that impact, Watson. And to what end, I cannot fathom."

Once more on course, Buchanan's ship now steamed slowly and almost silently down Southampton Water at half speed, past the docks and hospital on one side, past the beaches on the other, ready to make the turn into the S-shaped channel leading out to sea.

Amidst the raucous and almost disastrous send-off, the tooting of the tugboats' whistles, and four blasts of the great ship's sirens, we could only stand and watch this gargantuan ocean liner, a city unto itself, greater in length than the Singer building in New York stood tall, ease gracefully towards open water. Holmes and I, feeling quite dwarfed, remained speechless as we viewed the four proud funnels disappearing in the distance.

As I sit now and pen this narrative some ten years after the event, it is ironic to recall how, during the frenzy of that near accident, I regretted the absence of a writer like David Graham Phillips to record the impending collision as he had that of the *Victoria* and *Camperdown*; but since in fact the two ships before us had so miraculously avoided each other, I could only assume that the rest of Buchanan's journey would be uneventful and would therefore go unreported. Unreported indeed! Not able to foretell the future, Holmes and I had stood mute on the crowded dock, witnessing R.M.S. *Titanic* sail off on what the world knows now was her maiden voyage to oblivion.

Twelve

❧

CONCLUSION

"Truly, never is the human race so delightfully, so unconsciously amusing as when it discusses right and wrong."

–David Graham Phillips, *Susan Lenox*

"My Dear Mrs. Frevert," Holmes read aloud to me over afternoon tea a fortnight later when I was visiting him once again in Sussex. "The secrets surrounding your brother's death went down with his murderer aboard the *Titanic*. Dr. Watson and I ascertained, just as you had divined, that a conspiracy to assassinate your brother did in fact take place and that Senator Millard Pankhurst Buchanan was at its head. He admitted to his complicity when I confronted him here in London upon our return to England. That a circumstantial case against him could be constructed I have no doubt; that such a case could be adjudicated in our favour I have grave misgivings. With the death of Buchanan's secretary Altamont, there seem no leads available to confirm Buchanan's treachery. Besides, with Buchanan himself drowned, there seems little point in pursuing his culpability. After all, justice has been served. The murderer of your brother has been brought before a greater court than any you could ever hope to find in America or in England, and if there is a God in heaven, the assassin must stand guilty as charged. You have done honour to the memory of your brother, and your nation should be much cheered to have courageous souls such as yourself residing within her borders; but in the name of common sense, let me implore you to keep your celebrations as private as possible, for there are many police authorities who would not look kindly upon the carelessness—intentional or otherwise—of their own investigations being made public. Buchanan has found a watery grave; justice, as well as the waves, has brought him low.

"Think no more of fees. To help clear up so heinous a blow at freedom is payment in full.

Yours sincerely,
Sherlock Holmes

"Well, Watson, what do you think?" Holmes asked as he peered over the sheet of foolscap he was holding.

"Surely you're not going to post such a letter?" I responded. "Despite your caveats, Mrs. Frevert could easily take it to the police as some type of evidence and demand public justice. She might even present it to an unscrupulous newspaper. Mr. Hearst would love to get hold of such a story. Unable to prove the facts, you could become a laughing stock."

"You are a faithful friend, Watson," Holmes said with a broad smile. "Always trying to protect me. But rest assured. I wrote the letter and then decided, just as you did, that it revealed too much that couldn't be substantiated with Altamont dead and Buchanan presumed so. Instead, I sent Mrs. Frevert a telegram. Read this. Holmes leaned across the table and handed me a copy of the wire he had dispatched. *Mrs. Frevert* [it read simply]. *Rest assured. Justice has been served. Case closed.* It was signed *Holmes.*

"Much improved," I agreed. "Besides, your letter really didn't explain all that we have come to know."

"Ah, my good fellow," Holmes said between bites of one of Mrs. Hudson's biscuits, "ever the detective. And just what do you detect that I have disregarded?"

"Why, only the link between himself and so many other members of the United States Senate to which Buchanan admitted," I said.

"And if I had posted the letter, Watson, what good do you think implicating others of that institution would have accomplished?"

I thought for a few moments. It was a weighty question requiring a considered reply. "Surely, Holmes," I said at last, "a murder conspiracy involving members of the United States Senate deserves to be uncovered. After all, we have a dedication to finding out the Truth. That is why we have aided so many unfortunates in the past, is it not? Justice demands it."

Holmes smiled. "You know I detest sentimentality, Watson. Still, to your former observation, I assent. But not to the precept that the Truth must always be made public. Sometimes in the affairs of state, individual matters need to remain concealed to allow for the greater good. David Graham Phillips understood that obligation. He might not have liked it, but at least he understood. I believe it was Miss Emily Dickinson, the celebrated American poetess, who wrote, 'Tell all the truth but tell it slant, success in circuit lies.'

Not even Phillips himself advertised the large sum he was paid by Hearst for attacking the hypocrisy of the Senate.

"But more to the point, Watson, what do you think might be the international consequences—the damage to the relationship between our two mighty nations, America and England—if a British consulting detective and his compatriot successfully revealed to the American people that a prominent journalist had been killed at the behest of many in—and at the instigation of at least one member of—their most distinguished governmental brotherhood? Might England herself suffer not unlike the messenger in Caesar's time who was killed for delivering unhappy tidings? After all, look how Phillips was vilified for attacking the Senate. No, as I trust I have implied in my laconic wire to Mrs. Frevert, necessity suggests that we too put this case to rest."

"'Necessity'? 'International consequences'?" I threw his words back at him. "You sound more like *Mycroft* Holmes than his brother Sherlock!"

"Bravo again, Watson!" Holmes said. "I did indeed speak to Mycroft upon our return to England."

"I thought as much," I said, eyeing him with disapproval.

Rising from his chair, Holmes clasped his walking stick and pointed to the open French windows through which, despite the descending dusk, we could still see the ocean.

Grudgingly I joined Holmes on the gravel footpath as he ambled toward the chalky cliffs that overlook the sea. The small stones grated beneath our feet.

"You're quite right, Watson," he said. "Mycroft did indeed help me see the wisdom in keeping this story to our immediate selves."

"No doubt," I muttered.

"In point of fact, Mycroft tried to put us off this investigation from the very start when we met with him at the Diogenes Club in March."

I greeted this information with silence. Besides the omnipresent pounding of the surf below, only the crunch of our boots on the path and the cries of a few sea birds rent the peaceful afternoon that was fast turning into evening.

"It seems, Watson, that much of what we learned from our investigations in America was already known at the highest levels of our own government."

"Then why didn't Mycroft inform us?"

"Apparently the government feared that an attempt to thwart Mrs. Frevert might possibly explode in their faces. Besides, one never knows just what might turn up in a new investigation. His Majesty's Government did possess the barest outlines of the plot, but not the names of its perpetrators that we have now supplied through Mycroft and for which Downing Street is extremely grateful."

"Most accommodating of us," I said, unassuaged. It rankled me to think that we had been performing someone else's service. "But just because Mycroft wants us to remain silent—"

"On the contrary," Holmes interrupted. "It's not 'just Mycroft,' as you so simply put it. Mycroft's own instructions come from a higher authority in the government. In fact, the highest."

It never failed to surprise me whenever Holmes's and my activities caught the attention of the Crown; but here was obviously another such instance, and who was I to demur?

By way of answer I looked below me to the rocky white coastline that spread out in glistening stretches in either direction. My gaze followed the receding waves that were painted a fiery orange by the setting sun.

"We learn from nature, old fellow," my companion said as I stared contemplatively toward the horizon. "The water that blankets the *Titanic* and all her lost souls is like the mantle we human beings throw upon the Truth, neither one to be disturbed. How did Phillips describe the aftermath of that terrible naval disaster so long ago: 'The sea smoothed out again and began to laugh.'"

In the darkness I doubted that Holmes could see me shrug.

"Why not leave the final words about the conspirators to Mrs. Frevert?" Holmes offered. "It was she, after all, who had written on the stone over her brother's grave, 'Father, forgive them, for they know not what they do.'"

One need not have been Sherlock Holmes at that moment to detect the reluctance in my submission.

"I understand," I murmured.

And so we stood on the chalky cliffs as darkness fell, blanketing us and the sea alike. Circling far above us, some lost solitary gull shrieked in the night.

I did not hear from my friend Sherlock Holmes for a number of months following that last conversation; and when I did just before Christmas, it was not a letter that arrived in the post, but rather a number of cuttings from American newspapers. Much of the information these stories contained had, of course, been published by the British press. I did not require notification from Sherlock Holmes, for instance, to inform me that Woodrow Wilson, the former head of David Graham Phillips's *alma mater*, Princeton University, had defeated Theodore Roosevelt and William Howard Taft for the American Presidency the previous month;

but some of the news appearing in the cuttings from Holmes had not made its way into our periodicals, and when the articles were viewed together, they seemed to form a fitting *dénouement* to the story that had begun earlier that same year with the arrival of Mrs. Frevert in my surgery.

Street singers who were entertaining Mrs. Watson and me with Christmas melodies had just reached our windows when I opened the large brown envelope from Holmes. Because of its size, I had to shake it several times over the dining-room table in order to be sure the packet was empty. In all, six small strips of yellowing paper fluttered out. As I slid them around on the oak table to secure their proper chronological order, I felt I was manipulating into place the final pieces of some intricate puzzle.

The first story reported the proposal made the previous May 13 by the American Congress for an amendment to the United States Constitution requiring the popular election of senators. Thus, some six years after Phillips's 1906 attack on that body in his disputatious articles, reform seemed probable. Indeed, although I did not know it at the time, the people's right to vote directly for their senators would become law the next year when on 8 April, 1913–almost twelve months to the day following the loss of the *Titanic*–the Seventeenth Amendment to the Constitution was ratified.

A cutting from August 1912 told of Theodore Roosevelt's nomination for president by the Progressives' uniquely and appropriately nicknamed Bull Moose party after the Republicans had rejected him in favour of President Taft. Giving the keynote address at this third party's convention was none other than Albert Beveridge, who himself was standing for governor of Indiana as a Progressive.

The third cutting, and by far the longest, recounted a story that, had it not been for our own personal experiences with the homicidal factor in American politics, we would have found unbelievable. It reported the attempted assassination of Roosevelt on October 14 in Milwaukee. Wounded by a gunman, the former president was miraculously saved only because the bullet's velocity was slowed by passing through his spectacles case and the manuscript of a speech, both of which were tucked into an inside coat pocket. True to his spirit, the indomitable Roosevelt went on to deliver his scheduled address before allowing himself to be taken to hospital.

A fourth article told of Roosevelt's recovery; a fifth recorded not only his political defeat but that of Beveridge as well.

The last cutting in the little row of stories I had laid out on the table was the shortest of them all, a snippet from a social column reporting the entrance to a sanitarium the previous summer of Mrs. Carolyn Frevert. She was suffering from fatigue.

That there was no message from Holmes himself was not surprising. He knew that these final clippings would help me round out my account of the case, and so I concluded that he approved of my composing this narrative; but I also know that he, like myself, still regards it as an explosive story whose full details must continue to be withheld from public scrutiny for several more years. Thus, I shall add these last details only to complete the record and then hide it away until its telling no longer threatens so many actors still performing on the political stage.

It is now the fifth Christmas since the end of the Great War. Listening to this year's carollers, I sit with Mrs. Watson at my side before the glowing hearth, a light snow falling gently beyond our windows on Queen Anne Street. Like the recurrence of the seasons, it is an unending story, I think–that of concealing and uncovering and concealing once more. It is a drama bound to be acted again and again as long as Authority must convince the populace of Government's ability to control. I understand the necessity, but necessity can lead to expediency, and expediency in the political world can expose the most dreadful of human frailties. With murder and deceit as accomplices, it was just such expediency that so obviously resulted in falsely identifying for the historical record the murky role of one Fitzhugh Coyle Goldsborough as the lone assassin of David Graham Phillips.

London

23 December, 1922

SELECTED BIBLIOGRAPHY

The following books and periodicals will further elucidate many of the events referred to by Dr. Watson in his narrative:

Baring-Gould, William S., ed. *The Annotated Sherlock Holmes.* New York: Clarkson N. Potter, 1967.

Churchill, Allen. *Park Row.* New York: Rinehart and Company, 1958.

Filler, Louis. *Voice of the Democracy: A Critical Biography of David Graham Phillips.* University Park, PA: Pennsylvania and State University Press, 1978.

Garmey, Stephen. *Gramercy Park: An Illustrated History of a New York Neighborhood.* Routledge Books, 1984.

Hagedorn, Hermann. *The Roosevelt Family of Sagamore Hill.* New York: Macmillan Company, 1954.

Highsmith, Carol M., and Ted Landphair. *Union Station: A Decorative History of Washington's Grand Terminal.* Washington, D.C.: Chelsea Publishing, 1988.

Los Angeles Times. January 24, 1911. "Author Shot Six Times."

The New York Times:

January 24, 1911. "Author Phillips Shot Six Times, May Recover."

January 25, 1911. "Phillips Dies of his Wounds."

January 26, 1911. "Phillips Funeral Set for To-morrow."

January 28, 1911. "Throng at Phillips Funeral."

March 4, 1911. "David Graham Phillip's Will Filed."

June 23, 1911. "Mrs. Phillips Dies on Train."

January 6, 1954. "Algernon Lee, 80, Educator, Is Dead."

Phillips, David Graham. *The Cost.* Indianapolis: Bobbs-Merrill

Company, 1904.

_____. *The Plum Tree.* Indianapolis: Bobbs-Merrill Company, 1904.

_____. *The Treason of the Senate.* Chicago: Quadrangle Press, 1964.

Ravitz, Abe C. *David Graham Phillips.* New York: Twayne Publishers, 1966.

Rodgers, Paul C., Jr. "David Graham Phillips: A Critical Study." Ph.D. dissertation, Columbia University, 1955.

Tracy, Jack. *The Encyclopedia Sherlockiana.* New York: Avon Books, 1979.

Victor, Daniel D. "The Muckraker and the Dandy: The Conflicting Personae of David Graham Phillips." Ph.D. dissertation, Claremont Graduate School, 1976.

Viereck, George Sylvestre. *The House of the Vampire.* New York: Arno Press, 1976.

Also Available

The Further Adventures of

SHERLOCK HOLMES

SÉANCE FOR A VAMPIRE

BY FRED SABERHAGEN

Prologue

O f course I can tell you the tale. But you should understand at the start that there are points where the telling may cause me to become rather emotional. Because I—even I, Prince Dracula—find the whole matter disturbing, even at this late date. It brought me as near to the true death as I have ever been, before or since—and in such an unexpected way! No, this affair you wish to hear about, the one involving the séances and the vampires, was not the commonplace stuff of day-to-day life. Hardly routine even in the terms of my existence, which for more than five hundred years has been—how shall I say it?—has not been dull.

It is difficult to find the words with which to characterize this chain of events. It was more than grotesque, it was fantastic. Parts of it almost unbelievable. You'll see. Pirates, mesmerism, executions by hanging. Stolen treasure, murder, kidnapping, revenge and seduction. Women taken by force, attempts to materialize the spirits of the dead...

I know what you are going to say. Everything in the above list is a bit out of the ordinary, but still the daily newspapers, those of any century you like, abound in examples. But in this case the combination was unique. And soon you will see that I am not exaggerating about the fantasy. Some of my hearers may not even believe in the existence of vampires, may find that elementary starting point quite beyond credibility.

Never mind. Let those who have such difficulty turn back here, before we really start; they have no imaginations and no souls.

Still with me? Very good. Actually no one besides myself can tell the tale now, but I can relate it vividly—because, with your indulgence, I will allow myself a little creative latitude as regards details, and also the luxury of some help in the form of several chapters written decades ago by another eyewitness. He, this other witness, who is now in effect becoming my co-author, was your archetypical Englishman, a somewhat stolid and unimaginative chap, but also a gentleman with great respect for truth and honor.

As it happens I was nowhere near London's Execution Dock on the June morning in 1765 when the whole fantastic business may fairly be said to have begun. However, somewhere past the halfway point between that date and this, less than a single century ago in the warm summer of 1903, I lived through the startling conclusion. In that latter post-Victorian year I happened to be on hand when the whole affair was pieced together logically by—will you begin to doubt me if I name him?—by a certain breathing man blessed with unequaled skills in the unraveling of the grotesque and the bizarre, a friend of the above eyewitness and also a distant relative of mine. And this adventure involving vampires and séances was enough, I think, to drive the logician to retirement.

But let me start at what I will call the beginning, in 1765…

* * *

There had been laughter inside the crumbling walls of Newgate during the night; at a little past midnight a guard in a certain hellish corridor was ready to swear that he had just heard the soft giggle of a woman, coming from one of the condemned cells, a place where no woman could possibly have been. Naturally at that hour all was dark inside the cages, and there was nothing that could have been called a disturbance; so the guard made no attempt to look inside.

Some hours later, when the first daylight, discouraged and rendered lifeless by these surroundings, filtered through to show the prison's stinking, grim interior, there was of course no woman to be seen. There had been no realistic possibility of anyone's passing in or out. The cell in question contained only the prisoner, the tall, red-bearded pirate captain, still breathing, just as he was supposed to be—for a few hours yet. Breathing but otherwise silent, not giggling like a woman, no, he was still sane—poor chap. And the guard, as little anxious as any of us ever are to seem a fool, was privately glad that he had said nothing, raised no ridiculous alarm.

No one in the prison had anything to say about impossibilities that might have been heard or seen before the dawn.

An hour or so after that same dawn, upon one of those raw June British mornings suggestive of the month of March, a solemn procession left London's Newgate Prison. At the heart of the grim train emerging from those iron gates there rolled a tall, heavy, open cart in which rode three doomed men, all standing erect with arms chained behind them. Their three sets of leg irons had been struck off only an hour ago, by the prison blacksmith. Once out of the prison gate, the cart, departing sharply from its customary route, turned east. These prisoners had been convicted by the Admiralty Court, and such did not at that time "go west" with the ordinary felons to hang on Tyburn Tree. Instead, a special fate awaited them.

Astride his horse at the very head of the procession was the Deputy Marshal of the Admiralty. Red-faced and grave, this functionary bore in prominent display the Silver Oar, almost big enough to row with, symbol of that court's authority over human activity on the high seas, even to the most distant portions of the globe. Next came the elegant coach carrying the Marshal himself, resplendent in his traditional uniform, surrounded by his coachmen wearing their distinctive livery. After these, on horseback, rode a number of City officials, one or two of considerable prominence. But whatever their station, few amid the steadily growing throng of onlookers had eyes for them, or for anyone but the central figures in the morning's drama.

The high ceremonial cart in the middle of the parade came lumbering along deliberately upon great wooden wheels, which, though freshly greased, squeaked mildly. The three prisoners standing more or less erect in the middle of the cart had their backs to one another, and with their arms still in irons had little choice but to lean on one another for mutual support. The executioner— Thomas Turlis in that year—and his assistant rode standing in the cart beside the prisoners, and a Newgate guard walked beside each of the great slow-turning wheels.

The cart was followed immediately by a substantial force of marshal's men and sheriff's officers, mostly afoot. These walking men had no trouble keeping up; those who calculated the time of departure from the prison had assumed that only a modest pace would be possible. The narrow, cobbled streets made progress for a large vehicle slow at best, and today as usual the throng of onlookers grew great enough to stop the death-cart altogether several times before the place of execution could be reached.

All three of the men who were riding to be hanged today had been convicted of the same act of piracy. The tallest of the condemned, the only one with anything exceptional in his nature or his appearance, was Alexander Ilyich Kulakov, red-haired and green-eyed, rawboned but broad-shouldered and powerful, his red beard straggling over his scarred cheeks and jaw. Kulakov was Russian, but at the moment nationality did not matter. His Britannic Majesty's justice was about to claim all three lives impartially—none of them had any influential friends in London—quite the opposite.

The morning's procession carried its victims east, as I have said. A little over two miles east of Newgate Prison, passing just north of the great dome of St. Paul's, through Cornhill and Whitechapel, past Tower Hill and close past the pale gloomy bulk of the squat Tower itself, to Wapping, a district largely composed of docks and taverns, nestled into a broad curve formed by the north bank of the Thames.

And with every rod of progress achieved by the doomed men and their escort, it seemed that the crowds increased. Last night and this morning word had spread, as it always did, of a scheduled hanging. Hundreds went to London's various scaffolds every year, but despite the relatively commonplace nature of the event the route of the procession was thickly lined with spectators. As often as not, when the high cart stalled in traffic, folk leaned from windows or trees to offer the condemned jugs or bottles or broken cups of liquor.

Kulakov's usual craving for strong drink seemed to have deserted him. He stared past the reaching arms and what they offered, and ignored the excited faces; but his two fellow prisoners did their best, even with their arms bound, to take advantage of the gift. The executioners, with a practical eye to making their own job easier, assisted the pair to drink, now and again fortifying themselves from the same jug or bottle.

One of the Russian captain's former shipmates was well-nigh insensible with drink before the ride was over.

It was the other of the two English prisoners who, in that age when death was so often a social function, had a small handful of relatives present; these—weeping, expostulating, or stony-faced according to their several temperaments—tagged after the cart, and were jostled to the rear by the sheriff's men.

The authorities had long practice with such processions from Newgate; and this enabled them to time the arrival of the cart at Execution Dock to coincide almost precisely with the hour of low water in the tidal Thames, this being the only time when the gallows was readily accessible.

For hundreds of years, pirates and mutineers had been executed on this spot, while for occasional variety a captain or mate would be dispatched for murderous brutality directed at his own crew. On this morning, several of the fruits of last week's executions were still to be seen, each hanging in chains on its own post. Gulls and weather had already reduced the dead faces to eyeless, discolored leather and protruding bone, raking the passing ships with empty stares. Their continued presence was intended to impress the thousands of seamen on those ships as examples of the Admiralty's long arm and exact justice.

The posts displaying these veteran corpses had been erected along the riverbank at various distances from the now ominously empty gallows. The latter was no more than two posts and a crossbeam, the horizontal member being not much more than ten feet above the strip of muddy ground and gravel exposed now at low tide.

Somewhat closer to the gallows itself than last week's bodies, another set of three stakes, also ominously empty, waited for today's victims.

Crowding nearby land and water were spectators even more numerous than those along the route. Folk of high station and low were out this morning, their numbers not much diminished by the weather, which so far had not improved. Every comfortable vantage point, and some perches fit only for the stoic, even the acrobatic, had been occupied. The windows and terraces of taverns and other riverside buildings, as well as docks and jetties, were thick with onlookers. Scores of small boats passed to and fro, or had cast anchor in the river. The current was very slow just now, with the tide about to turn. A barge moored no more than forty yards offshore afforded rows of seats for those willing and able to pay. At a somewhat greater distance over the broad face of the Thames, the crews and passengers of a couple of anchored ships presented on decks and rigging rows of pale faces. Well beyond these larger craft, the shadowy shapes of docks and buildings on the south shore loomed out of cold mist and drizzle.

One of the watchers, ensconced in a high-priced seat in the window of a tavern built upon a nearby promontory, was a dark-haired, smooth-skinned woman of somewhat exotic dress and remarkable appearance. Despite the sunless pallor of her skin, her countenance was undoubtedly Asiatic. Today she was keeping to a position where she herself remained inconspicuous, her pallid face shaded from even this clouded daylight. She was sharing a table—though she was not eating or drinking—with a well-dressed, well-fed, stoutish man of middle age, named Ambrose Altamont, a commoner very recently come into startling wealth. The weathered condition of Altamont's face suggested that he was no stranger to the sea and tropic suns.

The table was bare before the woman—she had assured her new patron that she was not hungry—but the man had dishes and bottles aplenty in front of him. He was dining early today, by way of celebration, on lamprey pie—then considered a rare treat—and sampling good wine.

As nearly as I can discover, Altamont at this point did not, strictly speaking, know that the woman with him was a vampire. That fact and all its implications still lay over his horizon. He certainly understood that she was strange—for several nights now he had reveled in excitement over her exotic antics in his bed. Whatever the limits of her strangeness, whatever disadvantages were yet to be discovered, here was an attractive female who gave delight and satisfaction, beyond anything that he had ever previously encountered in almost fifty years of a thoroughly unsheltered life. Altamont might well have betrayed a business partner for her favors alone—even had there been no jewels.

The creaking high wheels of the tall cart fell silent as the vehicle eased to a halt on Execution Dock. While the massed guards cleared a space of spectators, the prisoners—their bodies stiff with confinement, two of them reeling with drink, all three chain-laden— were helped down. The severely drunken man had to be lifted bodily. Then, one at a time, the sober Kulakov first, the three men were led—or carried—down through mud and gravel to the rude platform, which consisted of only a few boards laid in mud beneath the gallows.

Waiting for them at that threshold of eternity was the chaplain, Mr. Ford, Ordinary of Newgate, ready to lead repentant sinners in prayer or persuade them that they should seek divine forgiveness.

No one today had thought to provide a Russian Orthodox clergyman; but if any had been there the Russian doubtless would only have snarled at him, as he did at Mr. Ford.

Under the circumstances whatever prayers were possible for Kulakov, the first victim, were soon said. Then a ready noose was placed around his neck and he was blindfolded.

Meanwhile, at the tavern table, the pale and sheltered but vivacious lady had allowed herself to be distracted from the show by a sudden impulse to admire yet again a gift she had very recently received. This was a wonderful bracelet, fine gold and silver filigree sparkling with red rubies and clear diamonds. This masterpiece of the jeweler's art came into view upon her white and slender left wrist when she deliberately drew back her full sleeve to reveal it.

"It fits you loosely," her companion commented, his voice rich with wine and satisfaction.

"I'll not lose it. Where are the other things?" she inquired softly. "Your brother has them, perhaps?" Her voice was small but determined, her English sounding with a strong accent, hard to define, but certainly as Eastern as her face.

Altamont winked at her, and smiled. "They're where they'll be safe for the time being—and you may lay to that." Turning away again, he squinted, in the practiced manner of a ship's captain, through his sailor's brass-tubed glass at the proceedings on shore.

Confident as Altamont was that no one could overhear their talk, he lowered his voice when he added: "My own suspicion—I've no proof of it, mind—is that they were meant as a gift for the Empress Catherine of Muscovy, from one of those nabobs in the East. Or they might have belonged to the Russian church, some of their clergy smuggling them abroad to keep them out of Her Imperial Majesty's hands. I hear Catherine's developed a taste for churchly property, as did our own dear Henry long ago." He shot his companion a sharp glance. "The Russian might have given you a better answer than I can give, as to who the first owner of your bangle was. Not that it much matters now."

The dark-haired woman did not seem to care. Indeed her fascination with the beauty of the ornament was as apparent as her lack of interest in its origins. "Then the other things must be just as rich as this?"

The man almost sneered, in his pride and his amusement. "Richer, by God! Half a dozen pieces in all, rings and necklaces, in the same style, but even more extravagant—a king's ransom. I am surprised you had no chance to see them on the voyage. You must have shared the Russian's cabin, sailing back to London."

The woman let her long sleeve drop, concealing jewels and precious metal. "Cap-tain Kulakov kept all well hidden."

"No doubt. I think he meant to keep such great treasure all to himself, and maybe to some of his men who knew of it. But to cheat his English partner—"* Altamont smiled and shook his head. "Well, greed, like pride, goeth before a fall. And now the Russian hath lost all; his treasure, his woman, life itself. Almost I could feel sorry for him—why are they taking so long about his stepping off?" He squinted through his glass again.

A prosperous man, Mr. Altamont, even before his recent dramatic

---

* The details of the efforts of the pirate partners to cheat each other have never become perfectly clear, nor are they essential to our story. A perusal of Admiralty records of the time indicates that alliances between pirates and politicians were by no means as uncommon as all right-minded people would like to think.—D.

accession of new wealth. He felt himself capable of handling even greater prosperity without undue difficulty. At the moment his countenance was alternating between frowns at the delay and a faint expression of abstract pleasure as he shifted from wine to hot buttered rum, while watching from his comfortable chair.

The pallid woman remained patiently seated with him. Though the air on this June morning had turned quite mild, she was glad to shelter here indoors; in her case it was in fact not chill nor damp, but the mild English sun that threatened.

On shore the experienced Thomas Turlis, and his assistant who was hardly less qualified, were proceeding about their business with deliberate speed. The junior member of the official team had already climbed to straddle the crossbeam, where he sat waiting until Turlis had guided his first victim halfway up the ladder, Kulakov's feet on the rungs awkward with the weight of chains and terror. Then, receiving from his senior's hand the loose end of the short rope already snug around the victim's neck, the assistant quickly and efficiently secured it tightly to the heavy crossbeam.

The red-haired man cried out, loudly and articulately, in the last moments while he waited for the noose to choke off his breath.

"*Al-ta-mont!*" There followed a string of violent un-English words, sounds carrying well across the water, between the two points on the curving shore.

"I understand very little Russian, really," the man at the table remarked comfortably. "Which no doubt is just as well."

"I un-der-stand a little, as with Ain-glish," the watching woman remarked abstractedly. "I spoke to him last night," she added after a pause. "He think he have give the jewels to you only for safekeeping, not?"

"You saw him last night?" Briefly her companion turned a puzzled but fascinated frown in her direction. "Really, I think that you did not, for you were pretty steadily with me. As I have good cause to remember, having got but little sleep." Lecherously Altamont displayed bad teeth. "But you know, I would wager my new fortune that it would not be beyond you to gain entry to a condemned cell—not when the guards are men."

"I spoke to him," the woman repeated. Not with an air of insistence, but as if she had not heard her companion's denial. "But he would not believe that I was real. I think thees Russian must be very—what is word?—su-per-sti-tious." Pulling her dreamy gaze back from the shore, she fastened it upon the man beside her. "Will you believe me, Al-tamont, when I try to tell you *what* I am?"

He made a small noise compounded of amusement and satisfaction. "I think I understand well enough what you are. So, you visited the condemned cell, did you, and had a chat? And what do you want me to think that you told dear Alexei? That we have both betrayed him? That the jewels are all mine now, while he is come to dine today on hearty-choke and caper sauce?"

The woman very slightly shook her head. "He did not need me to tell him that you keep the jewels." Perhaps she intended to offer some explanation about her activities last night, or drop more teasing hints; but at the moment her full attention, like that of all other watchers, had become focused on the shore.

For the space of a held breath the raucous cries of even the least reverent onlookers were silent. Turlis, the older and paunchier of the hangman pair, with his feet planted solidly in mud—the planks had been disarranged in Kulakov's last awkward stumbling—took hold of the ladder and, with a strong twisting wrench, deprived the bound man of all physical support. Except for that now afforded him by taut hemp, the smoothly clasping noose.

The drop was a short one, no more than three feet at the most, in this case not nearly enough to break the neck-bones, to tear and quickly crush out life and consciousness from the vulnerable soft tissue of the spine and brain stem. There was only the steady, brutal pressure of the rope to squeeze the windpipe, veins and arteries. Kulakov's powerful frame convulsed. His bound arms strained, his legs and feet moved in a spasmodic aerial ballet.

Hearty-choke and caper sauce.

The fact that Kulakov had been first to be hanged meant that comparatively few among the audience were paying his prolonged death struggle as much attention as it must otherwise have received; rather the fascinated scrutiny of the mob now rested in turn upon each of his colleagues.

Altamont commented knowingly to his companion that the knot of the rope had very likely slipped from the favored location behind the Russian's ear to behind his neck—but how could Altamont have known that, at the distance, unless he had made some private arrangement to have the knot deliberately adjusted in that wise? Trying to get the better of Altamont, as the man himself would have assured you, was likely to result in truly frightful punishment.

As for Kulakov, he had been denied his broken neck. So that he hung for a quarter of an hour, intermittently twitching and tensing in agony, all breathing not quite cut off.

"Are they not going to finish him?" Altamont's comment, coming after five minutes or so, was dryly lacking in surprise. "It would seem not."

It was common in such cases for one or both hangmen, when not entirely lacking in pity, to seize their client by the legs, and drag down with their full weight upon the poor wretch's body to assist his soul on its way out of it. But at the moment the executioners were busy. If any friends or relatives of the condemned were in attendance, that office might fall to them. But in Kulakov's case no one had come forward with any such merciful intention.

One after the other, the two remaining pirates followed their captain to the scaffold. The executioners gave no thought to taking down the body of the first man to be hanged, until the third was dangling, and they had paused to fortify themselves with rum. The two Englishmen went quickly, so there was no need for relatives to intervene.

When, in the chief executioner's professional judgment, the third man had been well and truly hanged, he gave curt directions to his assistant. Between them the two men loosened the knot holding the first body to the crossbar—there would be no wasteful cutting of the rope—and lowered their grim burden to the muddy shore. Already the feet of the hangmen splashed in water; at this hour the lower Thames was entering that part of its unending tidal cycle in which the rising weight of ocean a few miles distant forced the river swiftly back toward its source, as if it would convey the brackish tide up into the middle of the great island.

Now Kulakov's body, hands still chained behind its back, had been dragged some twenty-five or thirty yards from the gallows, to its next temporary resting place. There with some difficulty it was being chained upright, feet at ground level, to one of the three tall, empty stakes that had been driven deep into the muddy sands. By tradition, the freshly hanged at Execution Dock remained so mounted until their already lifeless lungs had been drowned thrice by the high tides.

One after the other, the Russian's now-unbreathing comrades joined him, were fastened to the trees which stood one on either side of his, forming a ghastly Golgotha. Surely, in some of the onlookers' minds, the tableau evoked thoughts of a certain antique and much more famous triple execution. But no one commented aloud upon the fact.

By the time the dead body of the third pirate was thus displayed, and the day's task of the hangmen essentially concluded, many of those watching had gone on about their business.

But perhaps they had missed something of importance. Did a murmur of morbid excitement pass through the remaining crowd when the central one of the newly chained corpses was seen to move? Could it be that the captain and ringleader of this pirate band was still not dead after having been hanged for a quarter of an hour?

Such an event would not have been without precedent.

We will assume that Altamont, in his dry way, even commented to his companion upon the most famous such case, which some of those watching Kulakov might have seen with their own eyes—that of William Duell, executed at Tyburn a quarter of a century earlier, in 1740. Duell, though only sixteen years of age when hanged, had been widely noted for his sadism. Convicted of rape as well as murder, his body was turned over to medical anatomists...but when finally placed on the dissecting table it displayed certain faint signs of life. The surgeons, ready to try a different experiment than that originally scheduled, applied their skills at healing and soon had the patient sitting up, drawing deep breaths and drinking warm wine.

Duell had cheated the hangman after all. Returned to Newgate, he was eventually ordered to be transported to America.

Hangings here at Execution Dock, with tide-drowning added as a flourish under Admiralty auspices, were somewhat more thorough. No one put up on one of these stakes for show had ever tasted wine again. Certainly the sharp-eyed Altamont did not find the signs of life so stubbornly displayed by today's first hanged man at all perturbing; rather amusing.

Altamont, alternately smirking and frowning over his latest glass of hot buttered rum, made a few remarks on the case of young Duell to his fair companion, who took a somewhat different view of such phenomena.

The woman said in her abstracted way: "I think we will not have to worry about Kulakov—he will die today. I spent but little time with him last night."

"Oh, he'll die today, and no mistake." The man stared at her for the space of several rummy breaths before adding: "Up to your mystification, are you, Doll? I've noticed you have a taste for riddles. But do go on with it—I like it well."

Altamont and the very un-English woman he called Doll—he had tried her real name once and found it unpronounceable—remained in their snug tavern window for an hour longer, until he had made sure with his own eyes that the swiftly running tide had raised the surface of the Thames well above that pale dot of a distant, red-bearded face. Then, humming a sea-song to himself, and more than content with the day's events so far, the prosperous observer called for his waiting carriage, offered his arm to his woman, and leisurely took his way to the Angel Inn on the south bank, where snug warm rooms awaited them.

Early next morning Turlis and his helper returned to the scene to check on their most recent handiwork. June at that latitude brought full sunlight well before many folk of any class or inclination were up and about. Both men expressed mild surprise on observing that the central stake of three was now unoccupied, the chains in which they had hanged the Russian's body for display now lying in the mud below, still looped and locked together but quite empty. Surely mere tide and current could not have done this—yesterday these experts had secured their trophy well. But there were obvious explanations. Either relatives had shown up belatedly to spirit his corpse away—or someone, even in this enlightened seventh decade of the eighteenth century, had coveted morsels of hanged man's flesh as an aid to practicing the black arts of magic.

The hangmen, discussing these possibilities, were momentarily distracted by the sound of shrill feminine screaming. The sound was repeated several times, carrying readily over the water, through the bright incongruous early morning sun, all the way from the south shore. Only momentarily distracted; at the river's edge in Wapping, such racket was common enough. Actually, what Turlis and his comrade heard were the screams of horror uttered by some innocent female servant who had just opened the door of a certain room in the dockside Angel Inn.

More than a hundred years would pass before any rational investigator connected that hanged man's disappearance during the night with the shocking sight which met the maid's eyes a few hours later. Not that the maid was startled by the walking undead form of Alexander Ilyich Kulakov—she was perhaps an hour too late for that. No, she had unsuspectingly come upon a corpse much more severely mangled.

* * *

Shortly after the midnight immediately following the execution,

Altamont had been awakened by something in his room. It was a supreme despair, more than terror, that choked off his first scream in his throat when he beheld what had roused him and now stood beside his bed. It was the figure of Kulakov, still wearing the prison clothes in which he had been hanged. The Russian's red beard was dripping water, his dead face a ghastly livid hue, his strangled throat, though no longer required to breathe, made croaking noises. But his limbs were free of chains, and his white hands were half-raised and twitching, groping toward the bed. The pirate's eyes, the only feature appearing to be fully alive in that corpse-countenance, were fixed on Altamont.

Doll in turn was awakened by Altamont's hoarse abandoned cry. On seeing Kulakov, she registered mild surprise—so, she had been wrong about Kulakov's dying a true death yesterday! It was obvious to her that the Russian, stimulated by Doll's repeated attentions on the voyage and in his Newgate cell, had, after all, become a vampire instead.

The woman immediately slid her compact, dark-nippled, quite un-English body naked from the bed. She smiled, and before her bedmate's uncomprehending eyes melted into mist-form and disappeared—only pausing long enough to pick up her jeweled bracelet from the bedside table, and slip it on her wrist. The bangle went with her when she vanished—we who are wont to travel in that fashion commonly carry with us a few small items, most commonly our clothing, when we go changing forms.

Kulakov paid little attention to either the woman's presence or her departure. The red rage filling his whole mind concentrated his attention elsewhere. In the next moment, the hands of the undead man had fastened their icy, awkward grip on Altamont. Then the vampire—new to the powers he had been given, almost as bewildered as his victim by his own seemingly miraculous transformation, and still unsure of how to handle it—plucked the treacherous, nightshirted Englishman like a louse out of his bedclothes, and cast him aside with stunning force. In the next moment Kulakov, moving in a kind of somnambulistic fury, groaning and grunting foul Russian expletives, began ransacking the room in search of his stolen treasure. Drawers, bags, and boxes were hurled about and emptied, furniture shifted in a grip of giant's strength. All in vain.

A moment later the searcher grunted in befuddled triumph, on discovering some small, hard objects sewn into a quilt or featherbed. Carrying his find to the moonlit window, smashing the dim smoky glass in a reflexive move to gain more light, (not that his newly empowered eyes really needed any more; but Kulakov did not yet understand this fact) he ripped the cloth to shreds. Inside, to his great disappointment, the searcher discovered only sand and gravel, what was to him mere ordinary dirt. In anger he hurled the torn cloth from him, letting its worthless contents scatter into the Thames below.

It flashed across Kulakov's mind that Altamont, rather than risk carrying the treasure about with him in London, had very likely given it to his brother for safekeeping.

And he turned to complete his vengeance upon Altamont.

The doomed Englishman had turned back to the bed and now had both hands under his pillow—in a moment they were out again, not holding gems and precious metal, but newly armed with a loaded pistol and a dagger. A tough, resourceful man, old Ambrose Altamont; but both weapons very quickly proved completely useless.

There was really not much more noise—the pistol was never fired—and those among the other breathing dwellers at the Angel Inn who were awakened by muffled screams and thumps only grumbled and went back to sleep. Soon enough—well before Kulakov really thought of trying to force him to tell where the jewels were hidden—Altamont had ceased to breathe.

Kulakov, having thus achieved a kind of victory, was suddenly overwhelmingly weary. Once more he returned to his search for the jewels that he still thought might possibly be here somewhere… struck by what seemed to him a good idea, he went to search in the connecting room.

Only a minute or two after the hanged pirate had stumbled out the door, the woman called Doll, a much more experienced vampire, reappeared in the room of carnage. Doll was as naked as when she left—more so, for she no longer wore her bracelet—and entered as she had left, in mist-form through the window. Around her in the predawn light, as she resumed a solid human shape, the other denizens of the Angel Inn still slept.

Picking her way fastidiously among great spatterings and gouts of gore, she stopped for an opportunistic snack, bending to bestow a sort of prolonged kiss upon the now-faceless body on the floor. There was, she thought, no use letting so much of the good fresh red stuff go to waste.

Only when she straightened up, neatly licking her lips clean, did she happen to glance out the window, and noticed to her horror that the cloth bag which had contained her earth, her only earth, lay torn open and emptied, caught on a spiky paling a few feet outside the window, just above the energetic river.

Kulakov was no longer in the room to hear her, but she screamed at him in her own language that he had slain her, scattering her home-earth thus.

Perhaps it will be helpful to some readers if I choose this point for brief digression: To each vampire, certain earth is magic. The soil of his or her homeland, is as essential as air to breathing human lungs. For a day, for several days in the case of the toughened elders of the race, the nosferatu *can survive without the native earth. After that, a twitching, unslakeable restlessness begins to dominate, and a great weariness soon overtakes the victim, culminating in true death. It is not an easy dying; the sharp stake through the heart, or even the scorching sun, are comparatively merciful.*

Kulakov in his confused state, still having no success in his monomaniacal quest to repossess his treasure, heard the woman's despairing cries and came back from the adjoining room.

Doll had put on her clothes again. Gibbering and pleading in her terror, she tried to bargain with him. She spoke now in her native language, which Kulakov had learned to understand: She told the Russian that she knew with certainty where the stolen ornaments were hidden, and that she would give them all to him in exchange for only a few pounds of her native earth.

Somewhere among the hundreds of ships in the great port, which had brought in by accident soil, plants, vermin from the farthest reaches of the globe—somewhere among all those far-traveled hulls, surely, surely there must be one whose cargo or bilge or windswept planking contained a few pounds, a few handfuls even, of that stuff more precious now to her than any gems or lustrous metal.

The Russian, his understanding still clouded by strangulation and rebirth, heard her out. Then he had a question of his own. He whispered it in fluent English: "Where are the jewels? They are not here."

Doll switched back to her imperfect English. "Are you not listen to me? I tell you where the treasure is, I swear, when you have help me find the soil I need. The jewels are not here. But they are all safe, in place you know, where you can get them!"

"I know." The pirate looked down at the red ruin on the floor. "*He* gave them to his brother, who has them at his country estate, somewhere out of town. His brother who helped him to betray me."

In near despair the woman clutched his arm, her long nails digging in, a grip that might well have crushed the bones of any breathing man. Once more she spoke in her own language. "Will you not listen to me, Kulakov? *I need my earth!* By all the gods of my homeland—by whatever gods you pray to in your Muscovy—I swear that if you help me find the earth that I must have, the treasure shall all be yours!"

The Russian mumbled something; perhaps he meant it for agreement. But he was almost stupefied. His own need for rest had suddenly grown insupportable. Overwhelmed like an infant with the necessity for sleep, he abandoned his solid form and drifted away, sliding out again in shifting mist-form through the window.

The woman, unable to obtain his help, began her own search, in desperation and in deadly growing daylight. But alas for poor Doll's hopes of immortality! Upon the whole long winding Thames on that June day there floated not a single vessel containing any of the special soil her life required.

But Russian ships, carelessly bearing with them some of the soil of Muscovy, though rare in this port were still discoverable. Kulakov by some instinct managed to locate the hidden, earthy niche he needed, in one of their dark holds.

New vampires, like new babies, will often require long periods of sleep. Three weeks later when he awakened, out of a long vampirish nightmare of being hanged, he was back in St. Petersburg, the capital of his native land.

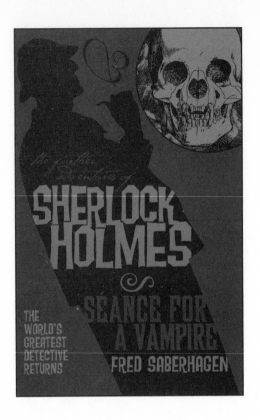

THE FURTHER ADVENTURES
OF SHERLOCK HOLMES
SEANCE FOR A VAMPIRE

Fred Saberhagen

When two psychics offer Ambrose Altamont the opportunity to contact
his deceased daughter, Holmes is hired to expose their hoax. The result
leaves one of the fraudulent spiritualists dead and Holmes missing. Watson
has no choice but to summon the only one who might be able to help –
Holmes' vampire cousin, Prince Dracula.

ISBN: 9781848566774

AVAILABLE JUNE 2010

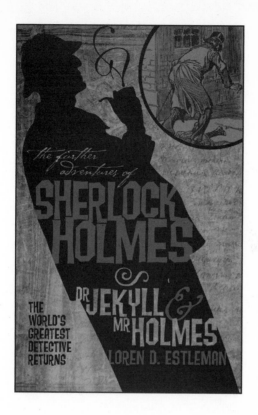

THE FURTHER ADVENTURES
OF SHERLOCK HOLMES

DR JEKYLL AND MR HOLMES

Loren D. Estleman

Sherlock Holmes has already encountered the evil young hedonist Edward
Hyde, and knew he was strangely connected with Henry Jekyll, the
respectable young doctor. It was not until the Queen herself requested
it, however, that Holmes was officially on the case of the savage murder
of Sir Danvers Crew. Here, then is the account of that devilish crime as
recorded by Dr Watson...

ISBN: 9781848567474

AVAILABLE OCTOBER 2010

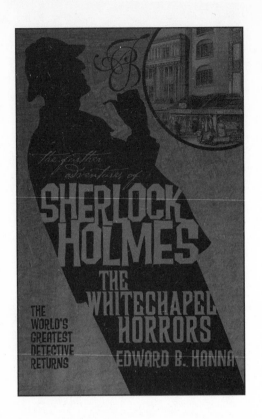

THE FURTHER ADVENTURES OF SHERLOCK HOLMES

THE WHITECHAPEL HORRORS

Edward B. Hanna

Grotesque murders are being committed on the streets of Whitechapel. Sherlock Holmes comes to believe they are the skilful work of one man, a man who earns the gruesome epithet of Jack the Ripper. As the investigation proceeds, Holmes realizes that the true identity of the Ripper puts much more at stake than just catching a killer…

ISBN: 9781848567498

AVAILABLE OCTOBER 2010